# NOWHERE TO HIDE

KERI BEEVIS

Boldwood

First published in Great Britain in 2024 by Boldwood Books Ltd.

Copyright © Keri Beevis, 2024

Cover Design by 12 Orchards Ltd

Cover Photography: Shutterstock

Every effort has been made to obtain the necessary permissions with reference to copyright material, both illustrative and quoted. We apologise for any omissions in this respect and will be pleased to make the appropriate acknowledgements in any future edition.

A CIP catalogue record for this book is available from the British Library.

Paperback ISBN 978-1-80415-151-8

Large Print ISBN 978-1-80415-152-5

Hardback ISBN 978-1-80415-150-1

Ebook ISBN 978-1-80415-154-9

Kindle ISBN 978-1-80415-153-2

Audio CD ISBN 978-1-80415-145-7

MP3 CD ISBN 978-1-80415-146-4

Digital audio download ISBN 978-1-80415-148-8

Boldwood Books Ltd
23 Bowerdean Street
London SW6 3TN
www.boldwoodbooks.com

*For my dear friend, Andrea Mummery.*
*And in memory of her beautiful gelding, Red.*

# 1

---

It was raining steadily as the train pulled into Norwich Railway Station and Callie Parker remained seated while the other commuters bustled around her, grabbing bags and positioning themselves in the aisle, all of them keen to make a quick exit.

The only luggage she had with her was the carrier bag she clutched to her side, and it contained all of her worldly possessions. A half-bottle of water and an untouched egg mayonnaise sandwich she had bought in London, her belly too jumpy to eat; a cheap, pay-as-you-go mobile phone; a silver picture frame – the one sentimental item she couldn't bear to part with – and a black, woven bag filled with cash.

Everything else – her credit cards and keys, her clothes, make-up and jewellery – had been left behind in Devon. She was thirty-four and her life was down to one bag, but this was her fresh start and there could be nothing to link her to what she was running from.

Eventually, the train emptied and she made her way to the exit, butterflies swarming in her empty stomach as she scanned her phone at the turnstile and glanced anxiously into the crowd.

Was he here? Would she recognise him after all these years?

The enormity of what she had done hit sharply, fresh nerves trembling their way through her from her head to the tips of her toes. She had abandoned everything, travelling across the country to a city she didn't know, to meet a man she barely remembered and hadn't seen in nearly a decade. Was she crazy?

Perhaps yes, but she had no choice.

'Callie?'

A hand touched her elbow and she flinched, stepping back abruptly.

The man who had startled her held his hand up in apology. 'I didn't mean to make you jump.'

Familiar, olive-green eyes held her gaze as he spoke and she tried to steady her breathing, not wanting him to notice how shaken she was. It was silly, she supposed, her embarrassment. They both knew what she was fleeing and she had nothing to fear from the man who stood before her. They may not have seen each other in years, but she was certain she could trust him.

Nico Adams.

His eyes hadn't changed, but the fine lines fanning from them were an addition. He would be, what, thirty-six now? A year or two older than her. And he wore it well. The natural waves in his golden-brown hair thick and slightly unruly and the stubble grazing his chin taking away the softness of youth. And despite the cool February temperature, his face had a tan.

'How did it go? Any problems?'

Callie's voice seemed to have deserted her, so she simply shook her head.

'Do you have anything else with you?'

*For God's sake, say something.*

She shook her head again, but this time managed to speak. 'Um, no.'

Could he detect the tremor in her tone? If so, he didn't say. He had always been quiet and thoughtful, never using more words than necessary.

Laurel, Nico's sister, thought it was probably because of his upbringing. No one fully knew what he had gone through before her parents had adopted him, she had once said.

'Come on. I'm parked outside.'

He sounded a little impatient and guilt heated Callie's cheeks, aware he had pulled himself away from work to come and collect her. She was already an inconvenience he didn't need in his life, and had there been another way, she would have taken it.

Clutching her carrier bag, she scuttled after him like a mouse, relieved when he didn't touch her again or try to talk to her as she followed, instead striding ahead. It gave her a few precious seconds to try to pull herself together before the car journey to where he lived.

Truthfully, she was stunned. Though she knew this plan inside and out, going through with it was altogether different.

She had started the day with everything and now she had nothing. And she was relying on the kindness of a stranger – because that was what Nico had become – to feed and clothe her, to put a roof over her head until she could find a way out of her nightmare.

The icy breeze hit them as they stepped out of the station. It was still raining, and he picked up the pace as he crossed the car park, clicking his fob at a black Jeep.

Callie hurried after him, aware she was getting soaked and didn't have a change of clothes. He was waiting by the open passenger door and she quickly climbed in, careful not to touch anything other than the seat belt, conscious of respecting his property.

The Jeep was different to what she was used to. It didn't look as if it had been wheeled out of the showroom, overly polished and the interior spotless. It was clean, but showing signs of wear and tear. Brown Buddha beads hung from the rear-view mirror, while sunglasses Nico didn't currently need sat in the central console. The scent of the vehicle was of worn leather and sandalwood.

As he went round to the driver's side, she drew in deep breaths, slowly releasing them as she tried to ease the knots out of her shoulders.

It was going to be okay. The worst bit was over.

Though they still had the drive ahead.

Laurel had said his place was about fifteen minutes from the city centre.

That was fifteen minutes of small talk with a man she barely remembered.

The nerves started churning again.

It was safer than what she was running from, Callie reminded herself as he got in the Jeep.

He glanced in her direction. 'You okay?' The rain had darkened the waves of his hair and he pushed it from his face.

No, she wasn't, but she lied. 'I think so.'

He nodded, starting the engine, and, to her relief, turned on the radio. She wouldn't be forced to try to make conversation with him then.

It was her favourite indie station playing, she realised, recognising the DJ's voice. Radio X. As a Kings of Leon track started, a little of the tension ebbed out of her. There had been little music in her life over the last couple of years and it hit her now how badly she had missed it.

She had been on tenterhooks waiting for today, for the plan to be put in motion, terrified it would somehow go wrong, and although it hadn't, she was bottling a dozen emotions. Unsure how to feel about any of this.

Had she made a mistake?

Should she have stayed?

Was there another way?

She knew the answer to each question was no, but it didn't make this any easier.

She had lost her home, her dog and her identity. There was no other way.

Her dog. She thought of him now. Giving up Chester was the toughest decision she had been forced to make and, months later, she was still heartbroken. There had been no choice, though. His safety had to come first.

Her anxious fingers fought the urge to toy with the ends of the blonde bob she wore.

She trusted Laurel and Laurel trusted Nico.

Callie had to believe she was doing the right thing. She used to trust her own judgement, but she had made so many wrong decisions lately, she had lost faith in herself.

She spared a brief thought for what she had left behind and the risks she had taken to get away. No one could ever find out she was with Nico. If the truth came out, she wouldn't be safe, and neither would he.

Fresh terror rattled through her, knowing how dangerous all of this was, that one false move could be her undoing, and her skin grew clammy with fear.

She understood what hell was. She had been there and looked the Devil in the eye. And there was no way she was ever going back.

## 2

The rain stopped as they were heading away from Norwich, the sun emerging from behind the clouds as Nico slowed the car, turning off the country lane into a driveway signposted Willow Brook Farm.

Callie looked ahead, curious as they passed through a tunnel of trees, their branches bare from a harsh winter. So this was his home.

Laurel had told her that Nico had inherited the property from his former employer, Teddy Bishop, a man who had been like a second father to him.

As they emerged the other side of the trees, the landscape opened up. To the right were half a dozen paddocks, separated by white fences, with stables beyond. A woman with a ponytail was in one, standing centre of the field as a black horse on a long rein trotted around her.

To the left, the landscape was open and rugged, with trees that became denser, merging into woodland in the distance. A small building sat on the edge of the thicket, reminding Callie of the house in the Hansel and Gretel storybook. Was that where she would be staying? Laurel had mentioned a separate cottage.

Up ahead was Nico's house. At least she assumed it was where he lived. Aside from the cottage, there were no other properties she could see.

She knew nothing about this place or Nico these days, other than what Laurel had filled her in on. Callie knew he trained horses, but that was it. In hindsight, she should have asked more questions when Laurel had offered to help her. But she had been so focused on what she was escaping from, she hadn't fully considered what she might be running to.

As they approached, Callie got a full view of the front of the house. A Tudor-style, two-storey property with a black and white striped exterior. It was a pretty building and well maintained, but there was nothing showy about it, and that relaxed her a little.

'I'll take you down to the cottage in a minute,' Nico told her, pulling the Jeep to a halt outside the house. 'We just need to make a stop first.'

It was the first time he had spoken since they had left the station, but the silence hadn't been awkward as she had expected. The radio had helped, but Nico didn't seem to feel the need to make conversation, which had given Callie time to work through her jumble of thoughts. Now she was curious why they were stopping and wondering if he expected her to follow when he climbed out of the car.

She didn't want to be presumptuous, aware it was a bad habit of hers, so instead she remained in the passenger seat, tension thrumming through her as she clutched the carrier bag.

Nico glanced over his shoulder when he reached the house, realising she wasn't behind him, and his eyes widened in surprise. 'Come on,' he urged.

Now she reddened, feeling foolish for staying in the car.

She was unfastening her seat belt as he unlocked the front door, pushing it open, but the apology she had become conditioned to give when she messed up or miscalculated never made it past her lips as she watched the dogs charge out of the house.

The first two, a fawn boxer and a black and white spaniel, initially held her attention, but then a smiley-faced Golden Retriever was charging after them, which had her pausing, double taking and catching her breath, for a moment unsure and confused.

It wasn't him. It couldn't be.

'Chester?'

For the first time in longer than she could remember, she reacted without thinking about the consequences, almost falling out of the car as the dog's ears pricked up at the name and he looked in her direction. In that moment, she was sure.

As he charged towards her, Callie dropped to her knees, sobbing as the blur of golden fur leapt into her arms, covering her in enthusiastic licks.

For several seconds, it was just the two of them and Callie was in shock that he was here. As she showered him with all of the love she hadn't been able to give him these last few awful months, her vision blurred, the tears now streaming down her cheeks.

Chester had been the breaking point. By sending him away, she had saved him, but her heart had broken. If there was any blessing in his departure, it was the realisation that she had to fight for herself.

Somehow, she had managed to get away and, even if she didn't dare believe her nightmare was over, it comforted her that she had her dog back.

As she hugged him tight, she glanced up at Nico. He was watching them both, as the other two dogs chased each other around in the drive, and she mouthed the words, *Thank you.*

How would she ever begin to repay him for bringing Chester back to her?

He didn't react, other than to nod. His green eyes dark and his expression unreadable, apart from the slight curve touching his lips.

Nico was a brooder, not a smiler. She remembered that detail about him now.

He was a careful man, measured in his responses, often deep in thought, and Callie recalled he wasn't prone to outbursts of emotion. Excitement and enthusiasm weren't on his agenda, but neither were anger or jealousy.

While staying with his and Laurel's parents over Easter, back in their university days, she had overheard their mum, Janice, saying Nico had gone through a tough time before he had been adopted and that his real mother had made him suffer unnecessarily.

Callie hadn't been earwigging, but Janice's words had stuck and she had always been curious, though she had never asked what had happened.

She was pulled from her thoughts when the spaniel wandered over, curious as to who she was, a wet nose pressing against her cheek.

'Meet Dash,' Nico introduced, as she made a fuss of the dog. He nodded to the boxer who was looking on curiously. 'And this is Shyla.'

'Are they both yours?'

Nico's mouth twitched again. 'For my sins.'

He was joking, dropping down to fuss Shyla, as the dog returned to his side. He clearly adored her. Dash, meanwhile, was living up to his name, now running around Callie and Chester, wanting to play.

Callie had so many questions and was still a little in shock. When she had asked Laurel to take Chester, she'd had no idea he would end up here with Nico. She had asked only that Laurel find him a loving home, believing she would never see him again.

'Laurel never told me you took him,' she said once they were back in the Jeep, driving to the cottage. Although the building was in walking distance, the rain had created large puddles and the track was full of mud. Callie glanced back at Chester, who was on the back seat, his tail thumping like mad.

'She wanted it to be a surprise.' Nico hesitated. 'She knows what you have given up and how hard it's been, and she thought you should have something familiar when you got here.'

Yet again, her friend had gone over and above for her. Callie knew there was no way she would ever be able to repay Laurel for everything she had done.

Nico pulled the Jeep to a halt outside her new home and her first impression was how dilapidated it was. Grey stone and single storey with a dark roof and white, shuttered windows. A sign beside the door told her it was called 'Stable Cottage'.

'I know it doesn't look much from the outside, but the structure is sound and it's well insulated,' Nico reassured her. 'I lived here for a while and it's heated by an Aga and a wood-burning stove. It's cosy.'

Although this was good, the enormity of everything hit her and fresh nerves choked her throat, while her leaden legs refused to move.

This was happening. She had escaped.

Still, she couldn't believe she was safe and feared she would always be looking over her shoulder.

If her hiding place was ever discovered—

No. She couldn't think that way, just as she dared not imagine the future and how it might look for her. She needed to focus on taking things one day at a time.

It both relieved and terrified her.

Sensing she needed space, Nico got out of the Jeep, taking Chester with him, letting the dog sniff around for a few moments before heading over to the cottage to unlock the front door.

Callie sucked in a breath, releasing it slowly to try to quell her roiling stomach, then forced herself to move. She could do this.

She *had* to do this because it was too late to turn back.

Nico had disappeared inside and she followed after him, distracted momentarily by Chester, who was on his way back out to look for her, seeming anxious that she had left him again. As the blonde lump of fur crashed into her, Callie reached out and held on to his collar, needing him as an anchor as much as he needed her.

'It doesn't look much,' Nico said, gesturing at the small living room they were in, 'but it has all the basics. The TV is digital and you're hooked up to a few channels, and of course you have Wi-Fi. The code is on the kitchen counter if you want to put it in your phone. I came down and lit the wood burner earlier to make sure it's warm enough for you.'

Callie glanced around the room. One small sofa facing the TV. There was a tiny table in the corner with two chairs pushed under it, and the walls were plain. No colour, no pictures, but he was right, it was cosy. The fire crackling and providing a warm sanctuary from the February chill.

She looked to the front window, relieved when she saw it had a slatted blind. Although they were out in the countryside, the cottage was surrounded by woodland and she didn't like the idea of anyone being able to look in.

'Kitchen is through here.'

He led the way into a smaller room. Dated, but clean. A shiny, modern kettle and microwave looking a little out of place on the worktop.

'You have the Aga and a fridge-freezer,' he explained, pointing to each appliance. 'No space for a washing machine, but you're welcome to use the one in the house. I'll get you a key.'

'Thank you.'

Callie didn't bother pointing out she only had the clothes she was wearing to wash.

At some point, she would have to find a charity shop and splurge some of her precious savings. Knowing how quickly they would dwindle terrified her. She hadn't yet figured out a plan for when she ran out of money.

Laurel had assured her Nico would look after her financially. 'He can afford it,' she had pointed out. 'And he wants to help.'

That was generous, but the whole situation made Callie uncomfortable. She was well aware nothing was given for free. What if at some point he wanted to collect?

She watched him open the fridge, surprised when she saw it was full, spotting milk, vegetables, eggs, juice and cheese.

'I had no idea what you like, so I got a bit of everything.' He shrugged, looking a little embarrassed. 'It should keep you going for a while. The freezer is stocked too and there's plenty of dog food in the cupboard under the sink.'

Unexpected tears clogged her throat and pricked the back of her eyes at his thoughtfulness. She blinked them away, clearing her throat before repeating, 'Thank you,' the nerves kneading a little deeper, reminding her how much she was now in his debt.

For a moment, there was silence and Callie was aware of the weight of his stare. When it lingered a little longer than was comfortable, Nico seemed to catch himself and moved brusquely on.

'One bedroom, through there.' He pointed, but made no attempt to show her. 'Laurel has put some clothes in the drawers for you.'

She had?

'And the bathroom leads off. You have toiletries in there.'

Callie sounded like a puppet as she thanked him for a third time, annoyed she couldn't think of anything else to say. Truthfully, she was exhausted and the enormity of what she had done was hitting hard.

'I need to get back to work, so I'll leave you to it.'

Of course he did. She had already upset his routine.

She nodded, disappointed, contrite and relieved when he gave her a nod before heading back through into the living room and to the front door.

'Call me if you need anything, okay?'

Nico's was one of two numbers stored in the cheap mobile phone. The other belonged to Laurel, though she had agreed with her friend they would keep their contact to a minimum. It was safer. Not just for Callie, but for Laurel too.

'I will,' she assured him, deep down knowing he, too, wouldn't hear from her unless it was an emergency. She would eke out the food he had left for her, making it last for as long as possible, and if she needed anything else, she would work out a way to get it without troubling him.

She watched him go, grateful to have Chester by her side. Although things had been a little awkward with Nico, now she was alone, it was somehow worse. The creaks and groans of the cottage as she locked the door seemed to only accentuate the otherwise deathly silence.

It was only building noise, she told herself. She was safe here. She had to be.

Taking a moment with her dog, Callie dropped down onto the worn sofa and pulled him close. Needing to breathe in his scent, overwhelmed and choked with emotion that he was back with her. His tail was thumping like crazy as he covered her in licks and having him with her gave her the extra strength she needed.

She waited until she was ready before exploring the rest of the cottage. Pushing open the bedroom door, she stepped into a room where a double bed with a carved wooden headboard and dressed in white linen took up most of the space. There was also one bedside table, a free-standing wardrobe, and a chest of drawers with a mirror positioned atop of it.

Callie stared at her reflection and the blonde bob framing her pale face. Dark shadows sat under her haunted eyes and they were petrified. She had tried her best to hide her fear, not wanting to worry Nico, but she could see from her expression that she had done a lousy job.

Her scalp was hot and itchy and she hadn't dared touch it all day in case she messed up and revealed her true identity to prying eyes. No one could see her now though and she carefully removed the wig, setting it down on the dresser, along with her plastic bag of belongings. Shaking her real hair free, she used her fingers to untangle the thick, auburn waves, going into the little adjacent bathroom in search of a hairbrush.

Laurel and Nico had taken care of everything, she soon realised, making sure Callie had all she needed, from clothes and toiletries to food. None of the fancy labels she had been used to, but that was a relief. There was something comforting about the cup of tea she made, and the apple-fragranced shower gel she used to bathe herself, keen to remove the grime of her journey and the sweat that had built up over the course of the day. The store-brand goods reminded her of childhood. As did the soft, slightly worn fabric of the pyjamas she changed into once she was dry.

As darkness fell, she drew all of the blinds and curtains, double-checking the front door was locked. hating that fresh fears surfaced.

The isolated location of Stable Cottage had initially felt safe, but now it was dark, she found it a little creepy, and letting Chester out to pee, she was aware of the low mist that had settled on the ground and the rattle of the breeze through the trees in the surrounding woods.

There was a sensor light, which illuminated the stone path and the patch of land to the front of the properly, and Callie lingered in the doorway as the dog did his business, arms hugging around herself to try to ward off the cold. And when he wandered a little further away, she called to him, not wanting to have to leave the safety of the cottage.

In the distance, she could see the lights of the main house and it offered a little comfort, reminding her that Nico wasn't far away.

Back inside, she locked the door, then fed Chester. While he ate, she binned the sandwich she had bought for her journey, glancing inside the fridge and realising she didn't have an appetite.

Instead, she decided to call it a night.

* * *

It was the dream that woke her.

She had been on the packed train, head down as she went over her route – Totnes to Paddington. Paddington to Liverpool Street. Liverpool Street to Norwich – but then she had glanced up and everyone was gone. A sense of unease had crawled over her skin moments before she heard banging coming from the door at the end of the carriage.

That was when she had seen him, staring at her through the glass, and she had screamed herself awake.

It took her a moment to realise she was in an unfamiliar bed and she pushed sweat-drenched hair away from her face, understanding it had been a nightmare. She was here in Norfolk. She had escaped.

Beside her, Chester whined, but as she reached out to stroke him, the noise turned to a low, ominous growl, and all of her nerve endings were on edge.

Her dog was upset about something.

Was someone outside?

She held him to her, unsettled by the low rumble reverberating through him. And then she heard it.

Knock, knock, knock.

She thought it had been in her dream, but now she realised it was in real life.

The unmistakable creak of the door handle turning had the hairs on her neck standing on end.

Someone was trying to get inside the cottage.

## 3

_____

### BEFORE – TWENTY MONTHS EARLIER

The problem with having a parent who has a successful career is that they often have high expectations.

Take my father, for example.

Michael Parker is a respected orthopaedic surgeon, a single-digit-handicap golfer, and a man who expects the best from everyone. He had wanted – no, *insisted* – my sister Phoebe and I follow in his footsteps and attend med school, but there was a slight problem with that, at least for me.

I am really squeamish with blood.

And when I say squeamish, I mean I can't deal with it, full stop.

Phoebe sliced her leg open when we were kids, catching it on broken glass, and she dealt with it better than I did. The memory of the blood gushing from the wound is enough to make my legs weak and my stomach churn. There was no way I could work in a hospital.

Instead, I studied media at university.

That was strike one with Dad.

Then, after I graduated, I took a job at the Lemon Source Agency, running their social media accounts.

That was strike two.

Dad is old-school and doesn't approve of the likes of Facebook and Instagram. It was difficult enough trying to bring him out of the dark ages by setting up a family WhatsApp group. It's me, Pheebs, her boyfriend, Ed, Dad and our stepmother, April. No surprise that Dad is the one who joins in least.

In a way, it was a blessing when he decided to move back to the States a couple of years ago, along with April. Don't get me wrong, I love him, but he does try to interfere and he disapproves of pretty much every decision I make. Phoebe is his firstborn, older than me by three years, and they have a much closer bond. I will never be able to compete with her, so I don't try.

As for April. She's okay, I guess, but we have never been particularly close. It always feels like she is going through the motions with Pheebs and me as it's the right thing to do, not because she wants to. Perhaps it's because we were both in our late teens when she came into our lives.

Phoebe and I hold dual citizenship, thanks to an American father and a British mother, and we have lived in the UK since I was nine. Sadly, Mum died of cancer five years after we arrived in England and April was on the scene two years later. It was a lot to take in.

I guess it wasn't easy for April either, and she has never been unkind. Things just feel a little awkward sometimes.

Having an ocean dividing us, and our interactions limited to WhatsApp, phone calls and the occasional visit is better.

Although it's just Pheebs and me now, we don't see much of each other. Phoebe and Ed live in Bath and both of them work at the Royal United Hospital, while I'm in Watford, close to my office and not too far from Berkhamsted, where our family home was. I like it here, and even though it's just me, I never feel lonely.

Dad might not have approved of my career choice, but I love my job and all of the people I work with. I may not have family close by, but I do have a big group of friends and my rescue dog, Chester, keeps me active. Perhaps that's why I haven't been bothered about my single status. I'm too busy for a relationship.

Of course it doesn't stop me occasionally lusting. Which is what I am doing right now, as the sexiest man on the planet stands in our reception area.

I had glanced up when I heard the door open, double blinking when I spotted him, and now I'm trying not to stare.

Heat floods my cheeks as he glances in my direction and our eyes meet, then, when he flashes a white-toothed grin and winks at me, my belly drops and my legs quake, and I nearly slide off my chair into a big puddle of drool.

His gaze lingers and I barely notice my boss, Tara, rushing out to greet him. I'm pretty certain my mouth is still open as they disappear into her office, the door closing behind them.

Right now, Tara Lemon is the luckiest woman on the planet.

Although we weren't introduced, I know exactly who the man is.

Duncan Stone.

He's a freaking A-list movie star.

Okay, well, a retired movie star. He stepped away from the film industry a couple of years ago, instead turning his attention to social causes. Funding a number of projects he said were close to his heart, particularly those involving underprivileged kids. Despite his own poor upbringing, he had managed to claw his way to the top, and he wanted to give the opportunities he had missed out on to those he believed most needed it.

On screen, he often played the anti-hero, both in gritty dramas and star-studded blockbusters, and he has brought that persona into the real world. A bit rough and ready, and not squeaky clean, but a celebrity keeping it real. A hero for the people.

'He was checking you out.' My work colleague and partner in crime, Juliette Bellamy, pops her head up from behind her monitor, her eyes wide and her tone excited. 'Did you see him wink at you?'

I try to act casual, ignoring the fact my tummy is somersaulting. 'He's Duncan freaking Stone. You've seen him on TV. He probably winks at everyone.'

'No, he couldn't take his eyes off you,' Juliette insists in her bossiest French accent. 'I could feel the chemistry.'

I ignore her, determined not to read anything into it. I'm not naïve and Duncan Stone is a practised charmer. He could have anyone he wants. While I am confident enough to know I am an attractive woman, I'm also smart and understand someone of his stature is not going to be interested romantically in me.

I have always thought he was good-looking, but I have to admit he is better in the flesh. Perfectly symmetrical features with the palest of blue eyes and a chiselled jaw. His dark hair is close cropped, which only serves to showcase his beautiful face. A face I had been staring at when he bloody winked at me.

I tell myself to get a grip, to keep my feet on the ground, but it doesn't stop me grilling Tara when the meeting is over. And I barely manage to contain my excitement when I learn he is a new client, and also there's a party the following week in London he is hosting. All of the staff at Lemon Source are invited.

'You need to help us with new outfits,' Tracy Novak from finance squeaks.

She looks hopefully at Juliette, who everyone knows is the clothes horse; the one who, thanks to her Nigerian and French parentage, is striking to look at, has skyscraper legs and can pull off any outfit. She is the go-to girl for fashion advice.

'Callie is the one we need to focus on,' Juliette says matter-of-factly, bursting Tracy's bubble. 'She caught his eye.'

I had, but only briefly, and I am under no illusions. Duncan Stone probably winks at a lot of women.

Still, it doesn't stop a little bubble of excitement growing as the date of the party approaches.

\* \* \*

Juliette has helped me pick a stunning coral dress and I wear my dark-auburn hair loose, the thick waves falling around my shoulders.

I don't expect Duncan to remember me, so my belly churns with delighted nerves when he catches my eye across the room, a smile spreading across his face as he gives me an acknowledging nod. Then, later, when he asks Tara for an introduction, I fight to keep my cool, terrified of making a fool of myself in front of him.

He is being polite and I wait for him to move on to other guests, surprised when he lingers after Tara is beckoned away.

'So, tell me, Callie. What's your story?'

That's a big question and one which sends me into a tailspin panic.

What *is* my story?

I assume he wants a brief version, and does he mean in a work capacity? Because why the hell would he want to know anything personal about me? He's only making polite conversation.

How do I make my life sound interesting in just a few seconds, especially compared to the one he leads?

Playing it safe, I stick to work talk. 'I help run the social media accounts for our clients,' I begin, wavering when his smile cracks into a grin. This wasn't what he meant?

'Yes, I know. Tara told me.'

She had? Duncan had acted like he knew nothing about me when Tara introduced us.

'I meant, I want to know *your* story,' he continues.

My skin heats as his startlingly pale eyes twinkle in amusement. Even in the dim light of the room, he is close enough that I can see the dark outer circle framing the blue of his irises. The scent of his aftershave, a piney fresh smell, is short-circuiting my brain and I can't believe he is standing here in front of me. That we are having a conversation.

If he was someone I had met in a pub or club, I would confidently read his approach as a come-on. But this is Duncan Stone. Former actor, philanthropist, one of the country's most eligible bachelors – because despite his high-profile relationships, he has never married – and I am Callie Parker. I don't move in his circle. We have nothing in common, so there is no way he is interested in me in a personal way.

A waiter passes by, a tray in his hand, and Duncan snags two glasses of champagne, handing one to me.

I accept it, taking a sip and using the moment to try to calm my nerves.

'That's a pretty big question,' I manage, hoping I sound cool instead of flustered.

'I guess it is.' He studies me for a moment and I squirm under the scrutiny. 'Okay. How about smaller questions instead?'

I nod, taking a second generous sip of my drink. Smaller questions I can handle.

'Are you from Watford?'

Another nod. 'I live there now,' I tell him. 'Though I grew up in Berkhamsted.'

'Do you have family living locally?'

'Not any more. My sister, Phoebe, lives in Bath and my dad moved back to the States.'

'Back? You said you grew up in Berkhamsted.' Duncan looks confused.

'I did. Well, mostly. My dad is American. I was born in Maine, but we moved here when I was nine.'

'I see.'

As he ponders his next question, I am aware of waving behind him. Juliette and Tracy. Juliette now giving me the thumbs up. I ignore them, my cheeks burning.

'Next question?' I ask, trying to be bold.

He considers, his brow furrowing. 'Okay. Hobbies. What do you like to do when you're not working?'

That one is easy. 'Hang out with friends. Go to festivals. Walk my dog—'

'You have a dog?'

I think of my big baby Golden Retriever, Chester, at home with my neighbour, Gina. Technically, he isn't fully a retriever. There is a little lab and spaniel in there too, and he isn't actually a baby. He was seven when I adopted him.

The plan had never been to get a dog and I had only been at the rescue centre with a friend who was donating some old blankets.

Of course we decided to say hi to all the animals while we were there.

Big mistake.

Chester's doleful expression had tugged at my heartstrings the moment I saw him and his story was so sad, his previous adored owner having passed away. After a couple of sleepless nights worrying about him, I went back to the shelter to fill in the paperwork.

I wouldn't have been able to do it without the help of Gina, who is retired and had offered to look after him while I was at work. Gina and her husband lost their little terrier last year and she was insistent I would be doing them a favour too.

'He is the best decision I've ever made,' I say now, my tone wistful. 'He wasn't planned, but I couldn't leave him in the rescue centre. I love him to bits.'

Duncan nods, but doesn't ask anything more about Chester, instead swiftly moving on. 'Right, pineapple on a pizza? Yes, or hell no?'

Maybe he isn't an animal person.

I shrug the thought away, telling myself it doesn't matter.

I can tell from the glint in his eye that he is flirting with me now and Chester slips from my mind as I finish the champagne, my confidence growing. 'Not my first choice of topping, but I don't hate it. What about you?'

'Food of the Devil.'

'So you're a pineapple snob then?' I confirm, grinning.

'Yes. Yes, I am,' he agrees, seeming amused by my comment. He finishes his own drink before summoning a waiter and replacing our empty flutes with full ones. Smiling, he toasts me. 'Okay. Final question.'

'Go for it.'

'Callie. Is that your actual name or is it short for something?'

I used to get asked this a lot, but not so much these days, as Callie now seems to be a name in its own right. Nevertheless, it's not my birth name.

'It's short for Micaela,' I say, screwing up my nose. 'But no one calls me that except my dad. His name is Michael and I think he had hoped for a son. He got me instead, so I guess he had to compromise.'

'I like Micaela,' Duncan says softly. 'It's a pretty name and it suits you. You should use it.'

For the first time tonight, I don't like the conversation.

'I prefer Callie,' I say a little stiffly.

It's silly, but he's touched a nerve and I don't like being told what name I should use. Callie was my mum's nickname for me, and after she passed away, it was the moniker I wanted to go by. I was always closer to Mum than Dad and, it might sound stupid, but it helps a little with the loss, making it feel like she is close by.

Of course, Duncan knows none of this and I have no intention of dumping it on him when we've only just met. It's personal and I doubt he would be interested anyway.

Perhaps there is something in my expression to warn him off the topic, or maybe it's the slightly awkward pause in conversation, but he seems to realise he has said the wrong thing, smoothly moving on. 'I know I said final question, but I have one more.'

I relax a little, feeling foolish. I overreacted. 'Go on,' I push, playing along.

'Favourite flavour ice cream?'

A fun question, and although I take a moment to consider, there is a clear winner. 'Chocolate fudge.'

Duncan's eyes lock on mine and there is heat in his gaze. 'What do you say about sneaking out of here?'

My eyes widen in surprise. Does he mean what I think he means?

'You want to leave the party?' He has caught me off guard and I almost stammer out the question.

'Are you game?' His smile widens as he takes our glasses, putting them down on a passing tray. 'Come on. There's somewhere I want to show you.'

* * *

Apparently, it is okay to leave your own party when it's in full swing. That is what Duncan assures me as we sit in a booth across from one another in the little café he has brought me to, long spoons dipping into the best ice cream I have ever tasted.

Perhaps it is so good because Duncan Stone is sitting opposite me, or maybe it simply is fantastic ice cream.

He knows the place well because the man who served us greeted him like a long-lost relative and he has a preferred seat.

The high-backed booths offer a degree of privacy from the other customers. Only one couple notices us and I am aware of them frequently looking over. Eventually, the woman plucks up courage to approach our table, shyly asking for a selfie.

Duncan is great with her and patient too, asking me to take the picture. He chats away with the woman, Susie, sounding genuinely interested in what she has to say, as I snap half a dozen shots.

'Thank you so much,' Susie beams at us both before heading back to the man who is waiting for her.

'I guess you must get that a lot,' I say, turning my attention back to my ice cream, which is now a pool of liquid in the bottom of the bowl. I scoop a spoonful up, savouring the creamy chocolate fudge flavour as I wait for his answer.

He shrugs. 'It goes with the territory and I guess I'm used to it. I wouldn't be where I am today if it wasn't for my fans. It's not a hardship to give something back to them.'

He has such a great attitude to his fame and there is nothing pompous about him at all. He was kind and respectful to Susie, and doesn't seem to have an ounce of arrogance.

I allow my mind to wander forward towards what comes next? Does he plan to kiss me? I imagine how it would feel to have his lips against mine, to have his hands caressing over my skin. To touch him. To taste him.

'Callie?'

I realise he is looking at me, and has asked a question, and my face flames as I look into his beautiful blue eyes. 'Sorry, what did you say?'

'You were miles away. What were you thinking about?'

'Um, nothing really. Just how nice this is.'

He looks amused and for a horrified moment, I wonder if he knows what I was thinking. 'I told you they had the best ice cream here.'

'They do,' I agree.

'Are you ready to go? I know we snuck away, but unfortunately I can't be missing for too long.'

He wants to go back?

My bubble bursts.

Of course he has to return to the party. He's throwing it for one of his charities and, although he made a speech at the start of the evening, they will expect him to be present and mingling with the guests. If he stays away too long, he is going to be missed.

'Yes, of course.' I keep my tone breezy, masking my disappointment.

'Thank you for escaping with me for a little while. I enjoyed it.'

'I enjoyed it too. Thank you for bringing me here.'

Okay, so I didn't get to kiss him, but how many women can say they've enjoyed an ice cream date with Duncan Stone?

\* \* \*

Back at the party, I barely see Duncan for the rest of the night, only catching odd glimpses as he works the room. On one occasion, we make eye contact, and he winks, giving me a sizzling smile.

'Where did you disappear to?' Juliette demands, appearing by my side and dragging me off to the loos, where Tracy and our other friend, Aarna Kapoor, are waiting. 'I know you snuck off, and a certain Mr Stone was missing in action too.'

I tell them about the ice cream trip, but make them promise not to say anything to anyone else, and Tracy squeals.

'I knew it. I told you he likes you.'

Does he? He never asked for my number.

Duncan isn't anywhere to be seen at the end of the evening, so I don't get to say goodbye. Instead, I reluctantly leave with the others for the journey home.

I stew over our encounter all weekend and when I arrive in work Monday morning, the office is buzzing with gossip from the party. Juliette has kept my secret, but it doesn't stop her giving me knowing looks throughout the morning. When the flowers arrive, she takes delivery of them, sauntering over to my desk with a big smirk on her face. A huge bouquet of roses, lilies and daisies.

My face heats, realising everyone is looking my way.

'Read the card,' Juliette demands, pulling it from the arrangement and thrusting the envelope into my hand.

Somewhere between embarrassed and excited, I rip it open and glance over the words.

I enjoyed your company Friday night. Now you know you can trust me with ice cream, will you trust me with dinner? Duncan.

A mobile number is written beneath the message.

'Oh my God, Callie.' Juliette is snooping over my shoulder. 'You're going on a date with Duncan Stone.'

'What?' This is from Ross, the designer who sits in the corner and who has conveniently taken his earphones out.

'Juliette!' I hiss.

'What?' She shrugs. 'He sent you flowers. It's not a secret. Everyone's seen them.'

I suppose she is right and a small part of me wants to scream out loud that Duncan Stone is interested in me.

Still, I am protective of his privacy.

'If you become his girlfriend, I want a tour of his house. The posh country estate one I saw in *HELLO!*,' Juliette says. 'Have you seen it? It's like a castle.'

'No, but then I haven't been stalking him online.'

*Liar.*

After the party, I went home, snuggled up with Chester, and read every article I could find on Duncan, in particular focusing on those featuring past girlfriends.

I wanted to know if he has a type.

It would appear not. The women he has dated have varied in hair colour, height and build, though all are very pretty.

I also know from my online stalking that he is forty-three and a Sagittarius, that he grew up in Mile End, part of Tower Hamlets in the East End of London, the only child of a single mother. They had lived in a grubby, two-bed council flat, with no outdoor space, and he had used his first big pay cheque to buy her a beautiful new home – be still my beating heart – one she lived in until her death last year. And, of course, I have seen pictures of the country home Juliette is talking about. It has turrets.

Everyone loves Duncan. From friends in the acting world and fellow philanthropists, to members of the public who have met him. And what they love most about him is he doesn't pretend to be perfect. He was the kid who came from nothing and he has made plenty of mistakes along the way. He ran with the wrong crowd when he was a teenager and was involved in vandalism and petty theft, and even after he cleaned up his act and got his first taste of fame, he had relapses. Getting drunk on set, punching a director, and then there was the infamous time he treated his mates to a drug-fuelled orgy with high-class call girls in one of London's top hotels.

He has bounced back from all of that, though, holding up his hands and apologising to the public, and while there are rumours he still has ties with some of the dubious characters he grew up with, he now generates nothing but good press. He is an honest man who is not afraid to apologise for his flaws. He wears his heart on his sleeve, and he doesn't have secrets.

Or, at least, if he does, he keeps them well hidden.

# 4

## NOW

It was the barking that caught Nico's attention.

He had let the dogs out to pee, immediately hearing the sound coming from the cottage.

Was Callie okay?

There were no lights on he could see, but the barking was ongoing. Chester sounding frustrated rather than excited. And now his two were picking up on it. Shyla with her head up, alert, while Dash was prancing around.

It was late. Gone eleven. She wasn't going to welcome a visitor.

But if there was any trouble...

Nico knew he wouldn't rest easy unless he checked it out.

* * *

It had been Laurel's idea for Callie to come to Willow Brook Farm, and initially Nico had resisted.

He remembered his sister's friend and had nothing against her, but she wasn't his problem. Teddy, his former boss, had been gone nearly four years and Nico had his hands full with the stables. He didn't need another project.

But Laurel had been persistent, and as he'd learnt more details about Callie's situation, he had gradually relented.

She had nowhere to go. And he did have the space. After he had moved into the main house, Stable Cottage had stood empty. He would have offered it out to the stable hands who worked for him, but they all lived locally so had no need for accommodation, and although he had toyed with renting it out, he had never got around to it. If Callie needed it, then it hurt no one.

And today, he had realised how badly she needed it.

Laurel's friend, the one she had roomed with at university, and who had come to stay on more than one occasion, had been confident and bubbly. The woman Nico had collected from Norwich Train Station was meek and terrified.

He had half-heartedly agreed to drive down and pick her up, again Laurel's idea, but Callie had turned the offer down. Seeing her today, he wished he had insisted, and remembering her haunted eyes when she had first stepped off the train had him picking up his pace now.

She was safe here. His place was in the middle of nowhere and he had kept a careful eye on the rear-view mirror on the drive out to Strumpshaw. If they had been followed, he would have known about it. There was probably a perfectly innocent explanation for Chester's barking. Still, he would feel better when he knew for sure.

He followed the path to the cottage, his long, easy strides quickly eating up the distance, knocking loudly on the front door and waiting for her to answer.

Inside, the dog continued to bark.

Perhaps he should have called out before using his key, but Callie had him worried, and he let himself into the living room, noting even in the darkness that everything was how it should be.

Chester was with him immediately, clearly distressed as he ran around Nico. The retriever had been anxious and a little jumpy when he had first arrived at the farm, but he had quickly formed a bond with the other dogs, particularly Dash, and, in turn, learnt to trust Nico. He was a senior and a little slower in his reactions, but seeing Callie today had given him a new lease of life and his tail hadn't stopped thumping. So what was upsetting him now?

'Callie?'

Nico kept his voice low, not wanting to startle her, though surely she couldn't be sleeping through the dog's barking.

Had she hurt herself?

The apprehension in his gut tightened when she didn't answer and he moved through the tiny cottage, hesitating when he saw the bedroom door was wide open. His eyes had adjusted enough to the shadowy light to see the covers were rumpled, but she wasn't in the bed.

Where the fuck was she?

He was reluctant to enter her personal space, but he was worried about her. Especially when Chester darted past him into the room, heading round to the side of the bed.

Nico followed and that was where he found her. Sitting on the floor, wedged between the wall and the bedside unit, knees drawn up into the foetal position and her face pressed against them, her hands clamped over her ears.

'Callie?' He spoke louder and, seeing her flinch, quickly crouched down before her. Was she hurt? Had something happened? He could see she was trembling and he reached out to touch her arm before thinking better of it.

'Callie.' He tried again, his tone softer. 'It's me. It's Nico.'

Chester was trying to push between them, his wet nose and

tongue in her face when she slowly raised her head, wide eyes looking up.

For a moment, Nico stared back.

The blonde wig was gone.

Although he had known about the disguise plan and remembered Callie had auburn hair, it still took him by surprise to see the darker waves framing her pale face.

'What happened?' he demanded, aware his heart was racing. She had scared the hell out of him.

She double blinked. 'Nico?'

'Are you okay? What happened?'

She stared at him for a moment. 'There was knocking.'

'What? Where?'

'Someone was trying to get in.' Her voice dropped to a whisper. 'I heard them try to open the door.'

Nico's first reaction was anger, but it quickly simmered down as he considered the reliability of the woman before him. There was no reason for anyone to be visiting the cottage this late at night, and he would bet everything he owned that they hadn't been followed after leaving the train station. He had been too careful.

Was this the product of a nightmare?

Had she imagined someone was breaking in?

He was sensible enough not to voice his thoughts. Whether it had been real or fictional, she was frightened and he didn't want to risk upsetting her further. Instead, he adopted the tone he used when working with a nervous horse, nodding slowly, aware he needed to earn her trust. 'Are you okay to come with me while we check it out?'

Her voice sounded small, almost childish in tone and a little uncertain. 'Okay.'

He stopped himself from offering her a hand to get to her feet, knowing it wouldn't be appreciated. Instead, he waited for her to follow, noting Chester was sticking close by her side.

Had the dog been upset because someone had tried to break into the cottage, or was it in reaction to Callie's behaviour? At this point, Nico was unsure.

A quick look over the door and lock told him nothing was untoward, which had him leaning more to the nightmare scenario.

It was understandable. She had been through a hell of a day. Was it any wonder her imagination was running riot?

Though he was convinced no one had been trying to break in, it wouldn't hurt to tighten the security at the cottage, if for no other reason than to put her at ease. The property already had a security sensor light, but cameras and an alarm would help give her peace of mind.

He decided he would look into it in the morning.

'Why don't you come and stay in the main house tonight?' he suggested. Although there was no danger here, it might make her feel safer.

He didn't particularly want a house guest, but one night wouldn't hurt, and it didn't sit comfortably just leaving her here.

'I'll be okay, but thank you.'

He had thought she would jump at the opportunity, so her answer surprised him.

'Are you sure? It's no bother.'

'I'll be fine.' Her smile was forced, lines pulling around her worried eyes. 'Whoever it was has gone.'

She was wearing flannel pyjamas that were too big for her, the shoulders falling down her arms and the bottoms too long, and it struck him how vulnerable she looked.

Nico made a decision. 'Okay, well why don't I stay here. On the sofa,' he quickly added, in case it wasn't already clear. 'Just to be on the safe side.'

Blue eyes flashed with sudden anger, but her tone was even. 'I said I'll be fine.'

That was when he spotted the stain of red colouring her cheeks.

She was embarrassed. Now the moment had passed, he could see she was mortified at dragging him out.

He didn't push it.

'Well, you have my number if you need me. Okay?'

She met his eyes, the pout of her chin slightly stubborn. 'Okay.' Then, checking her manners: 'Thank you. I'm sorry you came out here over nothing.'

It hadn't been nothing, but he didn't say that. If anything, it had given him a better understanding of the woman he was dealing with.

Nico had assumed that he could simply move her into Stable Cottage and leave her to her own devices. Now he realised that this was a bigger commitment than he had prepared for.

*Damn you, Laurel.*

She hadn't warned him what he was taking on. He knew about Callie's past and what she was running from, but he hadn't realised how deeply scarred she was.

Of course she was going to experience some PTSD. It was an oversight on his part that he hadn't considered that.

But she was here now and she was his responsibility. Whether either of them liked it or not.

# 5

Get to Norwich, try not to draw attention to yourself, and don't get in the way.

That had been the plan, but Callie had failed miserably on the first night, and she was mortified she had disturbed Nico.

He had been kind, but she had got the impression he hadn't believed her.

Whoever she had heard outside had been real, and for several terrifying minutes, she was certain she had been found. Now she was thinking things through rationally, she knew it was impossible they could have found her so quickly, but last night she had been in a blind panic.

She had promised herself if it ever happened, she would run like hell and not stop until she found safety. Now she understood her plan needed more work.

Instead of running, she had frozen, retreating into herself and letting the panic take over. If it had been them, she would be dead, or worse.

Which was how she knew it wasn't. Because they wouldn't have stopped until they had her.

Someone had been outside, though. She had heard them at the door, then walking the perimeter of the property, footsteps crunching against gravel. The fact they had tried the door was what unsettled her most.

After Nico had left, she had moved one of the chairs to stand in front of the door, the back high enough that the handle couldn't be pulled down. Still, she had struggled to sleep and the following day, she had been both tired and overwhelmed as the magnitude of everything hit home. She had stuck close to the cottage, heading out only to let Chester pee, reading the books and magazines she found in the living room, scared to turn on the TV or browse the net, fearful of what headlines she might stumble across.

Had the plan worked? Did they believe she was dead?

Nico would be keeping an eye on the news. If there were any developments she needed to know about, he would be in touch.

She had heard from him, but only briefly. His texts were like his conversation. He didn't like to use words unless they were necessary.

All okay?

She had apologised, still mortified, and assuring him she was fine.

His response had been five words.

Shout if you need anything.

She would try her best not to.

Instead, she took things hour by hour, exploring the tiny cottage in more thorough detail when she grew tired of reading, checking the locks on the windows and looking to see if there were any good hiding places should she need them. There weren't.

Her best bet, if she needed to get out fast, was the bathroom window. The bedroom one was larger, but it only opened at the top pane. The one above the toilet had an opening that pushed out. It wasn't the biggest space, but Callie could just about fit through it, and once outside, she would be able to hide among the trees.

She slept a little easier the second night, managing to keep the bad dreams at bay, and she woke refreshed and hopeful, before the familiar nerves started to creep in.

Not today. She refused to give into them.

She had allowed herself yesterday off to adjust and regroup, but today was Saturday and, as the sun was out, she wanted to get outside to explore. Yes, she would need to be careful, but as long as she stuck to country roads, she should be fine.

A long walk with Chester exploring her new surroundings would keep her occupied and hopefully tire her out.

The jeans she found were a little baggy and the jumper too loose, but the wellington boots fitted perfectly, while the anorak, gloves and woolly hat would at least keep her warm.

Clipping on Chester's lead, Callie locked up the cottage, pocketing the key, then, rather than cutting into the woods, she followed the trail Nico had driven in on. Now she was on foot, she could see there was a small stream running along the edge of the land.

That must be where the name of the farm came from, she realised, spotting the willows overhanging the point where it widened.

There was no sign of Nico's Jeep as she passed the big house, and Shyla and Dash weren't about either. In one of the paddocks bordering the long driveway, a woman with dark, braided hair was saddling a little palomino. She glanced up as Callie neared, her expression curious, but made no attempt to say hello.

Callie didn't want to invite conversation, but also she didn't want to be rude. 'Hi,' she said as they passed, Chester wagging his tail furiously.

Now she was closer, she saw the woman was younger than she first realised. Maybe late teens, early twenties. She nodded at Callie, the faintest hint of a smile touching her lips, as her gaze flicked briefly to Stable Cottage.

For a moment, it seemed she was going to say something, but then she appeared to change her mind, her focus shifting back to the horse.

Callie left them to it, familiar anxiety surfacing as she approached the top of the driveway, aware she was leaving the safe haven of the property behind her.

She stepped out onto the narrow country lane and as there was no path, she stayed to the side of the road in case of any traffic, keeping a grip on Chester's lead as he strained ahead, excited by the new smells. For an older dog, he had a lot of life in him.

The February sky was a cloudless blue and the crisp, cold air had her glad she had wrapped up warmly. Unsure where she was going and not wanting to get lost, she stayed on the same road, enjoying being outside with her dog.

Chester had barely left her side since they had been reunited and in turn, Callie was reluctant to let him out of her sight. The six months without him had been the hardest of her life and she couldn't believe they were back together.

Before they had moved to Devon to be with Duncan, this was how they had often spent a Sunday afternoon. On countryside walks, exploring together. He was her best friend and she had missed him so much.

The road took a few curves, but the scenery stayed the same. Fields and hedges, and thickets of trees, with occasional houses scattered along the roadside. They were mostly older-style properties. A few had been modernised, and several had caravans in the gardens.

Callie had been walking for maybe fifteen minutes when she heard the sound of a car approaching from behind her, and knowing how narrow the lane was, she shortened Chester's lead and moved up onto the embankment so it could pass.

It was the first vehicle she had seen on the road, which told her how remote the location was, and as it drew alongside her, she turned to acknowledge the driver, realising the side window of the Range Rover was tinted, meaning she couldn't see inside.

Her throat instantly tightened, every muscle in her body momentarily freezing before she started to tremble. People like Duncan and Rob drove cars with blacked-out windows. This vehicle looked out of place on the quiet country lane.

It wasn't. It couldn't be...

But then it was gone, speeding into the distance, and Callie was left to try to pull herself back together as Chester whined and tugged at his lead. Her legs shook as she stepped down from the embankment and she almost lost her footing.

Part of her was tempted to turn back to the safety of the farm, but she knew she couldn't keep giving into her fear. Determinedly, she pushed on.

Slowly, her heart rate returned to normal and she had just about shaken off the experience, a few minutes later, when she approached a bend in the road and, as the view opened up, she spotted the Range Rover again. It was parked in a lay-by of what looked like the opening to a field, several yards ahead.

Why had it stopped?

Dread sat heavy in the pit of Callie's stomach as she debated her next move.

The lane was empty and they were on a stretch of road where

there were no houses. There were trees to the right and a hedge fronting the field on the side the car was parked, giving her two choices. She could either carry on forward or turn around. But even if she did that, it was a good couple of miles back to Nico's place.

She slipped her gloved hand into the anorak pocket, feeling for her phone.

Should she call him?

He hadn't appeared to be home when she had left for her walk, so he might not be close by. And if he was, it would take him at least five minutes to get here.

She had already made a fool of herself in front of him once. What was he going to think if she called him out over a second false alarm?

Still, she would rather be embarrassed than dead.

Ignoring Chester, who had plonked himself down on the tarmac and was whining in protestation at the second hold-up, Callie pulled the phone from her pocket, wanting to sob when she saw she had no signal.

Panic coiled tight in her throat as she stared at the Range Rover. There was no reason for it to have stopped, and she imagined Duncan or Rob sat inside, waiting for the right moment to strike, knowing she was vulnerable and alone.

Urging Chester to his feet, she slowly backed up, keeping her eyes on the car, expecting a sudden movement.

They must be able to see her. How far would she get before they reacted?

It was time to find out.

Readying herself, she turned and ran.

**6**

---

Callie's heart was thumping, and despite the cold, she was dripping with sweat under the jumper. As she clung to Chester's lead, she willed the elderly retriever to keep pace with her.

At first, he had no issues, perhaps because he was enjoying what he thought was a new and fun game, but slowly he began to flag, and aware he was struggling, she had no choice but to slow down.

She glanced around, looking for anywhere they could hide, but there was nowhere.

Why the hell hadn't she stayed in the grounds of the farm?

In the distance, she spotted the last house she had passed. A pink cottage with several old cars parked outside. Could she stop there and try to get help?

The sound of an engine came from behind her, getting louder as it approached.

She didn't move to the side of the road this time. Instead, she picked up pace, hating that Chester was fighting to keep up with her, and focused on the house ahead, which suddenly seemed so far away.

'Excuse me?'

The voice threw her because she didn't recognise it.

'Excuse me? Miss?'

Callie slowed, turning.

The Range Rover had stopped, a head poking out of the driver's side window. Glasses up and perched on a bald head. It was an older man, and she blinked at him, for a moment unsure if she was seeing correctly. Not Duncan or Rob. She didn't know him.

'Can you help me? I'm lost.'

He was lost? Was that why he had pulled into the lay-by and had now turned around? Had she had overreacted, assuming the worst?

She approached the car warily. This man might seem harmless, and he looked at least seventy, but she didn't know him and they were out here alone.

'I think I came off the bypass too early. I'm looking for Lingwood.'

He sounded genuinely flustered, but, unfortunately, Callie couldn't help him.

'I'm sorry, but I'm not from around here, so I'm not sure.' She pointed to the pink cottage. 'The people in the house over there might be able to help you.'

The man peered at her for a moment, as if debating whether she was telling the truth. 'Okay, thank you.'

She and Chester stepped back as he passed them again and she watched him pull over by the pink cottage, now annoyed at her reaction.

Still, it was a sobering reminder that perhaps she should stick closer to the farm.

The last stretch back was hard work and took longer than the rest of the walk altogether. Chester had earned himself some of the dog treats she had found in the kitchen cupboard and a long nap, while Callie intended to have a shower.

As they headed up the driveway, she spotted Nico's Jeep, parked alongside an unfamiliar car, and then she saw him outside the house, talking to a man and a woman. Shyla sat patiently by his side.

Callie's path took her right past them and anxiety reared its ugly head at the thought of having to interact with the newcomers. Why were they here? Did Nico know them?

He and Laurel had devised a cover story for why Callie was in Norfolk, one she had rehearsed over and over on the train journey here, but now her stomach was heavy and her mind fogging over.

She was considering cutting across the field to avoid contact, but Dash took that decision from her, appearing from nowhere and charging down the driveway as he spotted them, happy barking as he ran. And Chester, finding a new lease of life, nearly yanked Callie's arm out of her socket in a bid to meet him halfway.

The newcomers and Nico both turned at the commotion and Callie understood there would be no escaping.

Flustered, she joined the threesome outside the house, aware of the weight of Nico's stare landing on her.

'Everything okay?' he asked quietly.

Callie nodded, watching as the man he was with bent down to greet her dog.

'Chester, old fella. How are you?'

She studied him as he ruffled the soft fur behind Chester's ears, talking to him as he made a fuss. Dark, curly hair that was greying at the sides, and dark eyes that were curious as they now looked up at her.

'You've been wearing him out,' he commented, before glancing at Nico, who didn't seem in any rush to make introductions.

'Hi, I'm Faith,' the woman said after a moment, breaking what was about to become an awkward silence. She smiled warmly. 'You must be new here.'

'Hi, I...' Callie's mouth opened and closed, her well-rehearsed cover story gone from her mind, and she was grateful when Nico finally stepped in.

'This is Callie, another member of the Adams clan. She's mine and Laurel's cousin and she's staying for a while.'

'Nice to meet you, Callie.' Faith said, rolling her eyes good-naturedly at the man. 'The dog whisperer here is Ethan. Nico's best friend and his accountant, and, for better or worse, my husband.'

Ethan straightened, shaking Callie's hand. 'You have my sympathy if you're staying with Nico,' he joked. 'I bet Mr Grouchy here isn't the easiest housemate to live with.'

Callie saw a smile touch Nico's lips, though he didn't retaliate.

'I'm staying at Stable Cottage,' she corrected.

'You are?' Ethan looked surprised. 'You kept that quiet, mate,' he commented to Nico. 'I hope you cleaned it out for her.'

'It's a nice spot,' Faith pointed out.

'Yeah, but no one's been in there in years.'

'It's fine,' Callie assured him. 'I like it there.'

She was about to make her excuses to go when Faith glanced past her and smiled. 'Here she comes.'

Callie turned, spotting a young girl of about nine or ten running towards them down the track from the stables. Was she their daughter? The girl she had seen earlier with the palomino horse wasn't far behind her.

'Be careful you don't slip on the mud, Olive,' she called out.

The child, Olive, ignored her, almost losing her footing as she joined the group.

'Anya warned you to be careful,' Faith scolded mildly, catching hold of her hand. 'Did you have a good lesson?'

Olive nodded as Anya caught up. 'She's a pro, Mrs Stuart.'

'Well, she doesn't get it from me,' Faith laughed. 'I can't stay on a horse. Ethan used to ride a bit.'

'It was a long time ago and I wasn't that good.' Ethan fished his key fob out of his jacket pocket, clicking it at the car. 'We should get going.'

'Maybe you need lessons too, Mr Stuart,' Anya suggested, winking at Faith and earning a snort of laughter from her, as Ethan looked aghast at the idea.

Earlier, the girl had seemed aloof, but now she was surprisingly chatty.

On her best behaviour for her boss, Callie guessed, catching Anya glancing at Nico, who had finally cracked a grin. It transformed his face, his cheeks dimpling and a lightness in his green eyes that she hadn't seen before, as his brooding scowl was momentarily banished.

'I've seen him ride. He needs more than a lesson,' he joked.

'And on that note, we need to go.' Ethan caught hold of his daughter's free hand, tugging gently as he pulled his family towards the SUV. 'I'll give you a call next week, Nico. Nice to meet you, Callie.'

'Yes, I hope you get settled in. I'm sure we'll see you again,' Faith said.

'Bye, Mr Stuart, Mrs Stuart,' Anya called after them. So far, she had taken no notice whatsoever of Callie, but now she pinned her with a dark, curious stare.

Nico must have noticed because he was suddenly introducing them. 'Anya, this is Callie. She's staying in the cottage. Callie, Anya is one of my stable hands, so you'll see her about a bit.'

'Nice to meet you,' Callie told her, hoping the smile she gave would be reciprocated.

It wasn't, and Anya's gaze remained cool. 'Hi, Callie,' she greeted her, before turning her attention back to Nico. 'I'll go start on the bedding,' she said, heading back to the stables when he nodded.

Deciding he was missing out, Dash ditched Chester, charging after her.

Callie watched her go. 'She seems young. Has she worked with you for long?'

'She's eighteen. And yeah, for a while. She's had a few issues. Being around the horses helped calm her down.'

He didn't expand on what the issues had been and it wasn't Callie's place to ask.

As silence fell between them, Chester let out a noise that was something between a yawn and a whine.

'I should get back.'

'Callie?'

'Yes?'

'Are you sure everything's okay?'

He sounded concerned and she paused, shoulders tensing slightly. Did he have a sixth sense or something? She toyed with telling him about what had happened on her walk. She could try to joke about the encounter, even if it had scared her. After what had happened her first night though, Nico was going to start believing she was the girl who cried wolf.

It was better not to.

'Everything's fine,' she said lightly.

'Do you need anything?'

'I'm good.'

'I picked up security cameras earlier for the cottage. Can I pop by later and install them?'

He had?

'Umm, yes, okay. Thank you.'

Callie hadn't expected him to do that. He had already gone out of his way for her.

Perhaps, she mused as she walked back to her new home, Nico had taken her concerns seriously after all. Either that or he just wanted to put her at ease.

Whatever the reason, she appreciated the gesture. Especially when she unlocked the front door, stepping into the small living room and immediately picked up on the feeling that someone had been inside.

She had become accustomed to trusting her gut instinct and when something was off or about to go wrong, she tended to sense it. As did Chester, whose nose was alert for new smells.

Nothing was out of place in the living room or kitchen, but then she went through to the bedroom, and that was where she spotted the signs.

She had fastidiously straightened the duvet when making the bed, the action ingrained in her, yet it was rumpled on the side where she had slept, as if someone had been sat there.

And that was when she spotted her photograph of her mother. The picture frame that sat on the bedside table had been twisted, as if someone had picked it up to look at, then placed it back in the wrong position.

Callie's mouth was dry. Who had been in the cottage?

*My cash.*

The thought came to her and, panicking, she opened the top drawer of the table, almost sobbing with relief when she saw the black bag. She counted through the money, her fingers shaking. None of the notes had been taken, and she let out a breath, the tension easing slightly in her shoulders.

Someone *had* been in the cottage, though. She knew she wasn't being paranoid. But if she told Nico, would he believe her?

He was the only other person with a key. She knew he had one, because he had used it to let himself in the night she arrived.

That had been different, though. He had no need to come here while Callie was out. And if for some reason he had, surely he would have mentioned it just now.

Unless he hadn't wanted her to know.

The ugly thought crept forward from her subconscious.

No. He was helping her. He was Laurel's brother. He could be trusted.

*Her adopted brother*, she reminded herself, recalling snippets of the conversation she had overheard from Laurel's mum.

*He's seen things.*

*No one knows what that poor kid went through or the scars it left.*

She was being mean, especially after everything he had just done for her.

Nico Adams had her best interests at heart. Didn't he?

## 7

BEFORE

'Odds or evens?' Duncan asks.

'Evens,' I reply, a smile on my face as I watch him roll the dice.

He likes to play games. I learnt that about him early on in our relationship. It's a bit of fun, he had told me, and keeps things fresh. The dice is a favourite of his, and he always carries them with him to add anticipation to the dullest of situations.

Where shall we eat?

What movie should we watch?

Where shall we go today?

I pick odds or evens. If I win, I choose. If I lose, the decision is his.

He always gets to set the question, that has never been up for negotiation, and as we have become more familiar with each other, these have become bolder.

If I win, I get to choose what you wear tonight.

If you lose, you have to wait on me all weekend.

To mix things up further, sometimes the number is an indicator.

You have to drink six shots of my choosing.

I get to spank you ten times.

Over the four months we have been together, I have learnt Duncan is good at getting his own way. He persuaded me to give up my house and move in with him within six weeks of meeting him, and because he lives in Dartmouth, down in Devon, in the turreted house I had seen online, he talked Tara into allowing me to work from home. I hadn't planned on doing either of those things so quickly, but he is smooth and convincing. What Duncan wants, Duncan gets, and I guess I have been caught up in his whirlwind.

So perhaps I gave in easier than I should have, but he is an addiction and difficult to say no to. Besides, we get on so well and his house, The Old Rectory, is big. A sprawling, old building set in several acres of grounds. It's just the two of us in the main house with Chester, but Duncan has a housekeeper, Shirley, who comes in four days a week, and his security man, Rob, lives in an attached annexe.

It is very much Duncan's house still, filled with his things and lots of photos of his late mother, and at times, I feel like I am a guest. I think it's because I am in awe at the size of the place and of Duncan himself. I'm sure it will gradually become my home too as I put my own mark on it.

I have extended an invite to Phoebe to come and stay one weekend, but she is always busy and we haven't been able to schedule a date yet. I want her to meet Duncan and get her seal of approval before Dad flies over in December.

He and Duncan are both big personalities and used to getting their own way, and it worries me a little how that is going to work out. I need to get Pheebs on my side.

I know I am the luckiest girl alive having a boyfriend like Duncan Stone, and I don't want my dad to mess things up.

I watch Duncan now as he rolls the dice on the bedside table.

We were out late last night meeting up with old friends of his and I was anxious, wanting to make a good first impression. Duncan is always telling me I have a lot to learn and I can sense his displeasure if I say the wrong thing or act inappropriately. I don't like embarrassing him. After all, he could have anyone, but he has chosen me. He often reminds me of this. Not to be unkind; he is looking out for me, aware that because he is in the public eye, people will judge me.

I think his friends liked me, but I was more than a little tipsy. The double gin had been to calm my nerves, but then Duncan had kept topping my wine glass up during dinner and I lost track of how much I drunk.

I was asleep this morning when he brought me a cup of tea and far too groggy to discuss how we should spend our Saturday.

'Are you hungover?' he had asked, teasing.

'A little,' I confessed.

'Perhaps you should have watched how much you had to drink last night.'

The accusation jarred. We both know he was the one topping up my glass all night and I quickly reminded him of that. For the briefest moment, his frown had darkened and a tiny flicker of unease stroked my spine, but then the smile was back on his face and as he pulled the dice from his pocket, I convinced myself I imagined it.

I watch the dice land now. A four and a five.

He gets to choose.

No surprise there, as he often wins. He must be lucky.

'So, what do you have in mind?' I ask, trying to keep my tone light. I would rather stay in bed.

He considers for a moment before nodding. 'Finish your tea,' he instructs.

I down the rest of my drink, before getting up and heading over to the giant, walk-in wardrobe.

'No need to get dressed. Come with me.'

There's not?

'Okay, well just let me use the loo first.'

My bladder is bursting. I could use a shower too.

'That can wait. Just come. Please.'

Chester, who has been asleep in his bed on the floor, looks up. Seeing us leaving the room, he starts to follow.

'Stay!' Duncan orders.

The dog halts, but he whines and looks at me.

'He can come,' I argue.

'No, he needs to wait here.'

'But—'

'Callie, please. I need you to come with me. He will be fine here.'

Unsure what is so urgent, I shrug and tell Chester to lie down. He does as he's told, though doesn't look happy about it. He and Duncan have never warmed to each other. I keep telling myself it's early days and to give it time.

Ignoring the stab of guilt, I follow Duncan from the bedroom and across the landing to the central staircase. The October morning is chilly and I wish I had stopped to grab my robe and slippers. The cotton negligee offers no warmth.

As we head down the stairs, I am wracking my brain, trying to work out what he has planned that is so urgent I couldn't stop to pee. If we're leaving the house, I need clothes. And even if his plan involves staying home, I want something warmer on.

It's a Saturday, so Shirley isn't in, and I'm glad. I like her fine, but it would be embarrassing if I ran into her while I am practically undressed.

I follow Duncan along the hallway to the huge kitchen. The wide, black and white tiles are cold beneath my bare feet. We pass the pantry and head into the back passageway that leads to the utility room, mud room and garage, and by now, my curiosity is piqued.

'What are we doing?' I ask, as he pushes open the utility-room door.

'You'll see. In you go.'

I do so without hesitation, immediately turning, ready with more questions. The slam of the door in my face makes me flinch and for a moment, I stare in disbelief, but then the lock catches and I grab the handle.

The door won't open.

'Duncan, what are you doing? Let me out.'

There is no response.

I try the handle again. 'This isn't funny. Open the bloody door.'

I am greeted with nothing but silence. Then I hear his footsteps. They are getting further away.

Has he seriously just left me in here?

It's a prank. It has to be. He will come back in a second and open the door with a grin on his face. Gotcha!

So I wait and my bladder burns. At first, adrenaline from the shock is keeping me warm, but as the minutes tick by, the cold takes hold. It starts at my toes, icy cold on the tiles, but quickly works its way up my body.

I start to pace the small room in an attempt to keep warm, rubbing at my goose-pimpled arms.

Shirley takes care of laundry, so I have only been in here once or twice. There is one window, but the opening is tiny, and no other doors. Just cupboards, a sink, and a washing machine. There is only one way out and it is locked.

As I left the bedroom without putting on my watch on and my phone isn't with me, I have no concept of time, and as I continue to pace, my confusion gives way to anger.

This isn't funny. It's not a joke. How dare he do this?

The sound of footsteps returning has me pressing against the door.

'Duncan. Let me the hell out of here!'

Silence, but I know he's outside.

I pound on the heavy wood. 'You've crossed a line. Open the fucking door.'

'No. You crossed a line, Mica.'

He stopped calling me Callie about a week after I moved in with him. He kept using Micaela, despite knowing it pissed me off, and I would glower at him each time. Often, he would trail off after the first two syllables. *Mi-cay.* Gradually, he started using Mica and I was sick of correcting him. I have reasoned that at least Mica is unique to him. His own special moniker for me, even if it bristles.

I almost don't hear him using it as he speaks now, because his tone is calm and reasonable against my anger.

'What?' I bluster, needing him to repeat.

'You crossed a line.'

'What bloody line? What the hell are you talking about?' I can hear the panic in my voice and try to dial it back with deep breaths. I just want him to let me out.

'You disrespected me.'

'What? When?' My heart is thumping and I am so confused.

'Last night in the restaurant. You were an embarrassment. I introduced you to my friends and you turned into a vulgar drunk. How do you think that made me feel?'

Is he crazy? He was the one pouring the drinks. I tried to stop him at one point, but he insisted on filling my glass. And now he's blaming me?

I try to keep my tone reasonable. 'I wasn't vulgar and I wasn't drunk. Yes, I was a little tipsy, but I told you I didn't want another drink.'

'That's typical of someone with a drink problem. Blame everyone else.'

'I don't have a bloody drink problem!' I snap the words in rage, unable to help myself. He is making me so angry. How dare he falsely accuse me? I like a drink, but it's not a crutch for me. I can easily go without.

'I think you need to be taught a lesson.'

What? Trepidation takes the edge off my anger. Although he sounds calm, there is a cruelty in his tone I haven't heard before.

'Duncan, please unlock the door. Let's talk about this face to face.'

'I don't think that's a good idea.'

'Yes, it is. You need to let me out. It's not funny.'

'I'm not trying to be funny, Mica. I'm fully aware this is not a laughing matter.'

Why is he doing this? He can't keep me locked in here.

I try the handle, then bash my fist against the wood, hurting my knuckles as fresh panic builds.

'Open the damn door!'

'I think you need to calm yourself down. You're scaring me.'

'I'm scaring you?' I am in shock. How can I be scaring him? I'm five foot five and he is over six foot and nearly double my weight. 'You're not the one locked in the bloody utility room.'

He is silent for a moment, and when he answers, his voice is emotionless. I barely recognise it.

'I think you should use this time wisely to get your anger under control. Consider your actions and understand why you are in there. Once you're acting rationally, I will let you out.'

My temper evaporates as fear takes over. He can't leave me in here.

And what about Chester? He needs feeding and walking.

I point this out now.

'He's a dog. He's fine,' is all I get back.

'Duncan, please don't do this. It's freezing in here, and I need the loo.'

'I'm sorry, Mica. Trust me. This hurts me more than it does you.'

'Let me out, please.' My voice cracks on the last word, humiliating tears blinding me. How can this be happening?

I continue to beg, but he doesn't respond. After his footsteps have faded, I sink to the floor, my head about to explode as I take everything in.

A short while later, I hear the whir of the mechanical garage door open and the engine of Duncan's Porsche, and I am on my feet again.

Is he going out? He can't leave me.

I open the tiny window and see his car drive by, Rob Jolly sitting in the passenger seat, and I yell and bang on the window, but then they are gone.

Over the hours that follow, I go from shell-shocked and scared to furious and humiliated. There is nothing in the room to help me keep warm. There is no tumble dryer and Chester's dog towel and our coats are kept in the mud room next door.

I can hear my goldy the other side of the door. He came running to find me as soon as Duncan left and I have no idea if he's been fed. He keeps barking and whining at me to come out, thinking I am hiding away from him, and it's wracking me with guilt as I talk to him, trying to reassure him that everything is okay.

How have I never seen this side to Duncan before?

He can't do this to me and get away with it. At some point, he is going to have to come back and let me out of here, and then our relationship is over. I can't stay with him. Not after today. Not after what he has done.

The real humiliation comes when I realise I can't hold my bladder any longer.

I am so uncomfortable and it's making my belly ache.

I had hoped Duncan would have been back to open the door, but perhaps it was his intention to place me in this predicament. After all, he had refused my request to use the loo.

Knowing I will have to use the sink, I force myself up and hop onto the counter so I am positioned above the basin, sitting on it like it's a toilet. Fresh chills tremble through me as I pee and my cheeks burn in humiliation.

The relief of an empty bladder is momentarily distracting, but as I run the tap and use bleach to try to get rid of the stench of my urine, I hate Duncan Stone.

I am so cold and my teeth have been chattering for hours. I am hungry too, and my brain is throbbing with the headache from hell.

Huddling back down in my corner, I wait. Chester has fallen quiet, though I know he is the other side of the door.

Eventually, darkness creeps into the room, but I don't want to move to switch on the light. I am too cold.

By the time I hear Duncan's car return, I am in complete darkness and immediately on edge.

What is going to happen when he opens the door?

What if he leaves me in here?

I hear a woof and the clipping of Chester's toenails on the hard floor, and I wait for the sound of Duncan's footsteps, but they are not forthcoming.

Anger comes, but I don't have the energy for it, and I'm scared that if he knows I am still mad with him, he will make me stay in here. I need to be compliant. At least for now.

When he does eventually return, I remain seated on the floor.

The constant shivering has tensed my muscles. I'm not sure I can stand, and I can barely feel my toes.

The door unlocks, the crack of light growing wider.

'Mica.' His voice is full of concern as he crouches down, studying me as if I am a wounded animal.

There is no trace of the man who left me locked in here, which only adds to my confusion. I honestly don't know how to react. Emotion takes over and I choke out a sob.

'Oh Mica. It's okay, baby.' He strokes my hair and wipes my tears as he soothes with gentle words and I could almost be mistaken for thinking that someone else had locked me in here. 'You're freezing.'

He is wrapping himself around me now and hugging me to him. Part of me wants to push him away. I can't forgive him for what he has done, and I don't want him touching me, but I am so cold and his body heat is like a radiator. I lean into him, needing more, and then he is scooping me up like I'm a little broken bird.

'I'm so sorry. We were only supposed to be gone for an hour. I had a call from Leon Clements saying he was in town and you know we've been trying to schedule a meeting, and how important it is. I didn't dare unlock the door while you were still so angry. I knew we needed to talk, so I figured we would when I got back, but one thing led to another and the meeting overran. I couldn't just leave. This project is too important, Mica.'

He is talking urgently as he carries me upstairs, needing to convince me how bad he feels. Leon Clements is an acclaimed movie director and Duncan has been trying to persuade him to film a series of commercials for a charity project.

But it's all irrelevant. He should never have left me locked in the room.

'Where's Chester?' I manage, my voice not much more than a whisper.

My dog is my priority right now. He has been left alone too with no food or exercise, and it worries me that he seems to have disappeared.

'He's fine. Rob has taken him out and then he's going to feed him. And I'm going to take care of you,' he says, carrying me into our bedroom, through into our en suite bathroom. The tub has already been filled and it bothers me that letting me out of the utility room wasn't his first priority. He lowers me into the warm water and I note he has filled it with my favourite fragranced bath soak. As the heat slowly thaws my frozen body, he eases me out of the negligee and uses a sponge to soap my back.

His movements are all careful and loving and I want to ask who the monster I encountered this morning was, but I can't stop crying.

After my bath, he gently dries me, wrapping me in a big, fluffy robe and moving me to the bed.

'Are you hungry?'

I was. I have been starving to the point of belly cramps, but now it seems to have passed and I just feel sick. Perhaps it is the shock.

I shake my head.

'You have to try to eat something, Mica. You haven't had anything all day.' He presses a kiss to my forehead. 'Wait here,' he says, before leaving the room, and, alone, I finally have a second to think.

Duncan is a big personality and I know he likes to have his own way. He is decisive and, dare I say it, he can be a little controlling, but that is only because he is used to being in charge. And it is balanced by kindness and generosity. He looks after what is his.

This morning, he was unbelievably cruel, yet now he is going to the other extreme, mollycoddling and smothering me with affection. But it doesn't forgive what he did. I don't care if Leon was in town. He should never have left me a prisoner in the house.

Chester bounds into the room, tail wagging furiously as he jumps up onto the duvet beside me, and my heart lifts. Duncan hates him getting on the bed, but in this moment, I don't care, and I hug my fur baby close, knowing he has suffered today too.

As I press a kiss against his neck, I glance at the clock on Duncan's bedside table, shocked to see it has gone 7 p.m. I was locked in the utility room for over ten hours. That is unforgiveable.

I watch him return to the room with a tray and he shoots a disapproving look in Chester's direction. For a moment, my stomach clenches, certain he is going to say something, but then his frown softens and he sets the tray down beside the bed. He has made me a toasted cheese and tomato sandwich and the waft of the food hits my nostrils, awakening my taste buds. My stomach growls. Maybe I do have an appetite. When he pushes it towards me, though, I shake my head.

He doesn't get to win me over with food.

Instead, I shuffle down under the duvet.

'I'm really tired.'

As soon as my head hits the pillow, I close my eyes.

I know we need to have a conversation about what happened this morning, but I can't face it right now. I need to consider where I can go if I leave here, and I want him to understand what he has done. We will talk in the morning.

I wait for him to leave, but he remains sat on the edge of the bed, his fingers lightly caressing my hair.

'You're angry with me.' He speaks eventually and I hold my breath for a moment, waiting for him to elaborate. 'You have every right to be, but know you won't ever hate me more than I hate myself right now. I crossed a line and did something terrible, and I am so, so sorry.'

Okay, so we're doing this right now.

My eyes open and I glance up at him. 'You hurt me and you

scared me. You left me locked in a room for hours. I don't care if you had a meeting and couldn't get away. You should never have left me in there in the first place. My dog was upset and I couldn't comfort him. I was cold and hungry, and I couldn't go to the bathroom. Why would you do that to me?'

I know he can hear the temper behind my words and I watch him closely, unsure how he is going to react. Today, he displayed the behaviour of a control freak. Of a gaslighting narcissist. This is not the man I fell in love with. What I don't expect is for his eyes to become bright with the sheen of tears.

'I was wrong and I'm sorry. I should have talked to you last night and told you how I felt. Instead, I let it build up and then this morning, I overreacted and did something stupid. I don't know what came over me and I'm so ashamed.'

As he should be.

It annoys me that he is talking about last night like it was my fault and I open my mouth to speak, but he hasn't finished.

'I was excited about you meeting my friends and I wanted everything to be perfect, for them to love you as much as I do. Jimmy made a joke before we left and asked if I wanted the number of his AA sponsor for you. I should have laughed it off, but instead, I was embarrassed and stewed over it all night. It was such a stupid thing, but I managed to blow it up in my head like it was some kind of big deal. I was angry with him and instead, I took it out on you.'

I am torn between humiliation and fresh anger. 'I don't have an alcohol problem. When have you ever seen me drunk before last night?'

'I think it was the shock of seeing you like that.'

'Duncan, you were the one who kept topping up my glass.'

'I know and I'm sorry. I'm just trying to explain to you why I reacted badly. It's not an excuse. But you know me. I have never done anything to hurt you. Something happened. It was like a switch. And, honestly, it scared me as much as it did you. I hate what I did to you. I love you so much and I never wanted to hurt you.' He is openly crying now, and I can see his remorse. I can't help but soften, even if I can't entirely forgive him.

'I need to sleep.' I close my eyes, unable to deal with this right now.

I hear him get up and whistle to the dog, who obediently leaves my arms to get down from the bed, and I think he is going to leave the room, but moments later, the mattress dips and he lies down beside me. I am facing the wall and instinctively tense when his body wraps around me. Two spoons.

'I love you so much, Mica,' he whispers. 'I'm going to spend the rest of my life making you happy and I promise I will never do anything to hurt you ever again.'

I can feel my resolve cracking.

Am I going to forgive him so easily?

He has accepted that what he did was wrong. And he is right. He's never given me cause for concern before. Although his behaviour this morning verged on abusive, this was an anomaly. Everyone loves Duncan and his ex-girlfriends speak highly of him from the articles I have read online. He dated the American model, Kacey Lewis, on and off for years and she has never said anything negative about him.

Do I want to throw away something that is mostly wonderful because of one awful day?

He is kind and generous and thoughtful, and he made a terrible mistake.

But everyone deserves a second chance. Don't they?

# 8

---

NOW

Two cameras. One for the front of the cottage and one at the back, outside her bedroom window, overlooking the woodland.

Callie watched as Nico installed them, wondering if they were supposed to protect her or keep an eye on her, as she thought back to the cameras at The Old Rectory. There were dozens around the house and she had learnt to dread them, aware they were all watching her.

But this was different. Nico was putting them up to help her feel safe...

Unless he was the one who had been in the cottage that morning. If he was snooping around while she was out, wouldn't this make it easier for him, knowing when she was coming or going?

Annoyed with herself for doubting him, she shook the thought away, but then, when he was done, he came inside and asked for her phone.

Callie's eyes widened. 'Why do you want it?'

'To put the app on your phone for the cameras.'

'On my phone?'

'Yes. You need it to view the footage.' His tone was patient. 'I can tell you what to do if you would rather link it yourself.'

Callie wouldn't have a clue where to start.

Reluctantly, she handed her phone over. Watching as he studied the device intently, thumbs moving over the screen and brow furrowed as he loaded the app.

She had first met Nico was when she had started university. She had been in her dorm room unpacking, jittery with both excitement and nerves, and curious who her roommate was going to be. Laurel had arrived with him in tow, and when they had first walked into the dorm, both heaving boxes, Callie had assumed he was Laurel's boyfriend, so had been secretly pleased when Laurel introduced him as her brother.

Back then, she'd had a bit of a crush on him. He had the whole brooding thing going on and earthy green eyes that had locked on hers intently when she spoke to him, which had caused a kaleidoscope of butterflies to start fluttering in her belly.

And he was nice to her too, helping her to bring the rest of the things up from her car, aware she had no family with her.

That was the problem with having an important surgeon for a father. Michael Parker was always in demand and he couldn't free up his schedule to drive Callie to Nottingham. It would be character building, he told her. April had never offered to take her, but then Callie supposed she considered it outside of her remit. Meanwhile, all of her dropped hints to Phoebe had gone unnoticed.

When the day had arrived, Callie had just sucked it up and driven herself. She surmised that it would be handy to have her car close, as well as a good mark of independence.

How things had changed.

Back then, she had been confident and carefree, and over that first year, she had become firm friends with Laurel, enjoying the term breaks when she was invited to stay with Laurel's family. It beat going home to an often empty house, and okay, part of the appeal was getting to spend time with Nico. Though that felt like a lifetime ago.

She had known Nico Adams for sixteen years now, but their paths had only ever crossed occasionally. Just because he was a face from her past and was helping her didn't make him trustworthy. And Callie knew her judgement was off when it came to attractive men.

'Will you be able to see the cameras?'

She hadn't meant to blurt the question out and only realised she had when Nico paused, looking over at her.

'Sorry?'

'The cameras, will you watch them... I mean the footage... will you have it. Be able to see it... on your phone?'

She cursed herself as she tripped over the words, but caught his flicker of hesitation before he answered.

'It's up to you. The app is on my phone. I can keep it on there or I can delete it. Whatever you prefer, Callie.'

If she hadn't asked, would he have told her, or would he have just kept the app and spied on her?

'Were you down here earlier?' She didn't want to doubt him, but she had to know.

When his eyes narrowed, she elaborated.

'Did you let yourself into the cottage while I was out walking Chester this morning?'

She watched his reaction for giveaways in case he didn't tell her the truth. There had been a weight of accusation in her words and she could see he was assessing, trying to figure out what was behind them.

If he was guilty, he was an accomplished liar, because he gave nothing away. 'No, I wasn't. Where's this coming from, Callie?'

She wanted to believe him, but she wasn't the best judge of character.

'Just forget about it.' She huffed out a sigh and looked away.

'Why do you think I was here?'

He wasn't letting it drop and she shoved her hand in her hair in frustration. She knew he had doubted her that first night. He was going to think she was crazy. And perhaps he was right.

'It's not important. I shouldn't have said anything.'

She snuck a glance up at him, immediately regretting it when she found herself caught in his sharp, green gaze.

'Has something else happened?'

'No, I—'

'I want to help you, but I can't unless you tell me.'

His tone was so reasonable and he made it sound simple.

'I think someone was here, inside.' She broke eye contact again, unable to look at him while she made the accusation, unsure how he would react. 'The lock wasn't damaged and you have a key.'

'I do, but I promise you this is the first time I've been here today.'

Was he angry that she didn't trust him? He sounded more curious.

'Does anyone else have a key?' she demanded.

'Not that I'm aware of. What makes you think someone was inside?'

Callie's face heated. 'The duvet was rumpled and my picture frame was moved.'

'Can you show me?'

He didn't believe her, she was certain of it, but she led him through to the bedroom anyway.

Pausing in the tiny hallway, she motioned for him to go into the room, hovering in the doorway as she pointed to the bed. 'See.'

He took a moment before commenting, rubbing his hand

across the nape of his neck, then turning to face her. 'Is it possible you left the bed this way? It's easy for the duvet to get creased.'

'No. I know how to make a bed.' And she had learnt over the last year and a half that creases were unacceptable.

'Okay.' He nodded. 'Well, what about Chester? He hasn't jumped up there?'

'No!' Callie's frustration was growing. 'And even if he had, it doesn't explain the picture frame. I left it facing towards the bed. Someone had turned it so it was towards the door.'

'Okay,' Nico repeated.

She wished he would stop saying that. It wasn't bloody okay. She was supposed to be safe here. 'I know you don't believe me.'

'I never said I didn't.'

'You're questioning me.' Her voice was rising with the edge of hysteria. 'I know how I left everything in here. Stop trying to make me doubt myself.'

'I'm not doubting you. I'm trying to help you.'

'You would say that while you're trying to make me think I'm going crazy.'

'Callie.'

Nico took a sudden step towards her, reaching out, and she flinched, jumping back. The action had his eyes widening and he seemed to take himself in check, moving away from her and putting his free hand in his pocket. When he spoke, his voice was calm, his words measured.

'I know you need time to trust me. I have to earn that. I get it.' He held up her phone. 'I'm going to put the main house cameras on here, okay? They cover all exit points and there are a couple in the house and over at the stables. You'll be able to see where I am. And now the cottage cameras are live, you'll be able to see if me or anyone else is approaching.'

Callie nodded, watching him carefully. He was saying all the right things.

'Do you want me to delete the camera app on my phone?' he asked. 'Then you'll be in control.'

She considered, then nodded, pleased he didn't try to change her mind, holding up his handset so she could watch as he binned the app.

'I want you to feel safe here. You are safe here. I promise.'

Was she?

If it wasn't Nico, then who had been inside?

The front door had been locked and there was no damage, which suggested the intruder had used a key.

If Nico was telling her the truth, then who had it been?

## 9

As winter thawed into spring, Callie settled into a routine. She walked Chester morning and evening, sticking to the grounds of the farm, too frightened to leave after her last experience, and she grew familiar with the people who worked for Nico. Anya mostly kept to herself, though she was never rude, while Jodie, the woman Callie had seen from the Jeep the day she'd arrived, and the other stable hand, Toby, who clearly had a soft spot for Anya from the way he was always following her around, were much friendlier, always saying hello if she passed their way, and sometimes stopping for a brief chat. If they were curious or had questions about why Callie was living at Stable Cottage, they didn't ask, and she assumed Nico must have given them the same story he had told Ethan and Faith.

She also became familiar with the horses. Several of them came and went, temporary residents who were here to be trained, but four of them belonged to Nico. There was a beautiful white mare, she learnt from Jodie was classed as grey, the little palomino who was often in a paddock with a cute-looking black pony, and finally, there was a handsome gelding. Red. He was a stunning chestnut colour with three white socks and a blaze running down his nose, and watching how patient Nico was as he worked with him occupied several of Callie's afternoons.

The rest of the time, she tried to keep herself busy. She cooked, she cleaned and attempted to make the little cottage feel like home. Picking daffodils and wildflowers that grew on the edge of the woods for the vase that sat on the kitchen windowsill, and overcoming her fear of listening to the news so she could have the radio on, the music and chatter banishing the silence. Nico had told her there had been a flurry of news coverage when the press realised her connection to Duncan Stone and that initially, Duncan had been very vocal, unwilling to believe she was dead. Gradually, though, the reporters had moved onto newer, more relevant stories.

Was Duncan still convinced she was alive or had he accepted she was gone?

They were questions Callie knew would continue to torment her, so she tried not to give them too much space in her head. Same with her family and wondering how they were coping. Although they had never been close, Callie's death must have had some impact on her dad and sister.

She had given up everything to escape Duncan and effectively no longer existed. Sometimes late at night when she couldn't sleep, the gravity of that hit hard.

She couldn't drive, leave the country, or open a bank account. And God forbid she became sick and needed a hospital. There were so many things with her situation that could go wrong. Somehow, she had to make sure they didn't.

Instead, she focused on the knowledge that staying would have been worse, and in the evenings, when her mind was more likely to wander, she read through the stacks of books that were in the living room and caught up on TV shows and movies.

And she watched.

Nico had put all of the cameras at Willow Brook Farm on her phone, and she regularly checked every single one of them, at first a little paranoid, wanting to know the location of everyone. At night, she focused on those at the main house, comforted that Nico was close by if she needed help.

She was still a little wary of him, but she no longer believed he had been snooping in the cottage. He was doing everything he could to try to put her at ease and she was slowly realising that he didn't pose a threat.

She didn't know who the intruder had been, and for several nights, she had struggled to fall asleep, terrified she would hear the turning of a key in the lock. Nothing more had happened and eventually, the incident was pushed further to the back of her mind.

Other than when she was watching Nico from afar as he worked, their paths only crossed a couple of times a week for laundry and shopping deliveries.

During her first trip to the house, she had been on edge, desperate to get her washing done so she could go, and she had taken Chester with her, turning down Nico's offer of coffee, choosing to go for a walk instead while her clothes spun. With each visit, though, she became more familiar with the routine, and a little more comfortable around Nico.

Then, once a week, like clockwork, he would show up on her doorstep with bags filled with groceries. At first, she had offered him cash from her precious stash of notes, but Nico had refused to take it. She didn't like being in his debt, but equally, she knew she had to eat.

He kept telling her to let him know if there were particular things she liked. To begin with, she hadn't wanted to put him out any more than she was already doing. But then he had reasoned he was going to keep buying her food anyway, so it might as well be stuff she liked. Eventually, she had relented, requesting a few ingredients she would need to make a couple of recipes she had found in a cookbook in one of the kitchen drawers.

She had never been a great cook, but the novelty of having some control back in her life, being able to eat what she wanted and when, and living in a place where she was allowed to make a mess hadn't worn off.

When she had unpacked the bags that time, she had found he had also snuck in a bottle of wine and chocolate. Taken aback, she had messaged him to say thank you.

In his typical concise way, he had simply replied,

Enjoy.

That had been the start of a trend. Little extras that he thought she might like. A punnet of strawberries or a pot plant, books from the library. And then there was the odd hand-me-down. Things that he said he didn't need and she might be able to make use of.

The first thing he had given her was a Kindle.

Callie's eyes had widened when he had handed it to her. 'I can't accept this.'

'It's an old one,' he had said. 'I bought a newer model, so you might as well have it.' He'd shrugged. 'It'll just sit in a drawer if not.'

It was basic and had wear and tear, but he had loaded it up with a ton of books, and it became her most treasure possession. Other hand-me-downs had followed. Recipe books, a dog bed for Chester that Dash and Shyla didn't use, a food mixer he no longer wanted, and Callie had appreciated them all.

Hearing his Jeep arrive now, she went to the front door and opened it, watching in surprise as he unloaded a bicycle from the back.

'I thought you might get some use out of this,' he told her, wheeling it over to the cottage.

He was being kind, but she couldn't accept it. He was already doing so much for her.

'It belonged to Teddy's late wife and came with the house,' he reasoned, when she started to protest. 'I'm not going to use it and it gives you a bit of freedom. I know you're stuck here without a car.'

Teddy, Callie knew, was Nico's former boss, the man who had left him Willow Brook Farm, and she guessed he was right. If it was just sitting around.

'Thank you.'

'It's a bit old-fashioned, but I've fixed it up for you and given it a good clean.'

He had done that for her? Callie's heart squeezed.

'Is there anything around here I can do to help?' she offered, feeling the need to give something back. She couldn't just keep taking.

Nico looked confused, so she elaborated.

'You're doing so much for me and I'd like to give something back.'

He brushed away her offer. 'There's no need. You're good.'

'Yes, but I want to.'

He must have picked up on the stubborn edge to her voice because he studied her for a moment before speaking. 'Do you know anything about horses?'

'Well, no, but perhaps I could maybe help muck out the stables.'

'I already have people who do that.'

'What about the house then?' Callie asked, changing tack.

'What about it?'

'Do you have a housekeeper?'

'A housekeeper?' he snorted, seeming both amused and

affronted. 'Of course I don't. Why on earth would I want a housekeeper?'

'It's a big house.'

'Which I'm capable of looking after myself.'

'Let me,' she pushed.

'Let you what?'

'Let me look after it. I can clean for you.'

'Thank you, but I don't need you to clean for me.'

He spoke as if she had suggested something ridiculous, and she was struck by the difference between him and Duncan, who had rarely lifted a finger and expected others to clean, cook and wait on him.

He turned to go.

'Nico. Please.'

Callie watched him falter.

'You might not need a cleaner, but I need this.' As he turned to look at her, she pushed on. 'I've been here seven weeks and I'm going stir-crazy. It's lovely you've been looking after me, but I want to start looking after myself again. I need a purpose and some self-worth. I can't go out and get a regular job, but I have to do something to keep me busy, and it will be a way I can repay you for everything you've done. I really want to do that.'

His expression was unreadable as he continued to stare at her, green eyes wide, and perhaps a little surprised at her sudden, passioned outburst.

'I don't need you to repay me.'

'You don't, but I do. I need this, Nico.' Her voice cracked as she spoke his name.

They had both known what the score was when she had agreed to come here. She had faked her death and there could be no trace of her existence for anyone to find. It was too dangerous.

Laurel was in touch with a friend of a friend, trying to find out if there was a way to get a new fake identity for Callie, but until then, she was stuck here.

It was the price she had paid for her freedom, though of course she was grateful to Nico for putting a roof over her head.

Finally, he spoke, his voice a little gruff. 'Once a week. I have cleaning products, but I'll get you whatever else you need.'

He got it at last, she realised, relief easing the tension in her shoulders.

'Okay, I'll see what stuff you have when I start and I'll let you know. I can come over tomorrow if that's okay with you.'

'It's fine.'

After he left, her mood was lighter. It helped that the weather was warming slightly and with the clocks having last week gone forward, the evenings were already drawing out. The spring brought with it hope.

Leaving Chester snoozing on the sofa, Callie decided to take the bicycle for a test ride. Her plan was to stick to the main pathways that led around the farm, but on a whim, she rode out of the top of the driveway, turning left and following the lane as it cut through the countryside.

She hadn't been on a bicycle in years and had forgotten how it felt to pedal hard, the breeze blowing through her hair, and the fields whizzing by, as the wheels gained pace.

When she arrived at a junction, she hesitated, wondering if she should turn back. She didn't want to get lost. But she wasn't ready to go home yet. Making a note of her surroundings, she stuck with the same direction, turning left again.

There were more houses on this road. Individual and expensive-looking, some modern builds and others retaining character. The road dipped as she passed under a railway bridge and she realised she was cycling into a more populated area, as a couple of cars passed her.

A place called Brundall, she noted. The houses were now closer together, and she passed a garage and a fish and chip shop.

She dismounted, her legs aching from using unfamiliar muscles, and bumped the bicycle up onto the pavement as she came to a row of shops.

One store caught her eye, Craft Angels, and she moved to the window for a better look, immediately taken by the treasure trove display of eclectic items. It seemed to be a mix of old and new: antique vases, jewellery boxes, and mirrors, sitting between bespoke jewellery and vibrant paintings.

Callie was immediately drawn to a canvas of golds and oranges, showing a setting sun over a river, and was imagining how it would look above the sofa in the tiny living room of the cottage. When sunlight shone through the window, it would catch the gold shimmers and make them sparkle.

The sound of raised voices inside the shop drew her attention. They were muffled, but she could make out that a man and woman were arguing.

Not wanting to appear nosy, she was about to step back from the storefront when the door opened and a woman stepped out.

'Just stay out of it,' she snarled back into the shop. 'It's none of your bloody business.' It was at that moment she turned, locking eyes with Callie.

Anya?

Callie started to say hello, but Anya glared at her, her cheeks pink with fury, before stomping off.

The man who came to the door looked harassed, his eyes widening when he spotted Callie. Quickly, a smile replaced the frown. 'Teenagers.' He shook his head as if they had just shared a joke.

'Is Anya your daughter?' Callie asked, as the door of a blue Renault Clio slammed shut across the road, Anya scowling at the two of them as she revved the engine before pulling away from the kerb.

'No. Thank God. My nerves would be shot.' The man's smile widened. 'She's my niece. You know her then?'

'She works at Willow Brook Farm.'

'Yes, with Nico Adams. Do you work there too? I haven't seen you around.'

'No, I'm from...' She had been about to say Devon, catching herself just in time. 'I'm visiting. Nico is my cousin,' she quickly added, remembering the lie. 'You have some lovely things here,' she told him, eager to change the subject. 'I love the painting in the window.'

It seemed to work.

'Thank you. That's one of my early pieces.'

'You're the artist?' Callie blinked, surprised. 'It's lovely,' she added when he nodded.

'Would you like to come and have a look inside? I'm Vince, by the way.'

'Callie.'

And yes, she did want to have a look, because she was intrigued. She loved shops like this. Plus, there was something about Vince that she instantly warmed to. He was rake thin and bald as a coot, but he had kind eyes that were a little too wide behind thick-rimmed glasses that reminded her of Jarvis Cocker. He looked younger than Jarvis though, and she guessed he was somewhere in his forties.

She propped her bicycle against the wall, figuring it would be safe there for a couple of minutes, then followed him inside the shop, glancing around in wonder at the many different things on sale.

'This place is amazing.'

'Thanks. We've been here for a couple of years now. I wasn't sure if it would work at first, but we do okay, and we're pretty successful on TikTok. That's drawn in a fair bit of trade. I wanted somewhere to display my paintings and I've always liked antiques. I try to showcase local craftspeople too. Something for every budget.'

Vince winked and Callie flushed. Her budget was non-existent.

She made a point of looking over a few pieces of jewellery while they spoke, and admiring his art again before edging her way out of the shop. 'It was nice to meet you,' she told him, getting on the bicycle. 'Next time, I'll bring my purse,' she lied.

It was a shame. She liked Anya's uncle and loved the shop, but it would be too uncomfortable returning and would look odd if she only ever went there to browse.

On the ride back to the farm, she was so caught up in her thoughts that she almost missed Anya's car parked on the side of the lane ahead. The Clio was pulled off the road in the entrance to a field, and seeing Anya stood by the bonnet, Callie slowed, wondering if she was having car trouble.

She didn't know the first thing about engines, but they were only half a mile from the farm. Nico might be able to help.

Anya hadn't spotted her, and Callie was about to call out when she realised the girl was on her phone. Calling her recovery service for help, probably.

Callie pulled to a halt behind her and waited patiently.

'So you'll be there, you promise?'

A pause.

'But where are we gonna go?'

Anya huffed a little in frustration, stepping away from the car.

'And you mean it? This had better not be some kind of trick.'

Callie bit her bottom lip, a little uncomfortable. This didn't sound like Anya was talking about her car. It was a private conversation and one she shouldn't be listening in on.

'You know I love you. I'll show you how much tonight. I can't wait either.'

Callie was considering how to leave without it being obvious she had been eavesdropping when Anya turned, seeming to sense she was there.

She looked horrified. 'Do you mind?' she snapped. 'This is personal.'

'I'm sorry, I wasn't—'

'Just go!'

Before Callie could react, Anya was stomping round to the driver's door and getting into the car, the phone still to her ear. As the door slammed, she muttered, 'Nosy bitch.'

So that had gone well.

Callie considered apologising again, but suspected it would fall on deaf ears. Anya didn't seem in the mood to be reasoned with.

Cheeks flaming, she pulled away, cycling back towards the farm.

\* \* \*

It was during her evening walk with Chester that Callie saw Anya again.

As the nights became lighter, she had started exploring the woods. They were part of Nico's land, and although he had no objection to the public using them, he had told her that not many people knew they existed. The road that ran alongside them was mostly a dirt track and less travelled, meaning only locals tended to venture in there.

As she wandered along the central path, stopping to pick wild-flowers, and Chester happily sniffed around, she heard voices. And instantly, she froze.

Her first instinct was to quietly get her dog and head back. She was only five minutes away from the cottage and she could be gone without anyone knowing she was here. It was already dusk, and there wasn't much light left anyway. She was best to start making her way back.

Not wanting to call out to Chester, she wandered over to where he had his nose in a bush, clipping on his lead and gently pulling him back. He had seen something in there that had drawn his attention, maybe rabbits or a squirrel, and he resisted a little before yielding.

As they headed back onto the path, she heard the woman's voice, raised and angry.

'I knew you would do this. I fucking knew it.'

She was with a man, because he started to speak, though the woman barely let him get any words out before she started yelling again.

'No, I won't calm down. I am sick and tired of your games.'

Was that Anya Callie could hear?

Curiosity took over and she stepped closer, despite remembering their last awkward encounter.

Who was Anya with?

She caught a flash of red, spotting a waving arm, then more of the girl as she took a step back, and Callie quickly ducked behind a tree, pulling Chester with her, hoping he wouldn't give their presence away.

'You promised and I trusted you,' Anya continued.

It must be the person she had been on the phone with earlier.

Callie couldn't see who he was, as he was blocked by the bushes, and she waited, hoping he would move forward. Toby, perhaps?

He started to speak again, but Anya was on a roll.

'No, I'm fed up with your excuses. I've had enough.'

The man reached for Anya and Callie caught a glimpse of dark-grey shirt, but nothing more to identify him.

Chester picked that moment to start scraping at the dirt, the noise cutting through the silence.

Anya's head shot up. 'What was that? Is someone there?'

Callie ducked back behind the tree, gripping the dog's lead tightly, barely daring to breathe. Perhaps she should just step out, admit she was there. But after earlier, she didn't want to be caught snooping twice.

'It's nothing, pickle,' the man spoke, trying to reassure. 'Come on, let's get out of here.'

Angry whispers followed and Callie remained pressed against the tree, hoping they weren't going to come and find her.

She heard the sound of footsteps and glanced in panic at the path. Should she make a run for it?

No, they would see her for sure.

To her relief, she realised they were heading away and finally, she dared peep round the tree again, wondering where they were, and glad they were already out of sight.

Still, she waited a few seconds before tugging on Chester's lead and heading back to the cottage.

Whoever Anya's boyfriend was, it was none of her business.

# 10

## BEFORE

My dad isn't a people person. He lacks patience, sets standards too high, doesn't suffer fools, and he has an air of omnipotence about him. Don't get me wrong, he is a brilliant and sought-after surgeon. But he is arrogant too and I have been dreading this meeting between him and Duncan.

Both of them have big personalities and I was terrified they were going to clash. Especially as Dad can be stuffy and formal, while Duncan is the lovable, cheeky charmer. I certainly didn't expect them to bond like old friends, and while I am relieved and pleasantly surprised, I am also cautious.

It's a couple of weeks before Christmas and we are out to dinner in Duncan's favourite restaurant. A place where the staff manage to act superior and sycophantic at the same time, and the cheapest bottle of wine could buy a week's worth of groceries. It has always struck me as strange that he likes to eat in places like this. The food and the atmosphere are so at odds with his roguish personality. When we come here, I feel he is slipping on a different skin, trying to look more refined than he is.

I always order the same thing – a vegetarian dish with wild

mushrooms that have apparently been foraged. It's the only thing I can ever understand on the pretentious menu, so I play it safe. Besides, I know it's something that is easy to eat in delicate mouthfuls, so at least I won't embarrass Duncan.

He is always berating me for being a messy eater. I never paid much attention to how I ate before meeting him, so it was mortifying to realise I slurp soup and can't twirl pasta properly. I am careful now with the food I choose, not wanting to make a fool of him in public.

As I pick at my dish and make small talk with April, Phoebe and Ed, Dad and Duncan ignore the four of us, caught up in each other's company, discussing the various projects Duncan is involved with and, of course, the hobby they share. Golf.

It's the first time any of my family have met Duncan. The visit I tried to organise with my sister never materialised and when she showed up at the restaurant tonight, I realised just how far we have grown apart.

We have never been close. Phoebe sees everything as black and white, while I recognise the layers of grey in between. And she struggles with empathy, often unable to connect or relate to other people's emotions or experiences. After Mum died, we briefly pulled together, but now she is almost like a stranger, our conversation polite and stilted, as if we've forgotten we grew up together.

Phoebe and Ed seem to like Duncan, too. Ed in particular is smitten and I know he has watched all of Duncan's films. He keeps staring at him and is becoming less subtle the more drunk he gets. By the time our desserts are put in front of us, it's all getting a bit embarrassing.

I try to catch his eye to draw his attention away as I push my sheep's milk mousse around the plate, wishing I hadn't ordered it. I didn't realise it has goat's cheese in it, something I can't stand, and I've only been able to stomach a couple of mouthfuls.

'How are things going now you're working from home?' April asks, distracting me. 'Do you miss being in the office?'

Truthfully, work is the one area of my life which isn't going so great at the moment and I had hoped to avoid talking about it. When Duncan asked me to move in with him, it was going to be difficult to keep my office job, as I couldn't commute from Devon, so I reached a compromise with Tara. She agreed to allow me to work remotely, as long as I attended the monthly staff meetings.

Initially, it worked well. The Old Rectory is huge and Duncan cleared a room for me that I could use as my office. Before I moved in, he renovated the whole space, repainting it in a calming grey and kitting it out with a new desk and an ergonomic chair.

I didn't realise what he had done until I moved in. It was all a surprise and I had been so happy at his thoughtfulness, I had brushed off my irritation at the cute little sign on the door that bore the name Micaela. He had gone to so much trouble, I wasn't going to nit-pick.

I was a hard worker and kept myself disciplined, making sure I was at my desk by eight-thirty and Zooming with my old workmates each day for the morning catch-up. And Duncan was great. He had his own things keeping him busy, but if he was at home, he was always careful to leave me alone.

But then he had a couple of charity dinners that took place on weeknights, that he was insistent I attend with him, and we had to stay overnight in a hotel in London. They went on far longer than he had promised, meaning I wasn't in bed until gone 2 a.m. The first time, I made sure I was up the next morning, logging onto the meeting with just seconds to spare, and yawning my way through it, but the next time, my alarm didn't go off and I overslept.

I could tell Tara was annoyed, but she didn't say anything. It took losing a huge file of my work, containing projects I had been working on and preparing for weeks, before she pushed me out.

'I'm sorry, Callie, but this isn't working. I need someone here in the office.' She hesitated. 'If you can't commute, I'm going to have to find someone else.'

She knew I couldn't commute. It would never work. I was devastated, as I loved my job, and I was also anxious. What would Duncan think when he found out. Would he be disappointed in me?

As it turned out, he was more than supportive.

'Maybe this is a good thing?'

'It is?'

'You won't have the tie of logging on every day or that monthly meeting you have to attend in person. It does restrict us.'

I guess I didn't see it that way. It was my job and I had already been granted special favours.

'Think of the freedom this gives us. We don't have to worry about leaving events early.'

Did he consider 2 a.m. early? We had been among the last to leave both of the charity functions.

'My job is flexible though. And I now have to find another one. It could be more of a tie.'

'Why do you need another job?'

'What?' My mouth had fallen open.

'Money isn't an issue,' he continued. 'You have me to take care of you.'

'But what am I supposed to do all day?'

'Enjoy your new home, keep me company.' I must have looked disappointed, because he quickly added, 'And maybe you could look after my publicity. I'll tell Tara I don't need her any more. You can handle everything.'

'I can?'

Wow, that had turned around fast. I had gone from the girl with no job to looking after Lemon Source's most lucrative client.

'You can. I promise. See, your day isn't so bad after all.' He pulled me into a hug.

'Thank you,' I whispered against his neck, breathing in his aftershave.

'I'll call a meeting with Tara,' he promised.

That was nearly six weeks ago and I have officially left Lemon Source, having worked a month's notice, but Duncan's meeting with Tara still hasn't happened. I have asked a few times, but he is evasive, brushing me off, and getting snappy if I push it.

I toy with the best way to answer April's question, conscious that I don't want my father to know I've been out of work now for several weeks.

'I like being at home, though I'm no longer with Lemon Source.'

'You're not?' I curse Dad's perfect hearing. I wasn't speaking loudly. 'So what are you doing now?'

There is an uncomfortable silence and everyone's attention is now on me, as they wait for my answer. My face burns.

'I, um...' I look to Duncan for help, but he sips at his wine, watching me with the same curiosity as the others. 'It wasn't working out,' I manage. 'Tara wanted someone office-based. I am going to help Duncan with his PR.'

Dad doesn't look impressed by this and his frown now falls on Duncan.

'Is this true?' he demands, gruffly.

Now, all eyes are on Duncan, but he isn't flustered like me. Instead, he calmly sets down his wine glass, taking his time before answering. Eventually, his gaze raises to lock on mine, and the pale blue of his eyes are icy cold.

'That's not entirely true now, is it, Mica.'

My mouth opens and closes. I want to call him out, but I have a sense of foreboding that it wouldn't be wise.

He shifts his focus to my father, all pally again. 'The truth is, Mica has been worried about you finding out, Michael. Lemon Source had to let her go. It pains me to say this, because I know she promised Tara that she wouldn't slack if she worked from home, but she wasn't giving the job her full attention.'

I am listening to his words, but struggling to register them. He is throwing me under a bus and making things sound much worse than they are.

'I didn't—'

'Micaela!'

Dad snaps out my name as I attempt to defend myself and I stop dead. I am an adult in my thirties, yet he still has the ability to make me feel ten years old.

I glance at Phoebe and Ed, but they are both staring at me in shock.

'Of course I can support her financially until she finds something else,' Duncan is continuing, his tone smooth. 'So there's no problem there. I think you enjoy being the lady of the manor and not having to work, don't you, sweets?'

He laughs at his own joke, while my father throws daggers at me, and I quietly seethe.

I don't want to make a scene in the restaurant, and I know from experience that anything I say now will fall on deaf ears. Instead, I stare sulkily at the table, still poking at my mousse.

What I had hoped would be a nice evening is now ruined.

'Mica, are you going to finish your dessert?' Duncan asks.

'I'm not hungry.'

I make a point of laying the spoon on the plate and staring at him, my gaze challenging. I am being childish, but I don't care. He has pissed me off.

'Fine.' I can hear his disapproval as he signals for the bill.

There is a brief disagreement over who will pay. Dad arguing that as Duncan insisted on paying for their hotel room, he should get to buy dinner.

Unlike me, he doesn't think it's odd that Duncan insisted the four of them stay in a hotel instead of with us, especially when we have all those empty bedrooms. Right now, though, I am glad they won't be coming home with us. The atmosphere here in the restaurant is bad enough and I can't wait to leave.

Duncan gets his way with the bill, and before parting, Dad arranges a friendly game of golf with him for the following morning at Dainton Park before he and April drive to Bristol to catch their flight to Paris. They are spending a few days there before flying home for Christmas.

I simply get a peck on the cheek and a reminder to start job hunting, while Phoebe looks on, a slightly smug look on her face. She has always liked making things a competition between us.

As soon as we are in the taxi for the ride home, I unbottle my pent-up rage on Duncan.

'Why the hell did you tell my family that Tara let me go?'

In the face of my anger, Duncan is calm. 'We'll talk about this when we get home.'

'No! We'll talk about it now,' I snap back.

'Mica.' There is a warning tone to his voice, but I don't care.

'Why did you do it? Why did you tell them that?'

'Because Tara *did* let you go.'

He is trying hard to sound reasonable and I catch him glance at the taxi driver. I realise he is uncomfortable airing our dirty laundry in front of him. The man recognised him when he picked us up, excited to have a celebrity in his cab, and Duncan is all about maintaining his perfect public image.

Well, that's tough, because I am on a roll now. He just humiliated me in front of my family and I am determined to make my point.

'Yes, because she wants someone in the office. You made it sound awful. Like I was slacking on the job.'

'You were.'

'I was not!' I snap back.

'You lost a whole file of work and you missed meetings because you overslept. I'm surprised she didn't get rid of you sooner if I'm honest.' Another glance at the taxi driver and he dials it back a bit. 'I love you, Mica. I do, but you can't blame me because you couldn't hold down your job.'

'Maybe if you hadn't dragged me out to those stupid charity events, I wouldn't have overslept. It's your fault I was out so late.'

'I didn't force you to do anything.'

Okay, maybe he didn't force me, but he was pretty insistent I go.

'We will talk about this when we get home,' he tells me again. This time, his voice is low. He doesn't want the taxi driver to overhear. 'Now stop making a scene.'

'But, Duncan—'

He reaches for my hand and squeezes it tightly. 'Stop. I mean it.'

His tone has me hesitating and I get an ominous feeling that I might regret it if I don't do as I'm told.

We ride home in stony silence, and as Duncan pays for the taxi, I storm ahead into the house.

'Good evening, Miss Parker.'

The voice makes me jump, and I swing round to see Rob Jolly standing in the doorway to the kitchen. He has been in the house today upgrading the security cameras and alarms, but I didn't expect him to still be here.

'Hi,' I mutter, caught off guard. His presence always unnerves me a little. Don't get me wrong. He has never been rude or unkind, but I feel as if he is keeping an eye on me. That he doesn't trust me.

Chester comes bounding through from the lounge, tail thumping, and I bend down to greet him, for a moment forgetting I am in a bad mood. But then Duncan follows me into the house and, remembering, I stomp upstairs for a shower.

'Everything okay?' I hear Rob ask.

'It will be,' Duncan replies, his tone clipped.

He doesn't follow me and I am grateful, as I need a few minutes to process his betrayal. He knows my relationship with my family is complicated and that I was nervous about the dinner. He was supposed to support me.

By the time the soapy water runs clear, my initial anger has turned into hurt and confusion. I simply don't understand his motive.

The bedroom is dark when I leave the steamy bathroom and, my focus is on fastening my robe, so for a moment, I don't see him sat in the corner chair. It's the clink of ice against glass that alerts me he is there, and it makes me jump.

'Duncan. What are you doing?' I flip the light switch on and now have a better view.

He is sat there watching me, jacket discarded and tie loose, a filled whisky tumbler in one hand and my dog obediently by his side. Although he looks dangerously handsome, the jitter in my stomach isn't lust. I recognise it as nerves. He hasn't answered my question and I don't like the way he is looking at me, a cruel smile on his lips.

'I'm going to let the dog out to pee, then go to bed,' I mutter, trying my best to still sound annoyed, so I don't betray my sudden unease. 'Come on, boy.'

Chester tries to pull away, whining as Duncan tightens his grip on his collar. He has never much liked my boyfriend.

'What are you doing? Let him go.'

'You embarrassed me tonight, Mica.'

Finally he speaks, but not the words I expected to hear, and I stare at him, shocked.

'I embarrassed you? Are you crazy? You humiliated me in front of my family.' My tone is more incredulous than angry. I can't believe he is trying to be the injured party.

'No, what I did with your family was tell them the truth. You can try to blame me for losing your job, but we both know that the buck stops with you.'

I stare at him dumbfounded, barely recognising the man before me. He isn't angry. He isn't shouting. His tone is cold, calm, and, dare I say it, reasonable, as if he is determined to make me understand. But there is something about his demeanour that frightens me.

'You wanted me to be complicit in your deceit. My first meeting with your dad and your sister, and you expected me to lie to them. What kind of person does that make you?'

'I never tried to make you lie,' I bluster. He is twisting everything around.

'And then you cause a scene in the taxi. I have a reputation to consider. I can't risk having my face splashed all over the tabloids because my girlfriend can't control her temper. Our personal life is private, Mica. We deal with problems behind closed doors.'

'It wasn't a scene. It was a discussion,' I snap back, my cheeks heating. Okay, perhaps I should've have waited until we were home, but I had been upset at what had happened in the restaurant. 'You hurt me tonight and I wanted to know why. And I never expected you to lie about why I left Lemon Source, but you didn't have to be so blunt about it. Besides, we both know the reason I don't have a job at the moment is because I'm still waiting for you to talk to Tara. Why didn't you at least tell Dad I had something lined up?'

Duncan's lips thin and his pale eyes heat. 'I think you proved tonight you are a terrible publicist. I need someone I can trust and depend on. And who fixes damage, rather than causing it.'

Is he kidding? He is seriously going to go back on his word?

'You promised.'

'And now I have changed my mind. You can't honestly expect me to employ you after your embarrassing display tonight.'

'But I need a job.'

I can't hide the panic in my tone and he picks up on it. We both know that being out of work for months isn't going to help my chances of finding something new.

'Well, I can't help you there, but you're right, you do need something to fill your time,' he agrees. 'I think you've had it far too easy since you moved in here and it's making you lazy and selfish. It's time you started to pull your weight and showed me a little respect.'

I stare at him, unsure how to respond. Why is he being so cruel? Tears prick at the corner of my eyes and, sensing my upset, Chester tries again to come to me, growing agitated when Duncan won't let him.

'Quieten down, you stupid animal,' he snaps, his sudden anger tensing every muscle in my body.

He turns back to me, swirling the ice cubes in his glass before taking a sip, his eyes never leaving my face. I clench and unclench my hands, as I stand before him, feeling like I am in the head teacher's office.

'Tomorrow, I am going to give Shirley her notice.'

'What? Why?'

'Having a housekeeper is a waste of money when you're swanning around here doing nothing. Looking after the house can be your responsibility.'

My jaw drops. 'You want me to be your cleaner?'

'I want you to clean *our* home. Perhaps the hard work might make you appreciate the fact that you live here for free.'

This was not how I anticipated this conversation going and I am lost for words. Emotions ball together in the pit of my stomach. Fresh anger and humiliation, but also doubt. I don't want to, but he has me questioning everything. Is it possible he is right? Have I been lazy and selfish, taking advantage of him?

I need some fresh air to consider everything that has just been said.

'Can you let Chester go, please? I have to let him out.'

'We're not finished yet, Mica. I want you to apologise.'

No way am I doing that. Okay, maybe I am a little at fault, but Duncan has to share a portion of the blame for tonight.

'Look, just let him go. He needs to pee.'

As if in agreement, Chester barks and strains at his collar. He is getting distressed.

Looking annoyed, Duncan rolls his eyes. 'Rob?' he yells.

'I'm here,' comes the other man's voice and I realise he is already on the stairs.

Rob has this knack of being there the instant Duncan needs him and it's a little unsettling. Like he is spying or eavesdropping on us.

'Take the dog out to pee, then lock him in the kitchen,' Duncan instructs, releasing Chester.

'No!' I protest, reaching out to my goldy, but before I can comfort him, Rob has hold of his collar and is pulling him from the room.

'Let him go,' I demand, heading after them as Chester continues to bark.

I don't make it to the door. Duncan is up and out of the chair, his vicelike grip closing around my arm and yanking me back towards him.

'Get off of me.' I tug at my arm. He can't manhandle me like this. My heart is thumping, but still I try to hold my ground. 'You can't lock him downstairs. He's used to sleeping upstairs with us.'

'Not any more. I am sick of you treating my house like a zoo. From now on, the bloody dog sleeps in the kitchen.'

'He doesn't have his bed.'

'He's a fucking animal.'

I fight to get away again, this time managing to wrench my arm free. I refuse to stay here for a minute longer and my plan, as I head for the door, is to get Chester, grab my purse and keys, and get the hell out of here. I don't care that I'm only wearing a robe, or that I'm over the limit.

The sound of glass smashes on the wall ahead and I realise in horror that the stain darkening the green paint is whisky. Did he seriously just throw his tumbler at me?

My heart is in my throat as I turn to him, adrenaline pumping through my veins. 'You're crazy. This is over.'

I can't describe the look that crosses his face as I spit the words at him, other than to say he looks wild, and like he really wants to hurt me. I need to get out of here.

He catches up with me as I'm crossing the landing, grabbing hold of my arm again, and as I turn to fight him off, a fist slams into the side of my face, my head snapping back in shock as I try to register the pain. And then he is releasing me and I am stumbling, the antique chest that stands near the top of the stairs in my path as I fall. Something cracks against my head and everything turns to black.

## 11

---

NOW

It was the picture frame that finally alerted Duncan something wasn't right.

For sixty-three days, she had been gone, and deep down, he had believed she was dead, even if at first he had clung to denial.

When that first stage of grief had passed, anger had taken over.

How dare she leave him? And purposely too.

She had known what she was doing when she had gone into the icy cold sea at Hope Cove. She wasn't the strongest swimmer, and it wasn't an accident, as the police initially thought. If she had have slipped, it wouldn't explain why she had removed her boots and coat. Both had been found on the rocks, next to her bag and ring.

When they turned to the possibility it had been intentional, they had looked closely at her relationship with Duncan and he had been forced to navigate some difficult questions. Tara Lemon had personally handled his PR and he was grateful he had stayed with her agency, knowing it would be difficult for Juliette Bellamy, Tracy Novak and Aarna Kapoor to speak out about one of their firm's clients.

He stuck to the narrative that Mica had been suffering with her mental health and he had been the loving boyfriend trying to help her, grateful when her father and sister bought the lie too.

Behind closed doors, he had seethed.

He had given Mica everything and this was how the ungrateful bitch had repaid him.

Bargaining had followed anger. He would give up everything to have her back.

They still didn't have a body. The coastguard said that the sea could be a harsh and unforgiving place, especially in a bitterly cold February, and it was possible she may never be found. The first few days had been a search-and-rescue mission, then it had changed to search and recovery. Eventually, it was called off.

Unhappy with the inconclusive result, he had hired his own team, paying for them to trawl the waters day after day. It was nearing the end of March when Rob had persuaded him to stop, telling him bluntly that he was wasting time and money, and that he needed to move on. That was when Duncan had finally sunk into depression.

Mica was out there somewhere, lost at sea, and until he had closure, he wasn't certain he could move on. It seemed the Parkers had already got to that point, though. They wanted to plan a memorial service, which was laughable. They didn't have a body.

Still, their decision was final. Duncan and Mica hadn't been married, which meant he didn't have control of the situation. Something he struggled with.

Acceptance never came. He was a bear with a sore head, barking at anyone who stepped in his path and incomplete without her. She consumed his every waking thought, as well as his dreams.

If she had understood him better, if he had worked harder to make her more compliant, perhaps it wouldn't have come to this.

Rob wanted to clear her things out of the house, convinced it would be the motivation Duncan needed to get his life back on track. He had resisted at first, the idea initially unthinkable, but eventually, he had caved. His charity work had fallen by the wayside, and although the public still adored him and had been supportive through his tragedy, they would only wait for so long. Somehow, he needed to find a way back to them.

Tomorrow, Rob was going to bag all of Mica's things up and remove them from the house. He was the only person Duncan trusted to do the job. The only one now who he trusted full stop.

The pair of them had known each other since childhood when Rob had been a couple of years ahead of Duncan at school. He, like Duncan, came from a broken family, and he had been one of the tougher kids. For whatever reason, he had taken Duncan under his wing and had his back in every situation.

Lacking opportunities – Rob didn't have a pretty face like Duncan, or any particular skill set – he had turned to petty crime after leaving school, and was in prison more often than out.

Duncan hadn't forgotten him, though, and as soon as he found success, he had offered Rob a job. The man was his confidante, his security and his closest friend. And Duncan knew he had his unwavering loyalty. He also had connections that had come in handy over the years.

It was during his third whisky that Duncan became wistful, needing to see Mica's things. He went upstairs to the bedroom, opening her walk-in wardrobe and stepping inside. It was the first time he had been in here since she had left. The idea too unbearable.

This was the room he had made for her, filling it with beautiful clothes, shoes and handbags. She had wanted for nothing and every rail and shelf contained only the best labels. He trailed his fingers over silk dresses and cashmere cardigans, recalling how he had liked to choose her outfits for her. He had always had a better eye for detail than she had, and although she had resisted at first, she had gradually yielded, accepting that he knew best.

She had embarrassed him once when the features team of a glossy magazine had shown up at the house for a photo shoot, and irritation still niggled his gut as he recalled how she had come downstairs wearing one of her old dresses, a cheap-looking cotton garment with a hideous pattern that did nothing for her figure or her complexion. He had politely asked her to change, but she had refused, and not wanting to cause a scene, he had silently seethed while forcing a smile for the camera.

Ever the professional, he had ensured they'd portrayed a picture of loving unity. The shoot was more about the house and its history than his personal life and he engineered it so Mica only featured briefly. The press had never been that interested in her anyway. He was the star. She just happened to be his girlfriend. A role that came with responsibilities.

After the crew had left, he made sure she understood what those were, holding her down on the bed while he ripped off the dress before going and gathering up a handful of her old clothes. She had tried to stop him when she'd realised his plan was to cut them into pieces and he had been forced to lock her in the wardrobe while he destroyed them.

He remembered how angry she had been, banging on the door and screaming at him, saying she was going to leave him, and fearful that she might, he had left her in the tiny room overnight, giving her a chance to calm down.

Before he let her out the following morning, he instructed Rob to take Chester for a long walk, knowing that Mica wouldn't leave without the dog. It gave him the precious time he needed to work her round to his way of thinking. A few kind words and gestures, a pity story with tears, telling her she was the only one who understood him. He knew her weak spots and how to manipulate them, turning himself into the victim.

It had all been for the greater good. Mica had underestimated his love for her and the lengths he was prepared to go to. He could have anyone, but had chosen her.

He had tried dating other celebrities, but it just didn't work. He liked things exact and there was always a power struggle. His relationship with Kacey Lewis had survived the longest, but it had been turbulent behind closed doors. Kacey had been his equal in many ways, but she wasn't subservient enough for Duncan's tastes, and if they had stayed together, they would have self-destructed. Everyone thought they had been the perfect couple and somehow, they had managed to come out of the relationship on good terms. Perhaps because they each recognised a dark soul and both had their secrets to keep.

After Kacey, Duncan had searched for a specific type of partner. One he could mould to his tastes. Mica had been perfect. He would lavish her and worship the ground she walked on. She would want for nothing. All he asked in return was respect and compliance.

For so many years, it had just been Duncan and his mum, Denise. He had never known his dad and his mum had been an only child. His maternal grandparents had died when he was still a kid and, after that, his mum had become his whole world.

The only time there had been a man on the scene had been when Cliff had lived with them. Duncan had been ten when the salesman had wandered into their lives and initially, he had feared the man. Cliff enjoyed a drink, and when he had a drink, he liked to slap Denise about. Duncan had learnt to hide away whenever she received a beating, covering his ears so he couldn't hear her screams.

When he was twelve, he had found out she enjoyed it.

She had cupped his cheek in her palm, her eyes shining

brightly. 'This is what true love looks like, Duncan. When you find the one, you will do anything for them, even when it hurts. Cliff gets a little too passionate at times, but it's just his way of showing me he loves me and making sure we stay together.'

After that, he had viewed Cliff though different eyes and the two of them had grown close. Cliff always quick to offer his own brand of wisdom, telling Duncan how men were smarter than women, that they required a firm hand. How everyone is in charge of their own destiny, and that life is the survival of the fittest.

When he decided to end the relationship, both Denise and Duncan were devastated.

'I would have done anything for him,' Denise had sobbed. 'One day, you'll meet someone, son, and you will know she is the one. I want you to promise me, when you find her, you never let her go.'

He had promised, but he hadn't believed her. He done his best to look after his mum. It had been so gratifying being able to give her all of the nice things she deserved after he received his first big pay cheque.

But then she had died too, cancer that spread too quickly, leaving Duncan heartbroken and alone. Of course he had plenty of friends, but they weren't family, and his mother's death left a gaping hole.

There had been plenty of women and relationships over the years, but none of them were marriage material. Then he'd met Mica and he had immediately known that she was different. There was something sweet and innocent and honest about her, and with her auburn hair and blue eyes, she reminded him a little of his mum. It was a sign.

Now she was gone too and he didn't know how to deal with this fresh loss.

Her perfume and creams were all laid out on a dressing table that was dominated by a huge mirror, and setting down his whisky, he picked up the expensive bottle he had bought her for Christmas, spraying it into the air as he stared at his reflection and the dark circles under his eyes. He briefly closed them as the scent of Mica filled the room, imagining for a moment she was still here with him.

'Why did you do this to me?' he whispered to no one, as tears dampened his cheeks.

He picked up the whisky glass, downing the rest of the smoky, amber liquor, needing to numb the pain. Tomorrow, he would get out of the house. He couldn't be here while his precious Mica's things were being packed away.

Rob wanted to get rid of everything, to give Duncan a fresh start, but would it be so bad to keep hold of a memento?

He scanned the dressing table to see if there was anything he wanted.

And that was when he noticed.

The picture frame. The one that had always sat there with the photo of Mica's mother. It was missing.

Surprise cut through the haziness of the alcohol and he blinked, suddenly more alert as he scanned the room, looking for anything else that might have gone. Everything was in its place, though, colour coordinated and neatly stacked, just the way he liked it. And, of course, he knew she had left her keys, phone and credit cards. They had all been found inside her handbag.

It was wishful thinking and perhaps a little foolish to believe she was still alive. She had nothing, so where would she go? Michael and Phoebe believed she was dead and she no longer was in touch with any of her old friends.

Still, as he turned off the light and left the wardrobe, the frame played on his mind. Mica was missing and so was the photo of her beloved mother.

He didn't believe in coincidences.

## 12

Anya hadn't shown up to work and Nico was in a foul mood as a result.

She was supposed to be in early, feeding the horses and getting them in the paddocks while she mucked out, so he had been dismayed, upon waking, to find out that they were still all stabled and she was nowhere to be seen.

The bad mood wasn't because he had to head out into the morning April shower, Dash and Shyla in tow, to do the job himself. Years of looking after horses meant he was an early riser, and he never thought himself above chipping in with the menial duties. They weren't just his animals. They were his life.

No, he was pissed off because he had put his faith in Anya, trusting her, and she had let him down.

He remembered how when he had met her, she had been a screwed-up sixteen-year-old with a huge chip on her shoulder and angry at the world. Not that he blamed her for her attitude. Everyone knew she was the daughter of Larissa Mitchell. A woman Nico had only met a couple of times, though he had heard all of the stories about her. That she had a drugs problem; that she had slept with so many men, she had no idea which one was Anya's father; that she resented her daughter and mostly fobbed her off on her brother, Vince.

People liked to gossip, but Nico had tried not to judge. At least until he had met Larissa himself. And from then on, he had been determined to help Anya.

She liked horses. He knew that much about her, as he often saw her making a fuss of them when they were in the paddock closest to the lane. Initially, she had disappeared every time he'd approached her, but finally he'd managed to get near enough for a conversation, letting her know it was okay to visit and spend time with his animals.

He got it. Remembering what it was like to come from a broken family and to have to rely on his own instincts. For a long time, he had been forced to fend for himself.

Could he help Anya? He understood difficult and frightened horses and knew how to work with them, to gain their trust. Would a teenage girl be that different?

The path hadn't been easy, but he had stuck by her, proud and justified in his actions when she had started to blossom, showing him she could be responsible and trustworthy. That was when he had offered her a job.

Not showing up for work was a stunt she hadn't pulled in a while, and he thought she respected him enough by now to not pull this kind of shit. But apparently he had that wrong, and he struggled to hold in his temper when leaving her a voicemail, asking her to call him.

The horses were all fed and in the paddock and he had just finished mucking out when Toby arrived, late for his shift also, and seeming a little distracted.

'I'm sorry, Nico. It took forever to get the bloody car to start.'

Nico glanced over at the kid's ancient Datsun, unsurprised. 'I keep telling you it's not going to last forever. I've said I will loan you the money if you want to get a newer car.'

'I know, and thank you.' Although Toby acknowledged him, he wasn't paying attention, glancing towards the stables. No doubt looking for Anya.

Nico knew he doted on her, and Anya knew it too. She often played on it, getting Toby to give her lifts or buy her drinks, and the poor sap did, crushed each time a new boyfriend came on the scene.

'She's not here.'

'What?'

'Anya didn't show up this morning. You haven't heard from her, have you?'

He had Toby's attention now, the boy's eyes going saucer wide. 'No. No, I haven't heard from her. Um, have you messaged her?'

'I left her a voicemail. If she shows up, let me know ASAP.'

'Of course.'

Leaving Toby to it, Nico headed back to the house for coffee and to take care of some paperwork before his newest client showed up.

Spotting Callie waiting on his doorstep had his brow creasing and for a moment, he worried if everything was okay. She never came over to the house unless she had washing to do, but there was no basket with her and she didn't have Chester with her either. Then he remembered. This notion she had that she needed to clean for him.

She didn't have to do that, but he had indulged her anyway. If feeling that she was being useful gave her a little bit of confidence and self-worth, and helped her to pull those shoulders back and hold her head a little higher, then he was fully on board. Anything that would reach the confident woman he knew was buried within.

Laurel had told him what Callie had endured, aware when he

had initially been reluctant for her to stay that it would be the way to cut through his defences. She knew that Nico didn't tolerate bullies and that he couldn't stand any kind of cruelty aimed at women, children or animals. Learning what Duncan Stone had put Callie through had left him raging inside.

Dash and Shyla reached her before he did and Nico greeted her with an easy, 'Hey' as he approached.

'Hey,' she repeated, her dark-blue eyes wary.

She had been at Willow Brook Farm for two months and still had that fearful look whenever he saw her. He wished he could get her to understand that she was safe here.

The earlier rain had stopped, but there were still puddles of mud on the ground, and the sun was daring to peek out from behind the clouds; the light catching the red of her dark-auburn hair. And although she appeared make-up-free, there was a hint of healthy colour in her cheeks. That was at least better. The deathly pale woman with the dark smudges under her eyes, who he had picked up from the station, had been banished.

'Have you been here long? I had to go down to the stables.'

'Just a few minutes. It's okay.'

'You're always welcome to let yourself in.'

She had a key and he had told her that before, but she never did. She was always so frightened of doing the wrong thing.

Still, they had made progress. She had conversations with him now, instead of giving monosyllabic answers, ones where she made eye contact and occasionally smiled.

Generally, he wasn't much of a talker, preferring to observe, but in recent weeks, he had found himself wanting to make an effort with her, hoping to coax out more of those smiles. And the look of delight on her face when he had given her Teddy's wife's old bicycle had made the hour he had spent cleaning it and checking it over time well spent.

'You'll find all the cleaning products in the utility room,' he told her, leaving the dogs outside to play as he led the way through the kitchen to the back of the house. Although she knew where the room was, he wanted to check she had what she needed.

When she had first come over to wash her clothes, he had shown her the room, surprised when she had lingered outside the door, seeming afraid to enter. She had been here several times since, so it caught him off guard when he opened the door, gesturing for her to step in first, that she faltered, looking worried.

Was it because he was with her? It was a small room. Perhaps it was the proximity. After that first time, she had only ever been in here by herself.

It needled a little that she was still scared of him. With every step forward, it seemed there was another one back.

Still, he reminded himself that patience was key.

Leaving her outside the room, as if it was no big deal, he started opening cupboards and pulling out bottles of cleaning products and cloths. 'The hoover is in the tall cupboard and you'll find a mop and duster in there too.'

'Thank you.' She hadn't budged from her spot.

'So, I guess I'll leave you to it,' he shrugged, stepping out of the room. 'I have some paperwork to do, so I'll be at the dining table. Give me a shout if you need anything, okay? And help yourself to coffee if you want one.'

He started to walk away.

'Nico?'

'Yes?'

'You haven't said where you would like me to clean.'

Was he meant to? He had never had anyone do this for him before, so he had no idea how it was supposed to work. And Callie wasn't a cleaner by trade. Did she know?

He must have been frowning in confusion because she elaborated.

'What I was trying to say is, are you happy for me to clean everywhere? Or are there any rooms you'd rather I stay out of?'

'You mean, like my bedroom?' he spoke without thinking, eyes widening when a blush crept into Callie's cheeks and she looked to the floor.

Fool.

He ran an agitated hand through his hair, backing away. 'Look, I've never done this before, so just clean what you think needs cleaning. I don't mind. And nowhere is off limits, okay?'

Turning on his heel, leaving before she protested or asked any further questions where he could embarrass them both, he let the dogs back indoors, then skulked through to the kitchen and filled the kettle, staring out at the view of the stables, with the paddocks in the foreground, as he waited for the water to boil.

He had hoped to spend time with Red this morning, but that was now looking unlikely.

The Irish Sport Horse had initially belonged to a lead huntsman, before being transported to a new owner in Norfolk for showjumping. He had struggled with the turns in the jump arena though, which was when Nico had bought him.

The gelding had been overexcitable when he had first arrived at Willow Brook Farm, refusing to stand still at the mounting block and off like a shot the second Nico was in the saddle. It had taken a few months to calm him down and get him to understand he didn't have to run everywhere fast and jump hedges, and now he was showing so much potential, he was exciting to work with.

Unfortunately, the paperwork couldn't wait and Nico had a retired racehorse arriving in a couple of hours, who had been causing all kinds of problems for his inexperienced owner.

And still there was no sign of Anya.

Irritation bristled again, souring the edges of his mood as he carried his coffee into the lounge.

Although he had updated parts of the house, this room still contained much of the original furniture. Leather sofas in a caramel brown and built-in shelves that still displayed Teddy's vast collection of books. Some of the photos remained too. Pictures of Teddy with his beloved horses, and one or two featuring a young Nico. The only additional frame was one he had added of Paul, Janice and Laurel – the family who had given him somewhere to belong.

A wide archway led through to the dining area and the enormous, rustic table. When the Bishops had been alive, they had eaten here every night and there had been many occasions when Nico had joined them. Now it was just him here, and as he dined alone, there was no use for it, other than as storage for all of his paperwork.

Ethan, who had been his friend first before becoming his accountant, liked everything in his life neat and orderly, and he despaired of Nico. Especially when it came to doing his books.

'You have to record everything properly for me,' he had complained on countless occasions. 'And stop doing things for free.'

He tried, but sometimes people needed a helping hand. He couldn't turn his back on them. Ethan was going to chew him out over today's client, as Nico had lowered his fee again, and he could already hear his friend's voice when he found out: 'I'm trying to make you money. Can you please listen to me?'

Nico did, sometimes. But, on other occasions, he couldn't help himself.

But then, perhaps that was why their friendship worked so well. It wasn't healthy to always agree.

While he wrote out invoices, Callie cleaned. He could hear her footsteps as she moved around the house and the hum of the vacuum cleaner, finding it strange having someone else here with him after so long of it being just him and the dogs.

Work kept him busy, and he wasn't interested in seriously dating, preferring the odd hook-up instead. There simply wasn't room for a relationship in his life and generally, he loathed distractions, so it surprised him that he found her presence in the house comforting.

She kept out of his way. Whether that was because she was trying not to disturb him or she wanted to avoid him, he wasn't sure, so he just left her to do her thing, staying out of her way too when he had finished.

He had just poured a second cup of coffee and was debating seeing if she wanted a cup, since she had ignored his offer to help herself, when the doorbell chimed, accompanied by a chorus of barking from the dogs.

Probably Ethan. His friend was self-employed and, as he lived just down the road, he often took breaks, calling in to annoy Nico.

As he stepped into the hallway, Nico spotted Callie through the open door of the downstairs cloakroom. She was on her hands and knees, scrubbing at the tiled floor. A waste of time as the room was never used, but, he supposed it didn't matter if it kept her happy.

Her gaze met his as he went to the door and he could tell from her expression that she was worried about who the caller was.

Was she always going to be this way? Looking over her shoulder, jumping at every little noise, scared that her past was about to catch up with her?

While it frustrated him, his heart also squeezed a little. Stone had really done a number on her. She deserved to feel safe. She also shouldn't believe it necessary to have to clean his damn floors.

Pushing aside his annoyance, he opened the door, finding a Stuart the other side. Just not the one he had been expecting.

'Faith?' he greeted her, surprised. 'Is everything okay?'

She had a wide smile on her face, so it clearly was.

'Olive's riding lesson?' she reminded. 'You'd forgotten, hadn't you?'

Nico had, but he remembered now. Olive usually had her lesson on a Saturday, but it had been brought forward so the family could go away for the second week of the Easter break.

'Where's Olive?'

'She's run ahead to see Anya.'

Nico cursed under his breath. This was another reason to be annoyed at the girl for letting him down. Olive adored her and now Anya was going to disappoint her too?

He was about to explain to Faith that she wasn't here, but she had already stepped into the house, her mouth dropping open when she spotted Callie in the cloakroom.

'You're getting her to clean for you,' she scolded, slapping Nico on the arm. 'She's your family. Not hired help.'

'I'm not making her do anything,' he scowled, moving back before she could hit him again.

Hearing the two of them, Callie got to her feet. 'It was my idea,' she told Faith, coming over to join them. 'Nico's letting me stay in Stable Cottage rent-free. It's the least I can do to say thank you.'

Faith seemed to have a different opinion on that, but Nico knew she liked Callie, so she kept it to herself.

'Callie Adams. You should be getting out and exploring the area,' she insisted. 'Norfolk is beautiful, but it's big. Do you have a car?' Without waiting for Callie to answer, she turned to Nico. 'If not, could she borrow the Jeep?'

'I don't drive,' Callie quickly pushed in. 'I don't have a licence.'

Not strictly a lie. Nico knew that she could drive, but she was telling the truth that she no longer had a licence.

'Oh, that's a shame,' Faith commented. 'Well, you can come out with me one day. A girls' day out. How does that sound? We could grab lunch somewhere. Maybe do a spa or shopping. We're going away for a few days, but then Olive will be back at school and I'll have some free time. What do you say?'

She was moving at a hundred miles an hour in that infectious, full-on way of hers and Nico could see the alarm on Callie's face.

'I don't know if... I would need to see... I—'

'She would love to,' he interrupted, watching her eyes widen in horror.

'Great, that's settled.' Faith turned to Callie. 'I'll get in touch when we're back. Do you want to give me your number?'

'I... um... I don't have my phone on me.'

If Faith didn't believe her, she didn't show it. 'No worries. Nico can message me with it. Right, I suppose I'd better go and say hello to Anya.'

'About that,' Nico said, halting her as she was about to leave.

Faith arched a questioning brow.

'Anya's not here. She didn't show up for work this morning.'

'She didn't?'

That was Callie and Faith in chorus.

'Do you think she's all right?' Faith added, sounding concerned.

'I think I am getting tired of giving her chances.' Nico huffed a bit. 'I honestly thought she'd stopped pulling this shit.'

'Don't jump to conclusions, Nico. There could be a reason. She wouldn't let Olive down like this. Have you checked with Larissa or Vince to make sure she's okay?'

He hadn't. He had just assumed the worst, and realised now that perhaps he should have made a call. 'I'll do it now. Why don't you go and get Olive. Toby and Jodie are around somewhere. Have a word with them. I'm sure Jodie will take the lesson.'

When Faith hesitated, he urged her, 'Go. I'll catch up with you in a few minutes.'

It wasn't that he wanted her gone so he could make the call. Callie was looking furious that he had committed her to a day out. He needed to explain why he had done it.

She rounded on him the moment Faith left, closing the door after her, then stomping after Nico as he headed into the kitchen.

'Why did you tell her I'd spend the day with her? You have no right to do that. You know I have to keep a low profile and I can't afford to go shopping with her!'

He had never seen her angry before and the American accent she had mostly lost was more pronounced. There was a steeliness to her deep blue eyes, and the colour that flushed her cheeks was from temper rather than embarrassment.

It was the most alive she had been since coming to stay with him.

'Yes, I know all of that.'

'Then why the hell, Nico? Why did you say it? I get to decide. Not you. I appreciate everything you've done for me here, but this is my life. I won't let you control me.'

Shit. Was that what she thought he had been trying to do? He wasn't her ex.

'Look, can you just let me explain.'

'There's nothing you can say that will excuse what you just did.'

'Callie. Please. Just listen.'

She quietened for a moment, but continued to pace in front of him, and he suspected she would go off like a rocket at any moment, so he spoke quickly.

'Faith is kind and well-meaning and smart, but she is also stubborn. I know her well enough that she wouldn't have taken no for an answer, and when you continued to resist, she would have become suspicious. Trust me, it is easier to agree now, then back out later.'

She stared at him, her expression wary, and he knew she was

trying to decide if he was telling her the truth.

'Only you, me and Laurel know why you're here, and it needs to stay that way. I love Ethan and Faith and I would trust them with my life, but secrets are better kept between as few people as possible. It only takes one slip-up or confiding in the wrong person for word to spread. That can't happen.'

'So you're saying you did it to protect me?'

Her chin was raised defiantly, and he couldn't decide if she was considering his words or getting ready to call bullshit.

'Yes.' He knew Faith well and he needed Callie to trust him on this.

'Okay,' she said eventually, her tone stiff. 'But you need to get me out of this. I can't go out with her. I need you to promise.'

He nodded, and when he spoke his agreement, he meant it. 'I promise.'

\* \* \*

It was late afternoon when Nico heard back from Vince Mitchell.

He had called Anya's uncle after failing to reach her mother. And part of him was relieved that Larissa hadn't answered her phone. Nico wasn't a fan and, having had to fend her off the first time they had met, she now scared him half to death. Vince, on the other hand, had an acerbic wit and a heart of gold. Two qualities that he appreciated.

When Nico had called him earlier, telling him that Anya hadn't shown up for work, Vince was annoyed, but he hadn't seemed too worried. He admitted to Nico that he and Anya had fought the previous afternoon – a fight, Nico would later learn once he got off the phone, that Callie had witnessed the tail end of.

It hadn't been anything serious. Since Vince's boyfriend, David, had appeared on the scene, Anya and he had grown close, with

Anya preferring to confide her secrets in David rather than her uncle. Vince was hurt at being excluded, especially when he'd discovered Anya was seeing someone and hadn't told him about it, and he had foolishly confronted her. Insults had been thrown and cross words exchanged, but, like Nico, Vince assumed she had taken off somewhere to cool down.

Now, though, he wasn't convinced. 'She doesn't have her medication with her,' he explained, his high-pitched tone betraying his panic.

'Are you sure?' Nico knew Anya was epileptic, which required her taking tablets twice a day to keep seizures under control. It was something she treated seriously, setting herself alarms.

'Yes, I went round to Larissa's and checked. Everything is on her bedside table.'

'And there's no chance she took a couple of tablets with her?'

'No!' Vince was getting frustrated now. 'She has a pill organiser for the different days of the week. The ones she should have taken today are still there. Look, Nico, I get that Anya was mad, but she's a sensible girl when it comes to her medication. She knows about the complications and how serious it can be if she doesn't take it.'

'Maybe she's with this boyfriend. Has David told you who it is?'

'No. He says she never told him his name. All he knows is that they were hooking up and she had fallen for him. She told him it was someone she has known for a while, but she had never thought of him as more than a friend until recently.' Vince paused for breath, and when he spoke again, the heat had gone from his tone. 'What if something has happened to her?'

Guilt gnawed at Nico's gut, as he remembered how angry he had been this morning, assuming that Anya had let him down. He should have contacted Vince sooner, instead of jumping to conclusions. Wherever Anya was, he hoped she was safe. If not, he wouldn't be able to forgive himself.

# 13

BEFORE

When I told my friends from work that I was moving to Devon, they had all been eager to come and stay, desperate to see Duncan's country home.

Despite making promises it would happen, I have been living here for seven months, and no arrangements have been made. I desperately miss them and there are times when our little WhatsApp group is the only thing keeping me sane.

There's Juliette, all French chic cool, with her cutting wit and wry observations; excitable Tracy, who finds the positive in every situation; and scatty Aarna, who is the biggest and most lovable klutz I know and has a brilliant, self-deprecating sense of humour.

I have asked Duncan a couple of times if they can visit, but he has been ready with excuses for why it isn't convenient. The second time I asked, I could tell he was getting irritated with me.

'I love you, Mica, but you're so selfish sometimes. You know how busy I am. Do you think I have time to entertain your friends?'

'You don't have to put yourself out. I can look after them,' I had pointed out. 'I just really miss them.'

'For Christ's sake. You're a grown woman. Not a child. Are you telling me you can't cope without your friends around? Stop being so pathetic.'

I stopped asking after that.

Therefore, it catches me off guard when he suggests they visit.

'I thought you might all like that catch-up,' he says.

Thrilled, I throw my arms around him. 'Thank you.'

It's exactly what I need. Much as I love Duncan, I have been struggling with depression recently, and this will be the perfect pick-me-up. The cold weather and constant darkness are affecting my mood. Things will be better when spring gets here.

I hate being unhappy because I know I'm lucky to be with him. Duncan reminds me on a regular basis that he could have anyone, but he has chosen me. At first, it was flattering, but now it is starting to make me a little bit paranoid. He is attractive and successful, and I try my best to be his equal, but somehow, I always seem to get it wrong, and he is always quick to point out when I do.

I have learnt to dread the social functions he takes me to. While he exudes effortless charm and confidence, I feel clumsy and stupid beside him, knowing everyone is probably wondering why he is with me.

It doesn't help that I am isolated out here in the countryside. Duncan likes to know where I am, so even while walking Chester or visiting the town centre, I check in with him. I don't know anyone else here, and although this house is enormous, sometimes I feel like I am trapped in a cage. Winter has been particularly difficult. Along with Duncan, it is ebbing at my confidence.

He can be picky, and he makes a lot of comments about my appearance, critiquing my hair or my clothes, or reminding me to be careful with what I eat, as the pounds can creep on.

He is doing it with my best interests at heart, but it can be overwhelming. I hadn't realised until I met him that I had so many flaws.

This is not how I envisioned life would be when I agreed to move to Devon.

Things changed after the night he hit me.

He still claims that he didn't do it intentionally. That he had seen me trip and reached out to catch me, his hand accidentally knocking my face.

I don't remember it that way, but after I gained consciousness, I was so confused, and I had both him and Rob, who apparently had seen the whole thing, telling me otherwise.

I remember we had been fighting and that I was upset about what he had said to Dad, but after I fell, Duncan's anger had evaporated, immediately replaced with concern.

What had happened was behind us and he was desperate to fix things.

There have been a couple of occasions now where he has really scared me and in the heat of the moment, I have wanted to walk out on him, but then he smothers me with so much love and kindness, and is the humblest man I know. He is a good person 90 per cent of the time. Do I want to give up the best thing that has ever happened to me because of that rogue 10 per cent?

Besides. He needs me. After both of those awful incidents, he has been at his most vulnerable. Opening up to me, talking about his childhood and how difficult things were for him and his mother, and how devastated he was when he lost her. I think it is the grief that occasionally sends him into a rage and I know it frightens him because he worries he can't control it. I have to stand by him and love him the best I can. If I keep him anchored, make him realise he can trust me and I will never let him down, I know I can help him heal.

We had such an honest and heartfelt talk after my fall, so it surprised me the following day when he announced at breakfast, he would keep Shirley on until after Christmas, to give me a little more time to recover.

His comment about letting her go had been said in the heat of the moment. Something he didn't mean. He didn't really expect me to look after the house, I had presumed. But apparently he did, and he was keen to get me agreeing with him.

'We don't need a housekeeper, do we?' He had phrased it as a question, as he bit into his toast. 'It's a bit indulgent, especially when I am trying to persuade people to give up their cash to help disadvantaged kids. The last thing I need is for one of the tabloids to print a story that I rely on other people to clean up my mess. You know they love to try to knock people off their pedestals. I don't need any bad press.'

I wasn't sure how to respond. 'It's a big house, Duncan.'

I must have sounded reluctant, because the next thing I knew, those damn dice of his were on the table.

'How about we settle this our usual way? If you win, Shirley stays. If I do, I have myself a new cleaner in January.' He winked at me then, as if it was a big joke.

'I don't think we should decide this with dice,' I argued. 'We need to discuss it some more.'

'Oh come on, Mica. How many people have a housekeeper in this day and age? I'm sure we'll cope. I can help too.'

Okay, so this had changed. Now we were a cleaning duo?

'You're going to help me scrub and hoover and dust?' I queried.

'Of course, why not? I'm not scared of a little manual labour,' he laughed, picking up the dice. 'So, what will you go for?'

'Evens,' I told him, caving. I should probably mix it up a little. I seem to go for evens a lot and I'm rarely lucky.

I watched the dice land, my stomach heavy as I saw the two and a three, and Duncan gave me a gloating smile.

'Fine,' I agreed, deciding it easiest to play along. It was still another week away. Plenty of time for him to change his mind. This was just one of his mad moments. I was certain he would change his mind about letting Shirley go. And it wasn't that I was too precious to clean the house, but the place is bloody enormous.

Christmas came and went. A sombre affair with expensive gifts I didn't want and huge Christmas trees decked out in red and silver baubles and ribbons, with hundreds of fairy lights making the branches twinkle. Duncan had hired a company to come in and dress them, and though they were beautiful, they were a little too perfect.

It was just the two of us and Rob for Christmas Day lunch. Phoebe was with Ed's family and Dad and April back in the States. We Zoomed on Christmas Day evening, Duncan all smiles as he placed his arm around me and bantered with my dad.

Then New Year was spent in London at the most glamorous party I have ever attended. I wanted to enjoy it, but I felt out of my depth, and while Duncan was the life and soul, I retreated into myself. No one was interested in me. It was the Duncan show, and as everyone else counted down to midnight, I was desperate to escape to the sanctuary of our hotel room.

Rob drove us back to Dartmouth on New Year's Day, then on the second morning of the new year, I was awoken by something landing on top of me.

'Wakey, wakey.'

'What are you doing?' I asked, rubbing my eyes.

'I've got you a present, for your first day in the job.'

My heart sank as I opened the package, finding a black apron inside. Lettering on the front read, *Keep it clean.*

'Come on. Get up and put it on.'

'I need to walk Chester before I can get started.'

'No need,' Duncan told me, as I glanced down at the dog bed

and realised it was empty. That was at least one thing he had relented on. Chester still slept upstairs with us. But where was he?

My heart thumped in alarm. 'What have you done with him?'

He laughed. 'Honestly, Mica. Your face. He's fine. Rob has taken him out. I want you to get an early start. You have a lot of work to do.'

He wasn't kidding and I worked my butt off that first day, not liking that he kept hovering near me, reminding me what to do or telling me I had missed a bit.

By the time I was finished, every muscle in my body ached.

'I thought you said you were going to help.'

'I did. I supervised,' he pointed out. 'Not a bad day's work, but you're not to Shirley's level. Still, I'm sure you will improve with practice.'

Cheeky bastard.

'You've seen how hard I worked today.'

'I did. And I expect you'll want an early night. Tomorrow, I want you to give all of the floors a good clean.'

My face fell.

Somehow, I had managed to convince myself this was a one-off, a prank, but no, it seemed he was serious. Surely he didn't expect me to clean the house permanently? This was just him being challenging and trying to push my buttons.

Although it was working, I tried my best not to show it, convinced he would eventually tire of this game.

So far, he hasn't and I am beginning to resent him. I am not going to spend my life being his cleaner while he sits around with his feet up. I am close to telling him this, but when he makes the suggestion that my friends can visit, my mood changes.

Things are about to take a turn for the better, I just know it.

I am quick to message the WhatsApp group and Juliette is the first to respond.

We were beginning to think you were never going to ask.

Tracy and Aarna are also quick to reply, and after a little back and forth between the group and Duncan, we soon have a plan in place. They are going to come and stay for the night the first weekend of February.

I am so excited at the prospect of seeing them, and Duncan knows it.

As I count down to their arrival, nerves start to creep in. I want so desperately for this weekend to be perfect, and aside from the cleaning, for which I am putting a brave face on, everything seems to be going smoothly. Our relationship is on track and our sex life is good. He is being sweet and attentive, the perfect boyfriend, but I can't shake the feeling that everything is about to derail.

The night before their visit, I can barely sleep.

Something will go wrong.

My friends will have to cancel.

Something important will come up and Duncan will say they can't come.

He will lose his temper.

*Please don't let him lose his temper in front of them.*

But none of those things happen, and suddenly they are there, getting out of Juliette's Mini, and I burst into tears because I have missed them so badly.

'Hey, what's up with you?' Aarna pulls me into a hug. 'I thought you'd be pleased to see us.'

'I am,' I sniff. 'These are happy tears. I'm just so glad you're here.' As I hug her back, I catch Duncan's expression. He is scowling at me. 'We're both glad you're here,' I correct, easing back.

None of the girls pick up on his mood or the fact he disappears back into the house, because we are all so busy catching up with each other, and them making a fuss of Chester, who has come out to meet them, tail wagging in excitement, and we have so much to say. By the time we drag the bags into the hall, Duncan is back, but this time full of smiles. The perfect host.

'Here, let me get those for you,' he insists, scooping up the luggage as if it is simply bags of groceries. 'I'll take these upstairs and show you your rooms. I'm sure you all want to freshen up before you have a look around. Mica, why don't you go and put the kettle on?'

He has them all on side, hanging on to his every word as they follow him up the stairs, though Juliette glances down at me, mouthing *Mica* and seeming amused.

I am so used to the name now, I forget she doesn't know it's what he calls me.

For a moment, I feel lost, standing wringing my hands together in the hallway. Chester nudges against me, his contact reassuring, and I spend a moment making a fuss of him before going through to put the kettle on as instructed.

Why can't I shake this ominous feeling that something is going to go wrong?

It's stupid really, because Duncan has made an effort for this weekend, asking one of his friends, who is a chef, to cook for us tonight.

After the girls have settled and we have caught up over tea, Chester and I give them a tour of the grounds and they excitedly bombard me with questions about life at The Old Rectory, asking what it is like to live with a movie star, if he is good in bed – that, of course, is from Juliette – if we have parties at the house, and if so, have I met any of his famous friends, and Aarna, who is the mystery and thriller queen, wants to know if there are any secret passageways or hidden doors.

There are none. At least not that I am aware of.

They also ask questions about work, and I say I am currently considering my options. I can't risk Duncan trying to embarrass me again.

Of course I don't tell them he has sacked his housekeeper and is making me clean for him. Perhaps I should, but I feel the need to provide the illusion of the life they think we have and to confess the truth would be too humiliating. There have been moments over the last few weeks when I have wondered if I have made a mistake in coming here.

I was so drawn in by Duncan and ridiculously flattered that someone of his stature was showing an interest in me, and when things started moving fast, I never stopped to question whether I should be trying to put the brakes on. I gave up everything for a man I barely knew, and some of the truths I have learnt along the way have been hard-hitting.

There might be rough, but there is also smooth, and I try to remember that now. It was his idea that I invite my friends to stay this weekend, so I know he can be kind and thoughtful. He is trying his best.

My friends have all brought pretty dresses with them for the evening. They consider this a special event and want to make an effort. Juliette suggests we get ready together, so I invite them to mine and Duncan's room, touched when he brings up a couple of bottles of chilled champagne and four glasses.

His friend, Kasem, has arrived to prepare the meal, so Duncan disappears downstairs to chat with him while we get ready.

Juliette arrives at the room first, stopping to make a fuss of Chester, whose tail starts thumping as soon as he sees her, then her jaw dropping when she sees I have a walk-in wardrobe. Her eyes light up as she steps into her version of Narnia, trailing her fingers along the rows of clothes Duncan has bought me, wowing and exclaiming '*Mon Dieu*' several times, which I know means 'my God' in French, as she checks out the labels.

I blush, aware my wardrobe is extravagant. I never asked for or expected any of these clothes and, if I am honest, I feel more comfortable in my own things. Duncan is a difficult man to say no to, though, and I haven't dared tell him it all feels a little too much.

'What are you going to wear?' she asks.

'I don't know,' I shrug, joining her.

That's not true. If I am entirely honest, I want to wear my go-to little black dress. It might be about ten years old, but I feel comfortable in it, and I know the cap sleeves and sweetheart neckline flatter me.

She pulls out a classy red jumpsuit that I have yet to try on. 'This is gorgeous, Callie.'

It is, but I screw up my nose. It's more her than me, and it will look great against her darker skin.

'Why don't you borrow it?' I insist. She will pull it off better than me.

Juliette doesn't even try to protest, her eyes lighting up. 'You wouldn't mind?'

'Of course not.'

She hugs me tight. 'You're the best friend. I hope he makes you happy.'

It strikes me as an odd thing to say. I have everything here: a gorgeous old house, designer clothes, a drop-dead handsome, ex-movie-star boyfriend. Why would she question whether he makes me happy?

She must feel me tense because she eases back slightly. 'He does make you happy, doesn't he, Callie?'

The fact she has phrased it as a question and is now looking directly at me for the answer has me wavering for a moment.

'Of course,' I manage to get out. 'Why wouldn't I be happy?'

'I'm just checking.' She smiles, as if to make light of her prying, and squeezes my hands in a comforting gesture. 'You know you can always tell me if you're not?'

The silence lingers between us. I desperately want someone to talk to, but what if I am making a mistake? Juliette is one of my closest friends. I should be able to talk to her.

'I miss you so much,' I tell her, unsure how to proceed. 'I love Duncan, but sometimes I wonder if...'

I trail off. A loud creak from the landing has both of our heads turning towards the open door, and as my shoulders instinctively tense, I see Juliette's eyes widen.

Breaking away, I go to the door, glancing both ways along the hallway, but no one is there.

What the hell is wrong with me? I am getting paranoid.

Giggling comes from a couple of rooms down and Aarna and Tracy step out of Aarna's room. They are both already dressed, but have bags of make-up with them.

My moment of panic passes. It's an old house and it makes noises. No one was listening in on my conversation with Juliette.

For a short while, it feels like old times. We have music playing, courtesy of Juliette's phone, and champagne flowing as we finish getting ready, and as we chat, there are plenty of laughs, as well as cuddles for Chester, who seems as delighted as me to see my friends. Juliette does everyone's eyeliner and mascara and she curls my hair. She looks stunning in the red jumpsuit and Aarna and Tracy look fab too. I am so glad my friends are here. Until today, I didn't realise how much I missed them.

In the end, I opt for my favourite little black dress. I know Duncan has bought me many beautiful clothes, but sometimes you just get attached to a particular item. I team it with a pair of beautiful heels and the cute little diamond earrings he gave me as a moving-in gift, but still I sense his disapproval when we head downstairs, and I swear his gaze darkens when he spots Juliette wearing my jumpsuit.

It is momentary and I wonder if I was mistaken when he is all smiles again, topping up everyone's glasses and acting like the life and soul of the party.

He is everyone's best friend as we have pre-dinner drinks before dinner is served, even making a fuss of Chester, and I gradually relax.

What is wrong with me? He doesn't have to do this, but he thinks so much of me, he is here, entertaining my friends. I know we have had our ups and downs, but he is making such an effort for me. I have the best boyfriend in the world and I need to lay off with the suspicion and start appreciating him.

Tonight is going to be perfect.

# 14

Everything is going smoothly, and as we sit at the dining table, I am finally relaxing, ready to enjoy this evening. The young waiter accompanying Kasem serves up our food, and as we tuck in, conversation flows easily.

Duncan seems determined we will have a good time and he is continually topping up our glasses. I haven't seen him this happy in a while and I am sure it is the infectious chatter that my friends have brought to the table. Sometimes, this house feels stuffy and unloved, but tonight it is full of warmth and laughter.

The Thai dish is delicious and after the plates are cleared, we are presented with a trio of desserts, comprising of a lemon tart, a fancy-looking trifle in a mini martini glass, and what looks like a caramel-topped cheesecake. It's not until I bite into it that I realise it's butterscotch, and there's a slightly salty taste to it, which suggests another ingredient.

My plate is almost empty when Tracy clears her throat, before asking in a small voice, 'Is there peanut in this?'

Everyone turns to look at her and I realise in horror that she is touching her throat, her face pale and sweaty.

We all know Tracy has an allergy. Duncan included. I was very specific and it's not something he would forget. Not when it's serious like this. There's no way it's peanut. She must be having a reaction to something else.

The waiter must have alerted Kasem because he appears in the doorway. 'Butterscotch and peanut butter,' he confirms, looking to Duncan. 'Like you asked for.'

'You asked for it?' Juliette is on her feet. She turns to me. 'Callie. You wouldn't have forgotten about her peanut allergy. I know you wouldn't have.'

I shake my head, dumbfounded, and look at Duncan. 'I told you she can't eat peanuts.'

The edges of his mouth tighten and, for the briefest second, his expression turns mean, but then he gathers himself. 'No. You didn't say a word. Jesus Christ. I've tried my best here, Mica. I never would have picked peanuts if you'd told me. I wanted tonight to be perfect.'

'But I did tell you. I remember.'

How dare he try to put this on me?

He takes a moment setting down his cutlery before glaring at me. 'No. If you had, I would've remembered.'

Is he doing this purposely or has he really forgotten? My cheeks burn as tears threaten.

'I'm sorry,' I whisper, realising the only way to smooth things over is to take the blame.

Wheezing from Tracy draws our attention.

Oh God, her lips have started to swell and she looks like she is struggling to breathe.

'Where's your pen?' Aarna doesn't wait for an answer, already rooting through Tracy's clutch bag that's sitting on the table.

'Have you injected her before?' Juliette demands.

They are gathered around Tracy and it takes me a moment to

realise I am still sitting at the table. I go to push my chair out, but Duncan's firm hand on my arm stops me. The next thing I know, he is up from the table and taking control of the situation, snatching the EpiPen from Aarna and, in one swift move, stabbing it into Tracy's thigh.

'I have a friend with an allergy,' he explains, as Aarna stares at him wide-eyed.

Everyone is concentrating on Tracy's recovery, so questions aren't asked until the ambulance arrives.

'You could have killed your friend tonight.' Duncan is furious as he gives me a dressing-down over the incident.

We are in the kitchen, while the paramedics check over Tracy in the lounge. Kasem and his waiter are quietly packing away their things and Juliette is pacing, looking agitated, while Aarna and I sit at the table.

Juliette had blamed Duncan for the incident, but he had put on quite a show, convincingly oozing a mix of sympathy, hurt, shock and outrage, insistent that Tracy's peanut allergy had not been explained to him.

His words left me stunned. I remember our conversation clearly, so how come he doesn't? Is he lying or does he genuinely not recall me telling him?

I don't know what to believe and although I protested my innocence at first, he is getting angry with me. If I push him too far, there will be consequences.

'Do you honestly have nothing to say for yourself?' he demands.

'Leave her alone,' Juliette snaps, while Aarna stays quiet.

I would give anything to not be here right now and I honestly don't know what to do for the best. I know I have done nothing wrong, but Duncan is in full denial. I fear things could turn nasty and I will pay a worse price.

He looks thunderous as he stares at Juliette. 'Her carelessness almost killed someone tonight. Take some responsibility, Mica.'

I swallow hard, aware tears are now falling, and I try to blink them away, staring at my hands on the table. 'I honestly thought I had told you, but maybe...' I trail off. 'I'm sorry.' I force myself to look up at Juliette. 'I'm really sorry.'

Her expression is stony as she stares at me. Is she angry that I've accepted responsibility or is she disappointed in me, believing it is my fault?

'I'm going to check on Tracy,' she says, her voice emotionless, and as she leaves the room, Aarna quickly scuttles after her. I don't think she wants to be left in the kitchen with Duncan and me, and I don't blame her.

Duncan's hand comes to rest on my shoulder, but it is not in reassurance. His fingers digging into my skin to the point it becomes so painful, I wince and pull away.

I hear him step away, talking quietly to Kasem, thanking him for his services, and apologising for what he refers to as 'tonight's embarrassing episode'.

It's not long before Kasem and his waiter, as well as the para-medics, are gone, and the mood in the house has hit a new low point. I apologise to Tracy as soon as they leave and she nods, but doesn't say much. I know the reaction to the peanut butter has left her feeling weak, and she excuses herself, heading up to bed.

Duncan insists the rest of us have post-dinner drinks and as we sit in the lounge, you could cut the atmosphere with a knife. He is barely speaking to me, and Juliette isn't talking to him. Aarna and I sit meekly with the brandies Duncan pours us, my hand on Chester's soft fur for comfort, and the awkward conversation in the room is peppered by periods of uncomfortable silence.

To my relief, Duncan eventually leaves the room and, moments later, I hear his footsteps on the stairs.

'What the fuck, Callie?' Juliette demands, the moment he is out of earshot.

My heart sinks. She's not letting this drop. 'I said I'm sorry. I don't know what else you want me to say. I feel terrible about what happened.'

'Why are you covering for him?'

'I'm not,' I protest, but the denial sounds weak to my own ears.

'I know you wouldn't forget about Tracy's allergy. So either you told him and he forgot or...' She trails off, but her insinuation is clear. She is considering that Duncan gave Tracy peanut butter on purpose, and I know Aarna now is too when I hear her gasp in horror.

There is no way Duncan would have done that. He shouldn't have made me take the blame for him, but still, it had been a mistake. I have to smooth this over and the only way I can do that is to convince my friends it was all my fault.

'I've been under a bit of stress lately,' I begin, feeling my way forward. 'And I keep forgetting stuff. I knew I had to tell Duncan and I thought I had, but it must have slipped my mind.'

'Bullshit.'

'It honestly isn't his fault. I'm the one to blame.'

Juliette and Aarna both stare at me and their disappointment is clear.

'I'm going to bed,' Juliette says after a moment, finishing her drink and putting her glass down on the coffee table.

Aarna hasn't touched her brandy. She hadn't wanted the drink in the first place. 'Me too,' she nods, getting up to follow. 'Night, Callie.'

Then they are gone and I let out a shaky breath, relieved to finally be alone with just my dog. I had been so excited to see my friends, but now I wish they had never come here. I just want them to go home.

Duncan never comes back down, so I assume he must have gone to bed, and I dread knowing I will have to go and join him soon. He is so angry with me. How is he going to react when it is just the two of us alone?

I put off going upstairs, instead sipping at my brandy, my hand trembling against the snifter, and fight to control my panic as I stroke Chester's soft fur.

Eventually, I can't delay it any longer and I clear the glasses, taking my time washing them up and returning them to the drinks cabinet before heading upstairs.

The bedroom is dark, but I can see still make out Duncan's shape under the covers. He is fortunately facing away from me. I settle Chester in his bed as quietly as possible, making sure he has his favourite stuffed teddy, before undressing and carefully getting under the duvet. I don't want to disturb Duncan, and I am relieved when I hear the grunt of a snore and realise he is asleep.

Still, as I lay there in the dark, my body tense as I replay the events of the evening, I know sleep is unlikely to come.

* * *

The morning after is just as uncomfortable as the night before.

I am exhausted from lack of sleep. Although it feels like I've had none, I did doze off eventually and Duncan was already up when I awoke. Unsure where he was, I stayed in bed for a while, delaying the inevitable awkwardness.

No one mentions what happened as we sit around the breakfast table, other than to ask Tracy if she is okay, but it is the elephant in the room that everyone is thinking about.

She is quiet and pale, despite telling us she is fine, and Juliette and Aarna are trying to make an effort, but I can tell things are off. Their smiles don't reach their eyes and the way my three friends came downstairs huddled together and whispering suggests they have been talking together about everything.

Duncan is the only one who seems to be in a good mood, which is one relief for me. He is chatting to everyone and back to being the perfect host as he serves the fry-up he has been cooking, either unbothered or oblivious when my friends suspiciously pick at the food he puts in front of them.

They mostly leave full plates, instead eager to leave, and I'm surprised to find they have already packed. As I go out to see them off, I can tell Juliette wants to have a word with me. It's not possible though, as Duncan hovers nearby.

Our farewell hugs are stiff and feel forced, and only their goodbye fuss for Chester seems genuine. While I am desperate for this awkwardness to be over, I have an overwhelming urge to cry, certain I am about to lose something precious.

The one genuine moment is when Juliette pulls me close, whispering into my ear, 'If you need me to come and get you, call me.'

I nod and she presses a kiss to my cheek. That's when the tears spill.

Duncan tucks me against his side, a perfect show of unity as we wave them goodbye, and as I watch the Mini disappearing into the distance, my stomach is heavy with homesickness.

Keeping his arm around me, he guides me back into the house and along the hallway towards the kitchen. He has fallen unusually quiet, but I am grateful. At least he no longer seems mad at me.

'What did Juliette just whisper to you?' he asks, the question coming out of nowhere and catching me off guard.

'Sorry?'

'Outside when you were saying goodbye. She whispered to you and you nodded. What did she say?'

He pauses in the doorway, turning me to face him so he can

watch my expression, and I am so flustered, I can't look at him, my gaze dropping.

'Nothing. She didn't say anything,' I manage. My face is too hot.

One moment I am staring at the floor, the next I am flying forward, my feet leaving the ground, but only briefly as my head smacks into the wall and I crumple into a heap on the hard tiles.

Dazed and in shock, for a second I think I have tripped, but then I realise Duncan has pushed me.

A sharp blast of pain throbs in my head and I blink, looking for him as I try to sit up. The plate I see hurtling towards me narrowly misses my face, and I flinch as it hits the wall, smashing into pieces. Bits of food splatter my face.

I see him then, slowly and with menace, walking towards me, and I try to duck away as he grabs hold of a clump of my hair, dragging me up to my knees. He is hurting me, his grip tight enough to bring fresh tears to my eyes.

'What are you doing?' My words are filled with panic.

'You're a liar, Mica. Do you think I'm stupid?'

'I'm not lying. I-I promise.'

The blunt force of his foot kicks me in the stomach, once, then a second time, as he shoves me to the floor again. I can't breathe, doubled up in agony and barely able to register what is happening. In the background, I can hear Chester barking, but I can't focus on anything but the pain.

'I invited your friends here, I tried to do something nice for you, and this is how you repay me? You've been an ungrateful little bitch all weekend. And now you are fucking lying to me.'

'Please,' I manage, but the word is lost on him. I have seen him angry before, but never in a blind rage like this, and I am scared.

'Did I give you permission to let that French whore wear your clothes?'

'No... no.'

'So why the fuck did she have your jumpsuit on last night?'

My heart is racing too fast. I'm sure I'm going to be sick. I curl up into a ball and whimper, unable to answer him.

'I bought those clothes for you to wear. Not to hand out to your friends. No wonder she didn't have any respect for me.'

He stomps away from me, pacing across the room, then back again, and the pure, unadulterated rage on his face has me preparing for another attack. It doesn't come, at least not yet, but I know he isn't finished.

'And I don't even know where to begin over your fuck-up last night with dinner. How dare you try to blame me because you are too bloody useless to pass information on? Do you know how embarrassing that was, to be accused in my own home in front of everyone? To be made to look a fool?'

But I had told him. I remember our conversation about the peanuts.

I dare not try to defend myself, though. 'I'm sorry,' I whisper.

'You're fucking sorry? Well, it's a bit bloody late now, isn't it? The damage is done. Look at all this wasted food this morning? I got up early to cook your friends a farewell breakfast and they barely ate it, because you've put ideas in their heads that I might have done something to it.'

I watch him pick up another plate and flinch, certain he is going to take aim again. He doesn't; instead, he comes over looking at me in contempt as he empties the contents over me. I squeeze my eyes shut as the slime of egg and beans runs down my face, the smell of bacon now turning my stomach.

Finished, he throws the plate to the floor, before picking up another and repeating the process. Lukewarm coffee and cold juice follows, seeping into my clothes and creating a sticky, uncomfortable puddle beneath me, but I dare not move, terrified that if I do, he will hurt me again.

When the table is empty, he ducks down beside me, his hand twisting in my hair again as he forces me to look up at him. 'What did she whisper to you?'

'I don't... she didn't—'

He pulls harder, making me cry out. 'This will get a whole lot worse for you if you don't tell me the truth.'

Tears leak from my eyes as fear rattles through me.

'She said... s-she told me... she said to call her if... if I n-needed her.' My teeth are chattering now and I wish they would stop, as I don't want him to see how frightened I am.

The change on his face is subtle, but he is close enough that I can see the tightening of his mouth and the hardness in his eyes. I can't breathe. Any moment now that last tenuous thread of control is going to snap.

'You nodded. You agreed?'

I dare not answer. Scared of what comes next.

'Do I make you unhappy, Mica?'

'No! I am happy.' My protest comes out too quickly. It's a lie and I suspect we both know it.

For a moment, he stares at me and I have no idea what he is thinking or planning to do next.

'Where's your phone?'

What? Why does he want it?

I hesitate and he shouts in my face. 'Where's your fucking phone?'

'On the... on the worktop.'

He gets up and I watch him look for it. Snatching it up, he puts it in his pocket.

'What are you... what are you going to do?' My voice is too small, too weak.

'I'm going out.'

With my phone? He's taking my phone? Panicking, I try to sit up. Everything hurts.

'Are you ready?'

The question isn't to me and I realise that Rob Jolly is standing in the doorway. He is not looking at me, instead his gaze is fixed on Duncan, as he nods in response. How much of this has he witnessed? And why has he not tried to stop Duncan? Is he seriously okay with this?

Duncan looks at me in disgust. 'Clean up this mess.' The anger has gone from his voice, but his tone is cold and hard-edged. 'When I get back, I expect this kitchen to be spotless.'

I watch him leave with Rob, and the second they are gone, Chester, who has been watching, agitated, from the corner of the room, his ears back, comes running over. He is disinterested in the food, instead prodding me with his wet nose and licking at my face. Still in too much pain to move, I pull him close, covering him in the slimy gunk from the plates, and sob against his soft fur.

The front door slams shut, but it's not until I hear Duncan's car leaving that I breathe a little easier.

What the hell just happened?

I can't stay. I have to leave.

Groaning, I roll onto my front, pulling myself up onto my knees. My head is pounding and I am sure I am going to be sick. The kitchen floor is a mess of spilt food and drink, and broken shards of crockery. Duncan expects me to clear this up, but time is too precious. I need to be gone before he returns. I will get in my car and go to the police. He won't get away with this.

My resolve lasts until I realise that, as well as my phone, he has also taken my car keys. With no landline in the house, he has effectively trapped me here. The only way to leave is on foot, and I am currently struggling to stand, let alone get out of the house. There are no close neighbours I can call on either.

Panic takes over, tears blurring my vision as each breath comes quicker than the last. I have to get out. What am I going to do?

His words ring in my ears.

*When I get back, I expect this kitchen to be spotless.*

I can't leave and if he comes back and the mess is still here... I am too scared to consider the consequences.

There is no choice but to bide my time. I need to get everything cleared up, then when he returns home and gives me back my phone, I will focus on getting the hell out of here.

# 15

---

## NOW

From what Callie had heard, the police weren't treating Anya's disappearance as suspicious, even though they were actively looking for her. The girl had a troubled past and it wasn't the first time she had taken off, but they were worried, as she had fled without her medication.

What if they had it wrong? Something sinister could have happened.

What Callie had seen that evening could change everything.

But it would also involve going to the police. And if she did that, she would be compromising her safety.

Duncan had friends on the force and she knew him well enough that he would have instructed them to keep an ear to the ground in case there was any word of her.

She couldn't risk him finding out she was still alive.

Unsure what to do, she had stewed over it, before finally confessing to Nico that she had seen Anya the night of her disappearance with an unidentified man in the woods.

Callie had been certain he was going to cart her off to the police station. Instead, his reaction had surprised her.

'I'll say it was me.'

His suggestion had come after a frustrated silence, probably because she hadn't told him straightaway. She knew he was worried about Anya but that he also understood her delay in coming forward.

'You'll tell them you were in the woods and saw Anya?'

'Yes.'

He would do that for her? Gratitude choked her. 'Thank you.' She was pensive for a moment. 'What do you think, Nico? Did someone hurt her or did she run away?'

She watched him scrub a hand over his face. 'Honestly? I don't know. I want to say she wouldn't run, but this is Anya. She's...' He trailed off, seeming reluctant to talk too much about the girl's past, even though Callie had heard enough from people to piece it together. She knew Vince was convinced his niece hadn't run and suspected foul play. Nico had spoken to him a couple of times.

Which she realised could be a problem. 'Isn't Vince going to wonder why you didn't mention seeing her with someone before?' she worried.

He hesitated, considering. 'I'll just have to say it slipped my mind.'

He said it casually enough, but they both knew it was a weak explanation.

The lying didn't sit easily with her, but it was the only way she could do the right thing and keep herself safe. So she went along with the plan, telling Nico in detail what she had seen.

While he went to the police station to give a statement, she waited at the cottage, trying to keep herself occupied: cleaning the tiny kitchen, scrubbing at the oven with vigour, and polishing the cupboards until they gleamed. Eventually hearing a knock at the door, she dropped everything, running to meet him, her words tripping over themselves. 'How did it go? Did they believe you? What did they say?'

'It's fine,' was all he said as he stepped inside. 'I told them everything you told me. It's done, and you don't need to worry about it any more.'

Callie's shoulders sagged with relief. In her head, she had conjured up so many scenarios, the worst being that they hadn't believed Nico, or that he had given away her hiding place.

He hadn't let her down.

It also made her realise for the first time just how far he was prepared to go to protect her. And with that, her guards lowered further. He was in her corner and ready to fight for her. She could trust him.

And that's how they came by their routine.

Nico asked her not to walk alone in the woods following Anya's disappearance. At first, his request sounded a little bit controlling, but she soon realised he was just concerned about her. Knowing she enjoyed the woodland walk, he started bringing Shyla and Dash over when she took Chester out, so they could all go together. The dogs playing while the two of them talked.

Other times, they met up with Vince and his partner, David, as well as other locals, heading out on searches in case Anya was lost and hurt, or worse.

If Vince wondered why Nico hadn't mentioned seeing Anya the night she went missing, he didn't say, and other than pressing Nico for any details he might remember the first time they searched, the subject was only ever mentioned in passing after that.

Callie liked Vince a lot, and she hated seeing the strain Anya's disappearance was putting on him.

As the weeks rolled by, the chances of finding Anya seemed to fade, the searches gradually dwindling in number until they stopped altogether. Everyone believed she had absconded with the man she had been seen with and even Callie had to believe it was possible. Only Vince clung to denial, until eventually David persuaded even him to stop looking.

And although at first Anya remained on people's minds, as April rolled into May, bringing with it blue skies, lighter evenings and an abundance of bluebells in the woods, signalling warmer days ahead, the teenager gradually fell to the back of everyone's mind. Even Toby, who had been withdrawn in the weeks after Anya's disappearance, gradually returned to his normal, perky self.

Nico didn't hire another stable hand, instead working with Jodie and Toby to pick up the slack, while gradually enticing Callie out of his house and over to the stables.

She was already becoming fond of his horses and growing in confidence around them, stopping to make a fuss of them whenever they were out in the paddocks. When he had first proposed she help with the feeding and cleaning of the saddles and bridles, instead of doing his housework, she had been a little daunted, but the idea quickly grew in its appeal.

It was calming being around the animals and she loved watching Nico's relationship with them, the quiet understanding they shared, and his never-ending patience.

He wanted to teach Callie to ride. She was still a little wary at the thought of getting on a horse, but maybe in time.

It was gradual, but she was becoming more and more comfortable around Nico Adams. That was why, when he proposed taking her down to Strumpshaw Fen one afternoon, she didn't hesitate.

'We can't take the dogs, unfortunately,' he told her, explaining that the place was a nature reserve and that the trails through woodland, reedbeds and orchid-filled meadows were filled with an abundance of wildlife.

Callie didn't like the idea of leaving Chester behind, but she trusted Nico, and the beauty of the fen captivated her, as did the bitterns and kingfishers that he pointed out. They saw swallowtail butterflies and a pair of marsh harriers dancing in the sky, and from the top of the tower hide, there was an unspoilt view across the reserve.

It was all so pretty, the conversation with Nico easy and the silences no longer strained, and for a while, her cares lifted and she believed she would eventually find a way to have a future.

When he offered his hand to help her cross a rough patch of ground, she took it without thinking, only realising what she had done when his warm palm pressed against hers.

Still, she didn't flinch or pull away. There was something comfortable and reassuring in his grip, and when he released her hand moments later, she found herself missing the contact.

After their visit to the fen, the trips out became a regular occurrence. Occasionally, they went alone, but mostly they took the dogs with them. New places that highlighted the beauty of the county, but never anywhere too populated that would leave her overwhelmed.

The county had many areas of wetland, with a network of rivers known as Norfolk Broads, and they visited several of them, at other times heading to the coast. Callie saw the ruins of St Benet's Abbey, a medieval monastery sitting on the banks of the river, and the seals on the beach at Horsey Gap, and then on one of the warmer days of spring, the jaw-dropping expanse of Holkham Beach, which stretched for miles where the tide had pulled out.

Nico had brought Red with them, towing the horsebox behind his Jeep, and while Callie looked after the dogs, she watched him mount the gelding with ease, nudging him into a gentle run before they tore off across the golden sand. As they disappeared into the distance, she made her way down to the water's edge, keeping an eye on the dogs as they frolicked in the waves. The sun warmed her face, bringing with it hope.

When Nico joined them again, Red was trotting elegantly along the surf, and it was evident they had been in the sea too, Nico's T-shirt damp and clinging to his body. As he allowed Red to pick up the pace again, the power and fluidity of both man and horse together, and the ripple of muscle in Nico's shoulders as he balanced effortlessly in the saddle, had something stirring deep in Callie's gut.

She was determined to ignore it, though on the ride back across the county, try as she might, she was aware of all the little details. The salty scent of sea air that mingled with wet-dog odour – something that perhaps should have been unpleasant but was a reminder of the day they had just enjoyed – the breeze from the open window slapping her hair against her face, and then there was Nico beside her: the scrub of stubble on his jaw almost golden in the sun shining through the windscreen, his hair mussed and curling at the edges where it was drying, and his green gaze steady whenever he glanced in her direction.

It was ridiculous. She was mistaking his kindness for something else. There was no denying that he was attractive, but another man in her life was the last thing she needed. And besides, he was never going to be interested in her in that way. She was a damaged and pathetic mess, and she was lucky he had taken pity on her.

It was so easy to remember Duncan's cruel taunts.

*You're lucky you have me. Do you think another man would put up with you?*

He had loved to remind her at every given opportunity that she was lesser than him. She lacked sophistication and intelligent conversation. Her hair was a mess and her breasts too small. Over the course of their relationship, he had managed to belittle and criticise her so much that his taunts had become so ingrained, Callie had lost all confidence in herself.

No, Nico would never look at her like that. She wasn't good enough for him.

Still, it didn't stop her thinking about him that night before she fell asleep, and the dream that she awoke from in the morning, in which he had featured prominently, had heat flushing her cheeks.

That same blush crept onto her face when she saw him at the stables later that morning, and she busied herself brushing the little palomino, Jerry, as Nico wandered over.

'Faith called last night,' he told her, and momentarily forgetting her embarrassment, Callie's heart lurched into panic. The woman hadn't given up on trying to get Callie on a girls' day out, despite Nico's attempts to deter her. 'She was pestering me for your number again.'

He still hadn't handed it over, managing to change the subject or conveniently forget each time Faith asked, and on the occasions the woman had shown up at the farm, Callie had hidden in the safety of the stables.

At some point, she was going to have to spend the day with her. If not, Faith would grow suspicious. It wasn't that Callie didn't like her. She did. Faith had a warmth about her and was easy to talk to. Callie just couldn't cope with a spa day or shopping in a crowd.

'Did you give it to her?'

'No, but her and Ethan are coming over for dinner tonight. And so are you.'

Callie's eyes widened. 'What?' she squeaked. 'I can't.'

'Yes, Callie. You can.' Nico's smile was wide, transforming his whole face, and for a moment surprising her into silence. His smiles were rare, but worth waiting for, and as her stomach flipped, she wished she was on the receiving end of them more often. 'I told her you're going through some stuff, so to lay off on the idea of a day out. This is the compromise. Faith has a good heart and she means well. You can meet her halfway.'

Callie remembered the dinners Duncan had made her suffer through with his friends. She had always been terrified of saying or doing the wrong thing, knowing she would pay the price later.

'I have nothing to wear,' she said, flustered.

'Wear whatever you like. There's no dress code.' There was the smile again, soothing the edges of her panic. 'It's just dinner,' he added, softly.

Just dinner.

She could do that, and she was grateful to Nico for making things easier for her.

'Okay,' she nodded. 'Are you cooking? Can I help with anything?'

Now his smile broke into a grin. 'I can cook. Just get over to the house for seven, okay?'

Callie had said she had nothing to wear, but when Nico opened the door to her, he was surprised by the effort she had gone to. The cornflower-blue dress she wore brought out the colour of her eyes and her thick, auburn hair hung in loose waves around her shoulders. When she had first come to stay with him, she had looked pale, underfed and terrified. Now there was a glow to her cheeks and a natural curve to her figure. Best of all, the haunted look in her eyes had mostly gone.

The more he got to know her, he could sense the free-spirited old Callie was still there. Just buried deep. He wanted nothing more than to bring her back.

The haunted look might have gone, but he could tell she was still nervous from the way she was clenching her hands.

'Remember, it's just dinner, Callie,' he said to her as she stepped inside. 'And nothing fancy.'

Dinner was lasagne. Classic and wholesome, and a nod to the Italian side of his heritage. Nico had never met his dad and the only thing he knew about him was that he came from Italy. It had been his adopted mum, Janice, who had urged him to embrace the culture.

Together, they had taken cooking classes and the lasagne was his signature dish. It was tasty, if clumsily thrown together, and presentation wise, it would have his ancestors quaking in their graves: large portions dumped on plates, with two bowls – one of salad, the other of garlic bread – in the middle of the table for his guests to help themselves to.

He didn't do dinner parties. This was for Callie, and he had made an effort, sweeping all of the paperwork to one side that had been cluttering Teddy's dining table and dumping it in a box that would have Ethan hyperventilating when he saw it. There was one course and a shop-bought dessert. He remembered Callie mentioning that she liked apple crumble, so had intentionally looked for one.

Whether she remembered sharing that little detail or not, the little 'hmm' of satisfaction she made when taking her first mouthful made the decision a good one.

What pleased him most as they ate was that there was no awkwardness. Nico had been worried that Faith was going to start pushing things – perhaps curious about Callie's past or wanting to know what it was she was going through – but she was the perfect dinner guest, keeping the conversation light and the wine flowing steadily. Even Callie, who had initially insisted on sticking to water, had relented and seemed to be enjoying the glass of wine Faith had poured her.

This was nice, Nico decided. Until Callie had moved into the cottage, he had been such a solitary man, preferring his own company, or that of his dogs and horses. Ethan was his best friend and dragged him out now and again, but really he had everything he needed here. He never considered the house lonely. Shyla and Dash were always about and he sometimes had the radio on. But having people in the house – no, not just people, they were his friends, Callie included – and the sound of their laughter, the lilt of conversation, made for a pleasant change. It reminded him of when Teddy had been alive.

It was after the plates had been cleared and Callie had finished washing up, even though he had told her she didn't have to, that Ethan produced the bottle of whisky he and Faith had brought with them. He found tumblers in Teddy's old drinks cabinet, pouring a generous measure and offering it to Callie, who promptly shook her head.

'Not for me, thank you.' She was still nursing her one glass of wine and was the most sober of them.

Ethan shrugged, pushing the glass towards Faith, before filling two more for himself and Nico.

'Nico says you've been working with the horses,' Faith said to Callie, as she sipped at her whisky. 'Be careful, he'll have you training them next,' she joked.

'Oh, I'm just helping out. I can't do as much as Anya.'

The moment the girl's name was spoken, the mood in the room changed. She hadn't been forgotten about, but she was seldom mentioned these days.

Nico still felt her loss, annoyed that he hadn't been able to help her, and he knew Faith and Ethan had been affected too. Olive had adored Anya and they had all tried to help her, to make her feel a part of something. In turn, she had let them down.

It wasn't Callie's fault that she had brought her up, but he could see she was wishing she hadn't, worried eyes darting from Ethan to Faith, then finally to Nico.

He shook his head to reassure her, mouthing the words, *It's fine,* but still she fumbled for the wine bottle in front of her, and when she topped up her glass, this time far more generously, he didn't miss that her hand was shaking.

Did she think she had done something wrong? That he was going to be angry with her? Was that how it had been with Duncan Stone?

It sickened him that Callie thought he might ever do something to hurt her.

'We should be talking about her,' Faith declared, finishing her whisky in one long drink and immediately pouring another measure. 'Anya, I mean. Why aren't we? She's not a dirty secret.'

'Faith—'

'No, don't "Faith" me, Ethan. I know she had a tough life. Lord knows Larissa Mitchell is a waste of space, but you don't just up and leave like that. We all tried to help Anya and how did she repay us? She let us down. I hope she realises that.'

'You think she definitely ran away?' Callie asked. She had ploughed through her second drink in record time and her glass was almost empty.

'Of course she did.' Faith continued on her rant, the frown line between her brows creasing deeper.

'But the man she was with in the woods...'

'So she had a boyfriend. I always thought she had a thing going on with Toby.'

In Toby's dreams, perhaps, Nico thought, remembering the stable hand's cute little crush. 'They were just friends,' he pointed out.

'Someone else then.' Faith sipped at her whisky. 'Which makes even more sense that they ran away together.'

'They were fighting. She sounded angry with him.'

Faith started to say something, but then she paused, eyes

narrowing at Callie, and Nico realised the slip-up at the same time Callie did, her face paling.

'I thought it was Nico who saw her in the woods?' Faith asked. 'Were you there too?'

'No.' Callie couldn't hold eye contact with her, distracting herself by reaching for the wine bottle again. 'I just remember... that's what he said.'

'She did sound angry,' Nico quickly intervened. 'That's what I told Callie, and the police.' He shot Faith a sharp look, warning her to drop it. Love her as he did, she was sometimes too damn nosy for her own good.

'Well, Vince said she had been in a bad mood. Anya told David she was seeing someone, but she wouldn't say who. Maybe she wanted to leave, but the boyfriend was having doubts.' Faith was theorising now, moving on from the slip-up, but Nico knew from the looks she kept giving Callie – who wasn't helping things by looking guilty as hell – that it was still on her mind. 'I think he was a little bit jealous that Anya had grown close to David.'

'I've never much liked David,' Ethan said, staring at his glass. His gaze raised slowly to meet Nico's before he quickly lowered it again. 'Considering he's only been with Vince a year, he likes to get his feet under the table and tell everyone what they should be doing. Maybe the police should be taking a closer look at him.'

Nico didn't have an issue with Vince's boyfriend, but then he had always appreciated people who were direct and didn't dress things up. You knew where you stood with them. 'I doubt David has anything to do with Anya running away,' he commented. 'He's always seemed okay to me.'

Ethan's lips twisted. 'Well, perhaps you're not the best judge of character,' he said darkly, waggling an eyebrow to let Nico know he was joking.

\* \* \*

'Do you ever wonder what Callie's deal is?' Faith commented on the taxi ride home, her mind working overtime.

'What do you mean?'

As always, Ethan had drunk more than everyone else, barely registering her comment, and when they arrived home, it would be her responsibility to get him into bed. It was like looking after a second child.

'Nico says she's his cousin, but have you seen the way he looks at her? He is definitely not having cousinly thoughts about her.'

'Well, it's not like they are blood related. Laurel is his adopted sister, remember?'

'Even so, it doesn't feel right. And why has Callie come to stay here, with him?'

Ethan shrugged, seeming uninterested as he looked out of the window. 'I thought you liked her.'

'I do. I just find the whole thing a little odd. How she's happy to stay in that cottage all the time. I tried to invite her out, you know, but she wasn't interested. If anything, she seemed half terrified at the idea.'

Nico had asked Faith to back off and she had agreed to, but it didn't stop her mind working overtime. She had always had an inquisitive nature.

'Perhaps she likes doing her own thing. Not everyone wants to be your friend, Faith.'

Ethan's words were slurred, but she still picked up on his bitterness.

The pair of them had always been a team, but just lately he was testing that, especially after he had been drinking, which seemed more often than not these days.

Ignoring him, her thoughts remained on Callie, with her wide, worried eyes and her often ill-fitting clothes. She was a pretty girl and could be stunning if she made an effort, but it seemed that beauty and fashion didn't interest her. Faith wished she could figure out a way to get closer to her. She had always liked having a project, and there was so much potential to work with. And, of course, there was the element of mystery.

She hadn't missed the moment when it had sounded like Callie was the one who had seen Anya in the woods. Nico had quickly stepped in, his explanation seeming reasonable enough, but there had been the exchanged look between the pair of them, as if they shared a secret.

Callie's phrasing had been odd. But why, if she had seen Anya, would she want to cover it up?

Yes, it was a mystery.

One Faith was determined to solve.

## 16

The plan was to stay sober.

Callie had been nervous about the meal at Nico's, her thoughts immediately going back to the dinners Duncan had forced her to endure. The ones where she never had anything in common with his guests, so had often been patronised or ignored, and at which she had spent the whole time terrified she might do something wrong and suffer the consequences later. If she stuck to water, she could keep her faculties about her and wouldn't have to worry about making a fool of herself.

She had fussed over what to wear, even though Nico had said it didn't matter. There wasn't much to work with, but the blue dress with its V neckline was a good fit for her figure and it was a little smarter than her usual jeans and baggy tops. With a lack of footwear, she had worn trainers to walk up to the house, and was glad she had kicked them off before Faith and Ethan arrived, daunted by Faith's effortless style and confidence as the woman pulled her into a hug, her expensive perfume clouding the air.

Still, Faith had done her best to put her at ease, making light conversation, and she hadn't mentioned anything about getting together again, much to Callie's relief. And dinner was a casual affair, exactly as Nico had promised, with little presentation, and Dash and Shyla working their way around the table, looking for handouts. She should have brought Chester with her, as Nico had told she could, and she now felt bad that she hadn't.

Everything had been going so well, but then, of course, she had opened her big mouth, bringing the mood down as the topic of conversation turned to Anya. That was when she had reached for the wine bottle. But the one glass meant to relax her had soon turned into three, the second two much larger, and by the time the Stuarts left, the effect of the alcohol was pleasantly dulling her senses.

'I'll walk you back to the cottage,' Nico told her, grabbing his jacket as she laced her trainers.

'It's okay, it's only a short walk.'

'I have to let these two out anyway.'

The dogs charged on ahead as soon as he opened the door and he waited for Callie to follow them before pulling it shut behind him.

As soon as the cool night air hit, the pleasant buzz she had been experiencing intensified, everything swaying.

'You okay?'

Had he noticed she was a little drunk?

It was so dark out here. Callie had left the porch light on and she could see it glowing in the distance, but between here and the cottage was just blackness. She was secretly grateful Nico had offered to walk back with her. It was creepy with the absence of street lights.

'I'm fine,' she lied, relieved when she realised he had a torch, the beam cutting a path of light ahead. Now she just needed her legs to work.

'So that wasn't too painful, was it?' he asked as they started walking.

'No, your friends are nice. Thank you for cooking for me, and I'm sorry about mentioning Anya.'

'You didn't do anything wrong.'

'I slipped up.' Callie was still kicking herself. 'I let you down after you covered for me. I'm such an idiot.'

Nico paused, looking down at her. With just the light from the torch, his face was cast in shadows, but she saw the frown line creasing between his eyebrows. 'Callie, you're not an idiot and you've never let me down. Stop beating yourself up about everything. I'm not Duncan.'

No, he wasn't. He was good and kind and far more patient than she deserved. He was nothing like Duncan at all, but the sharp reminder of the man she was running from and all that he had taken from her had tears pricking at her eyes. Would she ever be able to get back to who she had been before she had met him or was the damage irreversible?

She blinked the tears back, turning away, grateful now for the darkness, not wanting Nico to see she was upset. It was the wine. It was making her emotional.

As she stepped ahead, needed a moment to compose herself, she missed her footing, lunging forward. A firm hand on her arm stopped her from face planting on the ground and then she was back beside him.

'Are you okay?' He sounded concerned. There was no judgement that she had been drinking or nastiness telling her what a klutz she was.

She nodded, but didn't speak, surprised when he kept that steadying warm hand on her arm, and they walked the rest of the way in silence. It wasn't uncomfortable. Somehow it felt right.

Dash and Shyla were already at the door; Dash dancing around excitedly when Chester let out a bark the other side.

Callie eased away from Nico with reluctance. He had a sureness about him that not only made her feel safe, but also gave her a belief that she was capable too. He had overcome so much himself and it was difficult to imagine he had ever been the mixed-up, scared and defensive kid Laurel said he was when her parents first adopted him.

As she unlocked the door, Chester came bounding out to see his friends, and guilt poked at her again that she hadn't taken him with her tonight.

Nico had turned off the torch and they stood beneath the porch light together, watching the dogs play.

'Thank you for walking me back.'

His lips curved as he looked down at her. 'No problem. You going to be okay?'

She nodded and smiled back, remembering the silly crush she'd had years earlier. She had barely known him back then; he had just been Laurel's cute brother. Then, a few months ago, when she had come to Norwich, he had been almost a stranger. Now it felt like he was her home and it struck her that he was the person she trusted most in the world.

She could close her eyes and trace every line of his face, knew the exact shade of his irises: an earthy green, flecked with gold, and framed by ridiculously long lashes. And when he smiled, one dimple cutting higher in its cheek than the other, those gold flecks burned a little brighter and her world almost stopped.

That's what was happening right now. He was smiling at her and she was looking up at him, before the wine that she had promised herself she wouldn't drink made her do something really stupid.

She stretched up on tiptoes and pressed a kiss to his lips.

In her head, it had been the perfect moment, but what happened next had her wishing she could claw the seconds back.

Nico reacted as if she had just scalded him, flinching back, his expression startled, and Callie realised the implications of what she had just done. He was her rock, the anchor keeping her grounded, and she had just cut herself loose. What the fuck was she thinking?

Mortified, she tried desperately to fix things. 'I'm so sorry. I don't know what's wrong with me. It's the alcohol.'

Her cheeks were flaming and she wanted to flee inside.

'Chester, come on, boy.' She whistled to him, avoiding eye contact with Nico and shaking his hand off when he touched her shoulder.

'Callie, it's okay.'

He had recovered enough to try to reassure her, but it was too late. She knew. She had seen his horrified reaction.

'Please just go. I'm so sorry.'

Thankfully, Chester was old enough and wise enough to listen to her instruction, leaving Shyla and Dash and wandering past her into the cottage.

'Callie!'

She followed after the retriever, muttering another apology as she shut the door in Nico's face, aware she had just destroyed everything.

\* \* \*

Nico rose later than usual, allowing himself an extra half an hour in bed, glad he had asked Jodie to start early.

Not that he'd had much sleep. Callie playing on his mind for much of the night.

He should have insisted they clear the air, instead of leaving the situation to intensify. But, equally, he had needed time alone with his thoughts, so when he did talk to her, he knew the right thing to say.

Last night, she had taken a step he had not been expecting, changing the nature of their relationship. Nico understood his role; Laurel had asked him to look after Callie and to protect her. It had all been straightforward. What he hadn't counted on was that he was going to develop feelings for her.

And now he simply didn't know what to do next. Callie's safety was most important and he had to put that first, but if there was a chance she felt the same way he did...

No, it had been the alcohol. He had watched her knocking back the wine after the Anya slip-up, understanding she was nervous and embarrassed. It had skewed her view of things.

This morning, he would be finding out if his theory was true – that was, if she was still speaking to him after he had effectively pushed her away – because there was no way he was going to let her go walking in the woods alone. Not until he knew for sure that Anya was safe.

He drank coffee, showered, poured more coffee and ate breakfast, staring out of the window towards Stable Cottage, wondering if Callie was inside packing her meagre belongings, ready to leave, and debating what to do.

At a loss, he finally phoned Laurel.

'I fucked up,' he told her when she answered, already homesick from the honey-warm richness of her 'Hello, brother' greeting when she had answered his call.

They hadn't seen each other since Laurel had dropped Chester off. She had shown up at the farm with a furry-faced passenger and a car laden with things for Callie: clothes, toiletries, everything her friend might need over the coming months.

Laurel had orchestrated it all, persuading Callie to go along with her plan, to make a break for safety, and now he, Nico, had messed everything up.

'Okay, tell me. It can't be that bad.' She did that theatrical sigh: overexaggerated, but ready to fix everything.

But was this fixable? Nico hoped like hell it was.

'Callie kissed me last night.'

There was such a long pause, for a moment he thought she had hung up.

'She initiated it?' she asked eventually.

'Yes!' He tried to keep the exasperation out of his tone.

'Okay, well that's good. And you kissed her back, right?'

'No! Of course not. She'd been drinking and didn't mean it. Besides, you asked me to look after her. Why are you sounding like this is okay?'

He heard the slow rumble of laughter down the phone, irritation niggling as he realised his answer had amused her.

'Oh, Nico.'

'What?' he demanded sharply.

'The alcohol would have lowered her inhibitions.'

'Your point is?'

'You don't understand women at all, do you?' Laurel chided gently.

Nico ignored the dig. They both knew how his love life worked. Sex, he understood, but he never indulged in anything more than a fling. Relationships were alien to him, and the only ones he had ever formed were platonic ones, with Laurel and her parents, with Teddy and Ethan, and of course with his dogs and horses. He worked better with animals than he did with people, as this proved.

'Did you want to kiss her?' Laurel asked, her tone playful.

'She wasn't thinking clearly.'

'But what if she was?'

Laurel's five words stopped him dead and he fell silent as he processed them.

'You're her world right now, Nico. And you know she had a big crush on you when we were at university.'

'She did?' He was genuinely surprised.

Laurel didn't answer him, instead forcing his hand. 'You never answered my question. Did you want to kiss her?'

This time, the jokiness had gone from her tone and, put on the spot, he was forced to answer honestly. 'Yeah, I did.'

'Good.' She sounded triumphant, as if this had been her plan all along. 'So go tell her. Go on, get your bum down to the cottage and bloody tell her. You have no idea how much she needs to get her self-worth back.' When he remained silent, considering her words, she added, 'And let me know how you get on.'

With that, she hung up.

* * *

Twenty minutes later, Nico was at Stable Cottage with Shyla and Dash, knocking on the door, Chester barking when he realised his friends were outside.

Callie must have realised it was him, but still she looked flustered as she opened the door, Chester barging past Nico's legs in his rush to play.

Colour flushed her cheeks and in turn, Nico's face heated. He remembered Laurel's words and forced himself to push on. 'Last night, you kissed me. Was it just the alcohol or did you mean it?' he demanded, not at all subtly.

There was a moment of mortified silence before she started gushing an apology.

'I'm so sorry. I shouldn't have. I can leave if you want. I'll go somewhere else...' She trailed off, retreating back inside.

They both knew she had nowhere else to go.

Last night had changed everything though, and they were on a precipice. There was something skittish in her eyes and he sensed she was on the verge of fleeing. He couldn't let that happen, but how could he fix it?

Realising he was going about everything the wrong way, Nico made himself slow down, drawing in a breath before following her inside and trying again.

'I wanted to kiss you back,' he admitted, seeing her blue eyes widen and knowing he had her attention. 'Laurel asked me to keep you safe and that's what I have tried to do. But I wanted to kiss you.'

When she simply stared at him, looking surprised, he huffed a little, pacing the small living room, unsure what to do with his hands, and scared to get too close in case he spooked her.

'It never started out this way for me. I didn't let you come here thinking this would happen. It just did. And I know you've been through hell. I don't want to take advantage of you, I wouldn't do that. If it was the alcohol then it's cool and we can pretend it never happened. I don't want you to go. This is your home. But if it wasn't the wine and you do feel the same, then...' He tailed off, rubbing a hand over the back of his neck, uncomfortable with baring himself this way. 'Well, I guess I would be okay with that too.'

He wished she would speak. Say anything, just so he could stop rambling. He didn't normally use so many words.

Sensing more was needed, he took a careful step towards her.

She reminded him of a frightened horse, so he kept his movements slow and steady as he reached for her hands, gently closing his bigger ones around them. When she didn't pull away, he took that as a good sign.

This close, he was breathing in the scent of her. Something light and floral, maybe lavender, with a warm vanilla undertone.

'Not all men are like Duncan, Callie,' he said softly.

She gave a jerky little nod and he could see she was struggling with her emotions.

'I know,' she said eventually. 'I do know that. And I didn't come here expecting to...'

To what? Was that a yes, she did feel the same? Nico wasn't sure because she had stopped talking and didn't look like she was about to start again any time soon.

But then why would she? She had put herself out there last night and he had managed to embarrass her by pulling away like a jerk.

*Stupid, Nico.*

He had made her feel foolish, so now it was up to him to show her how he felt.

Deciding to hell with it, he let go of one hand and gently tilted her chin up with his forefinger so he could see her face. The doubts he had been fighting disappeared the moment he looked into her deep blue eyes and he mentally kicked himself again, before dipping his head and kissing her lightly, almost chastely, on the mouth.

She didn't react for a moment, but then her lips yielded, and as he instinctively deepened the kiss, drinking in more of that sweet taste of her, she moved her arms to link them around him. When she made a little hum sound in the back of her throat, pulling him closer, it pretty much undid him.

But he couldn't rush this. Everything had to be on Callie's terms, he understood that, which was why he fought against every instinct to move them through to the bedroom.

Instead, he broke away, his breathing a little laboured as he looked down at her.

Her eyes were shining bright, but now the embarrassment was gone and instead he saw lust – and was that hope?

A little self-conscious, aware this was new territory for him and that she meant so much more than a quick fling, he gave her a warm grin. 'Was that okay? That I kissed you, I mean? You have to tell me if it wasn't.'

Callie's lips curved into a smile that melted him inside. For a moment, there was no fear, no worry. She just looked happy. 'That was more than okay. All of it was more than okay.'

Behind them, Dash barked, as if he was giving his approval.

Callie's arms were still linked around Nico's waist and she seemed reluctant to part. 'I suppose we should take them out.'

She was right and the dogs had been good, playing outside while they waited. But they would need to be patient because he wasn't ready to end this moment yet.

He considered his schedule for the day, moving things about in his head. 'Have lunch with me.' Not giving her a chance to respond, he pushed on, 'There's a little pub down the road, The Shoulder of Mutton, and they do good food. It's mostly locals, so you will be safe there, I promise.'

Her eyes had gone wide with worry and for a moment, he thought she was going to say no, so she surprised him when she nodded. 'I would like that. Thank you.'

He gave into the urge to kiss her again, reluctantly easing back when Dash tried to squeeze between them. 'Okay, mate. We're now going.'

Nico considered himself a content man; he loved his work and had a quiet but decent life. As they headed towards the woods, the emotion warming his gut was unfamiliar. With Callie here beside him, knowing things had shifted between them, everything was brighter.

He watched her throw a ball for the dogs along the forest path, the glint of sunlight through the trees catching copper and gold tones in the deep red of her auburn hair, and when she turned and smiled at him, in that moment seeming carefree and happy, the haunted look she wore so often briefly banished, she reminded him of the old Callie.

He wanted this for her. He wanted to make her troubles disappear and for her to be worry-free. If he looked back at the moments that brought him the most pleasure, other than those involving his horses, they had been the recent times he had spent with Callie. Just walking with her and the dogs, sometimes talking, other times in companiable silence, or showing her some of the hidden gems in the beautiful county where they lived.

Yes, he wanted this for her, but he also wanted it for himself.

The vibrating of his phone in his back pocket was an irritating distraction and he was tempted to ignore it, but the responsible part of him caved.

Seeing Vince's name on the screen had Nico frowning and he answered the call quickly, dispensing with greetings.

'Vince?'

Quiet, muffled noises were the only response he received and his frown deepened.

'Is everything okay?'

Callie must have heard his question because she was wandering back along the path, the worried look back in her eyes.

'Nico.'

Finally, Vince spoke, and it was then Nico realised it was sobbing he could hear. His shoulders tensed. 'What's happened?' he demanded, a little gruffly.

He knew already. He realised that much later. Before Vince had spoken, before he told him the words none of them had wanted to hear, he had known. The dread already tightening his gut.

'It's Anya, Nico. They've found her body. She's dead.'

# 17

---

BEFORE

I don't recall exactly when it was that I started to fear Duncan. I can still remember a time when I wanted to be with him every waking moment, but now I automatically tense when I hear his footsteps, and wish I was far away from here.

Things changed after he had hit me for the second time. I realised then I should never have forgiven him the first time it happened, believing his lies it had been an accident. I wouldn't do it again.

My plan had been to contact Juliette as soon as I had my phone back and ask her to come and get me, but it seemed he had anticipated this. Unlike on previous occasions when he had returned home after hurting me, when he had had been full of heartfelt apologies and promises that he would try harder to control his rage, there had been no contriteness.

That day, my head had been thumping and my stomach was painfully sore, the bruises already showing, but I had managed to clean the kitchen as asked and he had skulked around it inspecting my work before I was able to make my escape to the bedroom.

I looked at the phone, quickly learning that the WhatsApp group I had with my friends had gone. Frantically, I scrolled through my contacts, panicking as I realised he had deleted their numbers.

'Is there a problem?' he asked innocently, as he walked into the room, hearing my gasp of shock. We both knew what he had done.

My heart thumped, unsure if it was better to call him out or pretend everything was okay. Either option could work out badly for me.

'I wanted to check my friends arrived home okay,' I said meekly, deciding that lying to him wasn't a good idea. 'But our chat is...'

'Gone?' He had the nerve to phrase it as a question.

'And their numbers,' I managed, ashamed of the tremor in my voice.

'Yes, those have gone too.'

I fought to keep the panic from my tone. 'Why?'

'Because I don't want you contacting them again. They're not welcome back here.'

'I don't understand.'

'They were rude and disrespectful to me in my own home. They're a bad influence on you, Mica, and you have no need for them. Your life now is here with me.'

It wasn't until later that I discovered the full extent of what he had done.

My contacts were deleted, together with our WhatsApp conversations and my call history, but the vile words in Messenger that Duncan had sent Juliette, pretending to be me, were still there for me to see.

I have thought long and hard before sending this message. You embarrassed me this weekend with your rudeness to Duncan.

We let you into our home and you were confrontational and disrespectful. He is a good man and did not deserve to be treated so badly. I am guessing it is jealousy. You've always been the one to land on your feet, the one who men look at, but it's a shame that they can't see the ugly soul behind your pretty face. It's not about you this time, is it, Juliette? I am finally having my moment and you don't like it. Is that why you tried to get into my head before you left, whispering to me and making out my relationship is in trouble? How dare you? I thought you and Aarna and Tracy were supposed to be my friends, but you've shown your true colours. I wish I had never invited you here. You're just a bunch of stupid girls who will never amount to anything. I am happy here with Duncan, so crawl back to your sad, pathetic lives and don't ever contact me again!

Tears blurred my vision. I wanted to tell her it was all a lie, but I couldn't, because Juliette had blocked me. The words beneath Duncan's message informing me that,

This person is unavailable on Messenger.

Panicking, I tried Aarna and Tracy. Duncan hadn't contacted them, but Juliette must have shown them her message, because they had blocked me too. I was also blocked on Instagram.

There had to be a way to reach them, to explain I'd never written those words.

I needed to get back to Hertfordshire and talk to Juliette, make her understand, and I needed out of this relationship now. In that moment, anger superseded fear as I stormed downstairs.

'You can't do that!' I raged, finding him in his office.

He glanced up at me, unfazed.

'How dare you send messages pretending to be me? You had no bloody right. They are my friends. You've crossed a line, Duncan. You've gone too far. I can't forgive you for this.'

'Juliette needed to be put in her place. You'll thank me for this one day.'

'Thank you?' My tone was incredulous. 'You're crazy.'

'Calm down, Mica. You're overreacting.'

'Don't you dare tell me to calm down. I need to go home and fix this, and I'm not coming back. We're over.'

I never made it as far as the door, a hand in my hair jerking me so hard backwards, my teeth snapped together. I would have fallen to the floor if Duncan didn't still have a hold of me. I screamed for him to let me go, but his fingers twisted tighter into my hair, my scalp burning, as he dragged me back into the room, and forced me face first down on his desk. I tried to pull away, but managed only to twist my head slightly so my cheek pressed against the cool wood.

'Let me go. Get off me.' I was still angry, but the panic in my voice was evident.

Ignoring me, he picked up his monogrammed letter opener with his free hand and leaned close to my ear. 'Apologise,' he whispered softly.

'Duncan, please. You're hurting me.' My eyes were watering with the pain.

He pressed heavily against me, pulling harder. His breath hot on my cheek. 'I want you to apologise.'

The hand with the letter opener moved closer towards my face, the sharp end in my eyeline, and fear rattled through me. 'Please stop.'

'Apologise, Mica.'

'I-I'm sorry,' I stammered. 'Please.'

'I can't hear you.'

'P-please. I'm sor-sorry.'

He eased back slightly and I gasped for air. The respite was brief, though, as he turned me around so I was facing him. When I tried to raise my head, his fingers twisted against my scalp again, while the weight of his body held me in place. He grazed the cold metal of the letter opener down my cheek with his free hand.

'You are not going anywhere, do you understand?'

'Y-yes.' In that moment, I would tell him whatever he wanted to hear. I just needed him to let me go.

'And you are never to try to contact those bitches again, do you hear me? If I find out you have, I will make sure you regret it. And if you ever try to leave me, I will find you and I will kill you.'

The last two words were spoken so softly, it took a moment for me to register what he had said. As they sank in, ice-cold terror tightened in my gut.

With his fingers wrapped in my hair and holding me down, I had no choice but to look up at him and I could see that the pale-blue eyes I had once found so attractive were now cold and empty, and that the warning was real.

'I mean it, Mica. You are my world and I need you here with me. If you dare to betray me, I won't rest until you're dead. And I will make sure you suffer before you die.'

His words were chilling and shook me to my core. I had no doubt he meant them.

\* \* \*

Over the following days, the house became my prison as Duncan took to watching me like a hawk. I had planned to message Juliette on her work email, to try to explain, but I was so frightened of Duncan finding out, I didn't dare.

Convinced I was going to take off, he monitored my every

move, regularly taking my phone off me to check if I was talking with anyone, then getting Rob to put even more cameras up around the house. He even made Rob follow me on the rare occasions I left the grounds of The Old Rectory – for security reasons, he had insisted, concocting some elaborate story about a potential threat he had been warned of. I didn't believe him and I knew he was keeping tabs on me, but what could I do? I knew better than to question him.

With no means of escape, I scrubbed and cleaned the house we shared, trying my best to keep things as he liked them, not wanting to give him any cause to grow angry with me.

And so the charade has continued. He has now isolated me to the point that I am struggling to recognise myself. My confidence is at an all-time low and I can no longer remember why I ever found him attractive.

He has a big sexual appetite, and while he was always a little bit selfish in bed, up until things went wrong, we had a decent enough sex life. Now I dread going upstairs at night. It's not just that I have fallen out of love with him, his touch repulsing me, but lately, I feel as if I am just his plaything, to use how he sees fit, and he has been revealing kinks that I am growing increasingly uncomfortable with.

He still likes to play with the dice, but these days, I seldom get a choice. They are simply things he wants to do and the numbers are sometimes an indicator for the length of time or intensity.

Despite his warning, I know I need to get away. This can't be my life.

If I go to the police, though, will they believe me? Everyone loves Duncan and he is good friends with many senior officers. They consider him to be family. It is too risky.

I have also been tempted to reach out to my family and tell

them the truth about what is going on, but knowing we're not close and they are all big Duncan fans, I have so far held back, but last night he choked me so hard, I was convinced I was going to die, and the polo neck of the jumper I am wearing now is disguising the bruises from his fingers.

That is why I am waiting for Duncan and Rob to leave for their golf game. When they are out together, it's the only time I can relax. Well, to a degree. Those damn cameras are still watching me. But today, I will try to fool them.

Once they are gone, I am going to drive to my sister's. Phoebe has to help me. She is all I have got.

'We have people coming for dinner tonight,' Duncan tells me before he walks out of the door. 'I want this place to be spotless by the time I get home.'

'We have?' Not that it matters. I don't plan on being here.

He lets out a sigh. 'I already told you this, Mica. I wish you would listen.'

Except he didn't. I know because I do listen. Too fearful that if I don't, I will get something wrong. This is one of his little games. He likes to surprise me with dinner guests. I think it amuses him to keep me in the dark for as long as possible, then send me into a mad panic getting the house ready.

'Wear that red dress I bought you for Christmas, the one with the polo neck. And tie your hair up into a topknot. It might fool them into thinking you're sophisticated.'

That's the other thing. He now dictates how I look. I am his puppet.

The door shuts on his snide barb and I am finally alone. I don't waste any time, getting the laundry basket and taking it upstairs to the walk-in wardrobe in the main bedroom. It's one of few places in the house where I know I am not being watched.

It is in here that I pack a few things into a bag, before placing it into the basket and covering it with what will appear on camera as dirty washing. The bag is small and I know I can't take much, but I honestly don't care. I just need a few things to tide me over.

I have rehearsed this, but still I am riddled with fear that something will go wrong, that I am going to get caught.

Terror chokes me so badly at one point, I almost back out.

Down in the utility room – another camera-free zone – I remove the bag, leaving the basket of washing on the worktop, and add the tins of dog food I have managed to hide behind the laundry detergents, then I whistle to Chester. I grab my car keys and we head out via the back passageway, going into the garage. As soon as the car leaves the garage, it will be on camera, so I know I will need to move quickly.

It's half a mile to the gate and I floor the accelerator of my little Polo, clicking my fob, my shoulders sagging in relief as the gate opens. Duncan should be at the golf club by now and surely won't be checking the cameras. I should hopefully have a bit of a head start before he realises I am gone.

It's a three-and-a-half-hour drive, but I don't stop, not even to let Chester pee and stretch his legs, and my mouth is dry with both fear and the fact I haven't had anything to drink since breakfast. My gut is empty and jumpy with nerves, but I don't think I could eat even if I tried. I just want to put as much distance between me and Devon as possible.

Duncan is going to guess where I have gone. He has managed to isolate me from my friends, and although we are not particularly close, Phoebe is the only family I have in England.

I just need her to help me, for my big sister to tell me what to do and how to get myself out of this awful mess I am in.

As I near Bath, it occurs to me that she might not be home. What if she is on shift or, worse still, has gone away somewhere?

She doesn't keep me up to date with her plans.

I let Chester have a few minutes in the little wooded area near where she lives, before we head to townhouse she shares with Ed. My stomach is tight with nerves as I knock on the door and when it opens and she is standing before me, I burst into tears.

Her expression goes from surprise and slight disdain when she sees I have my dog with me, to one of concern. 'Callie, what are you doing here?'

I can't speak, so overcome with emotion, and when she pulls me into a hug – a rare occurrence for her, she isn't a tactile person – I completely break down.

It is not until we are finally inside the house, and I am sat on the sofa with a glass of water in front of me, that I finally manage to string a sentence together. I hold onto Chester for support. 'It's Duncan. I have to get away from him.'

'What? Why?'

'He hurts me.'

Phoebe's mouth drops open and for a moment, she seems lost for words. I watch my capable sister with her stunned expression, and wait for her to say something. Her shocked, dark-blue eyes are a mirror of my own, but that is where the similarity between us ends. She has our father's longer nose and her hair, although red, is almost a strawberry blonde, while mine is much darker. She always wears it tied back, in a low knot at the nape of her neck, never a strand out of place.

I have only been to her house a handful of times and it is rather bland and sterile, with white walls and lacking the soft furnishings and personality that make a place a home. That is my sister. She doesn't do clutter.

'You've had a fight,' she decides. It's an observation, not a question, but I start shaking my head vehemently.

'No, it's worse than that.'

I try to tell her what a monster Duncan is and the terrible things he does to me.

'But you were happy,' she insists.

'I was. At first. But then he started to change.' My sentences are punctuated by gulps for air as fresh tears start to fall.

'Here, drink the water.' Phoebe picks up the glass, pushing it into my hand. 'You're hyperventilating.'

I do as told while she looks thoughtful, considering everything I have just said.

'People change, you know. It's only natural to try to impress someone at the start of a relationship. I know Ed did with me. When we first met, I had no idea that he doesn't clean the shower after using it or that he has to use every utensil when cooking. He's a monster in the kitchen. I'm sure Duncan thinks you've changed too. It's okay to disagree with each other. You just have to work together and learn to accept each other's flaws.'

Why is she not listening to what I have been saying? I told her about the terrible fights and how he has isolated me from my friends. About how he has hit me.

My sister excels at making up her own narrative. She can also be detached, but perhaps that is part of being a good surgeon. She can switch off emotionally from her patients.

But she can't do that to me. I need her.

Desperate to make her understand, I lower the neck of my jumper and show her the bruising around my throat.

Finally, she pauses.

'How did you get that?' she asks, sounding confused.

For such a bright woman, Phoebe can sometimes be a little slow on the uptake.

'Duncan.'

'He did that to you?' Her eyes widen, appearing at last to have gripped the gravity of my situation. 'When did he try to strangle you?'

'Last night in bed.'

Her eyes widen. 'I'm confused. So you were asleep and he tried to kill you?'

'No, Phoebe. We were, you know... having sex.'

I can't look at her when I say the last word. It's not that I'm a prude, but my sister is, and we have never had the type of close relationship where we can discuss things like that.

'He choked you during sex?' Her tone is a little flat.

'Yes, he likes doing that.'

'But you let him?'

This isn't going as planned. I try to explain I don't get a say, that Duncan does as Duncan wants and I am forced to go along with it, but I can see she's not listening.

I must have said something right though because she agrees I can stay, despite not liking having Chester in the house. Ed is working a late shift, but perhaps when he comes home, I can get him to help me make Phoebe see sense. I need their help if I am going to escape Duncan, but there is no way I intend to discuss my sex life with Ed.

Phoebe makes me a cup of tea and leaves me to drink it while she does a few chores. I am so tired and my eyes are stinging from crying. It's not long before they fall shut.

When I wake, I am curled up on the sofa, a blanket covering me, and it is almost dark outside. I realise I have been asleep for the best part of three hours and it is nearly 5 p.m. Chester is snoozing on the floor beside me.

I can hear my sister in the kitchen and smell tomatoes and garlic. My stomach rumbles, though I think I am too jittery for food. But Chester needs to eat.

I go through to join Phoebe, taking one of the cans of dog food I brought with me and sort my boy's dinner.

As he tucks in, Phoebe urges me to try to eat too, putting bowls of pasta on the table, and after picking at a few mouthfuls, I realise I am ravenous. As we eat, she makes polite small talk, but seems uninterested in talking about Duncan. It's as if we never spoke about him earlier.

It bothers me that she won't look me in the eye either. Is it because of what I told her about the choking? Is she embarrassed I overshared?

She is clearing away the plates, insistent she doesn't need my help with anything, and I have just gone back through to the living room, when the doorbell rings.

My first thought is that it's Ed, but I'm sure Phoebe said his shift doesn't finish until late. Besides, he lives here. Why would he need to ring the doorbell?

That is when the first hint of unease crawls down my spine.

I hear the door open and the sound of hushed voices, then, moments later, Phoebe is poking her head around the door. This time, she is looking at me in pity.

'He only wants to talk,' she says softly, speaking to me as if I am a child.

My eyes widen in horror as I realise who the visitor is and panic claws its way into my throat. It isn't him. She wouldn't do this to me, not after everything I told her.

'We had a good chat when he called me earlier and I'm sorry you've been going through a tough time, Callie. He just wants to help you get better.'

What the hell has he told her?

My gaze darts around the room, but there is nowhere to escape to. I feel like a caged animal, pushing my way as far back into the corner of the sofa as possible, as Duncan steps into the room.

On the floor, Chester looks up and his ears go flat. He knows I am distressed.

Duncan's face is carefully sympathetic and his eyes are red. Has he seriously been crying or is he faking it? I honestly no longer know.

'Mica, you've had me so worried.' His voice drips with concern.

He comes towards me and I want to run. I fight the urge to scream out about how much danger I am in, remembering his threat that he will kill me if I ever try to leave him. If I cry for help now he is here, how will he react? What will he do? I am too scared to find out.

Instead, I cower pathetically and tremble, and as the pasta roils in my belly, I am certain I am going to throw it up.

He sits on the sofa beside me, pulling me towards him. I am stiff as a board, despite quaking inside, and he must sense how frightened I am as he draws me into an embrace.

Phoebe hovers in the doorway, wringing her hands together as she watches, and I can tell that she has swallowed whatever bullshit he has fed her. I look at her pleadingly, trying to make her realise she has made a terrible mistake. She has to do something to fix this.

'Please,' I beg her in a small voice 'I want to stay here.'

'He's going to take care of you,' she tells me, oblivious to the danger I am in. 'You have to trust him.'

'No, I—'

'It's okay, Mica,' Duncan soothes. 'I know you're confused, but we're going to get you the help you need. I promise, baby.'

He plays the part of the concerned boyfriend so well, it's no wonder I fell for him in the first place. If only I had realised who he was beneath the mask.

Within minutes, he is trying to guide me up off the sofa.

'No, no. I don't want to go,' I protest more vehemently. I can't leave this house with him.

'I won't leave you here. If you hurt yourself again, I'll never forgive myself.'

*What?*

'It's okay,' Phoebe agrees. 'I didn't know you were struggling like this. Let him help you.'

Struggling? What the hell?

I try to resist, but he is bigger and stronger, and as he forces me out of the front door, Phoebe asks him to keep her updated.

I want to flee back inside her house, but I know Duncan will just come after me and my sister will let him. He fooled me, and now he is fooling my family. I could try to run, but if I did, where would I go? If I went to the police, it would be my word against his, and he is clearly more convincing.

When I spot the cars, I realise Rob Jolly is with him. That they have brought two vehicles. Instead of taking me to his Porsche, Duncan leads me to Rob's BMW. My Polo is still parked across the road, but it seems he has no intention of taking it.

'Drive her home,' he says quietly, sitting me in the passenger seat and fastening my seat belt. 'And take the scenic route. I'm going to go on ahead with the dog.'

My heart thumps. 'No!' I shout, realising Duncan has Chester. What is he going to do to him?

I try to push open the door, but it is locked.

'Please let me see Chester,' I beg Rob as he gets in the driver's seat.

He doesn't respond, stony-faced as he watches Duncan put Chester in his car, then go to give Phoebe a hug. He looks like he is reassuring her that everything will be okay.

Then Duncan is in the driver's seat of his Porsche and pulling away. Tears are streaming down my face as Rob follows. Within a few minutes, Duncan is taking the turn for the motorway, while we stay on the B roads.

Why has Duncan taken Chester? What is he going to do to him?

Maybe it is just to keep me compliant.

I tell myself this, but I don't believe it.

And as we head back towards Devon, I can't help but worry what fate awaits me too.

## 18

When we eventually arrive back at The Old Rectory, it is almost 10 p.m., and Duncan's car is parked outside. The house is lit up, and seeing him standing in the open doorway waiting to greet us, I want to stay in the safety of the BMW.

Rob releases the locks, but I remain seated for a moment, terrified about what is waiting for me inside.

It is the need to find Chester that finally pushes me to get out and my legs tremble as I approach Duncan nervously, conscious that my dog would normally come running out to greet me.

'Where is he?' I try to sound commanding, but the tremor in my tone gives me away.

He cocks a questioning eyebrow, forcing me to elaborate. We both know who I am talking about.

'Where's Chester? Please give him to me.'

He stares at me for a moment, his expression unreadable.

'He's fine,' he says evenly. 'Come on inside, Mica. I've cooked a nice dinner for you.'

I'm not hungry. Even if I hadn't eaten at Phoebe's, I'm too nervous. Besides, it's late. Why does he want to have dinner now? I dare not say any of these things, aware this situation is already bad enough.

He places a hand on the small of my back, guiding me into the house. 'Go upstairs and have a shower. Clean yourself up. Your dress is laid out for you. Dinner will be ready in about fifteen minutes.'

I do as I am told, my stomach churning. Even the soothing pelt of warm water can't relax me. Duncan is acting so calm and he hasn't yelled at me yet for leaving. I feel I am being lulled into a false sense of security and my nerves are on edge, knowing he could blow at any moment.

My dress is on the bed. Red and figure hugging, with a mid-length hem and a polo neck collar, managing to be demure, yet a little sexy at the same time. It's the same one he had instructed me to wear before he left to play golf this morning, which reminds me he had invited people for dinner.

Are they still coming at this late hour? Or did he cancel?

Unsure what to expect, I get dressed, then, with shaking fingers, I knot my hair the way he likes it, adding diamond studs to my earlobes. They are ones he gave me for Christmas and I am hoping that if he sees me wearing them, it will please him.

Knowing I had better not keep him waiting, I go downstairs to meet my fate.

\* \* \*

'Eat your dinner, Mica.'

We are sat in the big dining room, just the two of us facing each other across the table, and it's a formal affair. Candles are lit and he has even laid out napkins, the lights dimmed to give an ambient glow, and soft classical music plays in the background.

Duncan is looking handsome in a navy suit, the top button of his shirt undone, and his hair styled back from his face. If his fans could see him now, they would be swooning. But they don't know him as I do, and although I am trembling, butterflies swarming in my gut, it's not with excitement or anticipation.

Something bad is going to happen tonight. I can sense it.

I pick at a carrot, reluctant to eat more of the strong-flavoured, fatty meat on my plate. I don't like game, which I suspect this is, and Duncan knows that.

I dare not say anything, and seeing him keep looking at my plate, I suspect he won't let me leave the table until I have finished.

It takes a while, but finally I manage to eat the disgusting meal between sips of water. It sits heavy in my stomach as I finally put down my knife and fork.

He has a smile on his face. 'There, did you enjoy that?'

'It was lovely,' I lie, knowing I have no choice but to go along with the charade.

'Do you have room for dessert?'

I honestly think I will be sick if I eat anything else. 'I don't think I have room, but thank you. May I please see Chester now?'

I look at Duncan, hoping that as I am being compliant, he might take pity on me.

Instead, his bellow of laughter makes me jump.

What is so funny?

I stare at him. 'Please let me see my dog.'

'You've been a good girl finishing your dinner, Mica. I'm impressed. I'm guessing you've never had mutton before.'

I shake my head, wondering where this is going. 'No, never.'

'It has a distinctive taste, doesn't it?'

A disgusting taste, I want to say, but I keep my mouth shut.

'I'd heard it's similar to dog meat, and now I've tried both, I think I have to agree.'

The words register, but still I doubt them.

'What did you just say?' I ask quietly, my mouth dry.

He grins broadly at me, before wiping his mouth with his napkin. 'Keep up, Mica,' he laughs. 'I said the dog meat we just ate tastes like mutton.'

It's a joke. A horrible one. He doesn't mean it. Chester is safe. He has to be.

But where is he? Why won't Duncan let me see him, and why was he so insistent on having this bizarre late dinner? I stare at him across the table, at the smug and satisfied look on his face. At the cruel amusement in his eyes.

*Did he just make me eat my dog?*

My reaction is instantaneous, the contents of my stomach violently emptying all over my plate. I can't stop puking, heaving until my gut is empty and my throat is raw. Weak with the exertion, my eyes watering, I clutch the edge of the table, barely aware that my fingers are resting in vomit, and I glare at him.

He is going to be angry with me for throwing up everywhere, but in this moment, I don't care. 'Where is Chester?' I demand.

I won't believe he is dead. I know Duncan has a mean streak and that he has threatened me before, but he wouldn't go this far. I have to believe it.

His look of delight at my anguish forces me to accept that perhaps I am wrong.

'You wouldn't hurt him. Please tell me he is okay.'

I start to sob, utterly distraught.

What have I done? I should have stayed. I should have tried harder.

It takes a moment to realise that Duncan is laughing again. This time, he is so amused, he is having to wipe tears from his eyes.

'You bloody idiot. I had you going there, didn't I?'

I look at him in confusion.

'Do you actually think I would kill your stupid dog? Jesus, Mica. What kind of monster do you think I am?'

I can't answer that. In this moment, I honestly don't know what he is telling the truth about and what is a lie. I am a shaking, nervous wreck. Either he is a psycho, or he has just made the sickest joke ever.

'Where is he?' I whisper.

He huffs and rolls his eyes before getting up, glancing in disgust at the mess I have made. 'You had a bit of an overreaction, don't you think?'

When I don't respond, he tuts.

'Come on. Come with me.'

I am reluctant to follow, unsure where we are going and what awaits me. Is he taking me to Chester? He hasn't said.

We head to the back of the house and as we enter the corridor that leads to the garage, I hear muffled barking.

My heart leaps. Is he in there?

Duncan opens the door, Chester's barking is now frantic, and I step into the garage looking for him, upset to see he is in a dog crate. One that is too small for him. He has enough room to turn, but that's just about it.

'What are you doing? Let him out?'

I run to the crate and drop to my knees, reaching through the bars. I need to touch Chester to know he is real and this isn't some kind of trick. He is happy to see me, licking my face, but I can tell he is distressed.

I turn to Duncan and beg. 'Please, you can't keep him in here.'

'This is where he sleeps now, Mica.' He slowly walks towards us. 'I should have taken a firmer hand over this when you moved in. I don't know what I was thinking, letting him in the bedroom. I was too soft on you. Well, that changes now.'

'It's too small,' I protest, despair creeping into my tone 'You can't do this to him.'

He sighs in irritation, but I hear a key jingle in his pocket. 'Fine. I will let him out, but just for tonight. If I do this for you though, I want you to do something for me.'

'Okay,' I agree without hesitation. All that matters in this moment is freeing Chester from the crate.

'I haven't said what it is yet.'

Honestly, I don't care. I just want Chester safe. I assume whatever Duncan wants involves sex. I will go along with it as I always have. It's unlike him these days to even give me the choice.

'It's fine. I'll do whatever. Just let him out. Please.'

'Promise me, Mica. I don't want you trying to back out.'

Dread at what he has planned now coils in my belly. What am I agreeing to? But then I look at Chester's face and I know I don't have a choice. 'Okay, I promise.'

Duncan nods, and I watch as he unlocks the crate, Chester charging out and into my arms. He is all that matters. I have him with me for now.

'Okay, get inside.'

For a moment, I assume he means back into the house, and that he wants to go upstairs, and I reluctantly start to get up.

'No!' He barks out the word and I jump. 'Not indoors. Get in the crate.'

I look at him slowly, certain I misheard. 'Sorry?'

'I want you to get inside the crate, Mica.'

I stare at the tiny cage. He's surely not serious. 'I... I can't.'

'You just promised me you would do whatever I asked,' he reminds me.

I did, but I never expected this.

'I won't fit,' I try to reason.

'You will. Now get in.'

'Duncan, please.'

'Get in the fucking crate. NOW!'

I cower away as he yells in my face, covering me in spittle, and I cling on to Chester.

He can't lock me in there.

'Mica, I am going to count to five. If you are not inside that crate, things are going to get ugly, both for you and the dog. Don't test my patience.'

'Please don't do this.'

'One.'

I look at the crate. It's so small, I won't have room to move.

'Two.'

'Please,' I beg again. 'Ask me to do anything else.'

'Three.'

He's not backing down and I fear what will happen if I disobey him.

'Four.'

'Okay.' I reluctantly release Chester, realising I don't have a choice.

I am on my hands and knees, and manage to get my head and shoulders inside.

'All the way in,' he orders from behind me, and I carefully push the rest of my body into the tight space. It is cramped, with little room to move and when I try to lift my head, it hits the top of the crate. I draw my knees up to my chest – the most comfortable position for now – and wrap my arms around them. I can't stay in here. It's too uncomfortable and there isn't enough space.

I start to tell him this, but to my alarm, the door slams shut, the key turning in the lock.

'Okay, I did it. Please let me out.'

He's not listening to me. Now he has me where he wants me, my pleas fall on deaf ears.

'Come on,' he instructs the dog, and to my horror, he heads towards the door.

'Duncan.' I am panicking now. 'You can't leave me in here.'

Chester looks back at me, unwilling to leave, and Duncan snaps at him to follow, coming back and dragging him by the collar when he doesn't listen.

'Please don't go.'

The light turns out, plunging the garage into darkness. Then there is the unmistakable click of the door closing.

'Duncan!' I scream his name as fear trembles through me. I don't have enough room to move and it feels like I am suffocating. It takes me a moment to realise I am having a panic attack. My skin is clammy despite the coolness of the garage, my limbs fighting the bars, desperate to break free. I gulp for air, trying my hardest not to give into the terror.

It takes a while, but eventually my heart rate slows. It is then that I notice the cold. The February fog creeping in through the cracks in the garage door. My skin is covered in goosebumps, my teeth chattering, and with just the flimsy material of the dress, I have no protection.

I hug myself tightly and beg for Duncan to come back.

\* \* \*

I must have somehow drifted off to sleep and I awake with a start, for the briefest moment wondering where the hell I am, then, as I try to move, to stretch out, I come crashing back to reality.

I am so cold, the kind of icy chill I fear I will never warm up from, and I ache from where the bars of the crate are pressing uncomfortably against my legs and spine. My mouth and throat are dry and filled with a foul, bitter taste, reminding me that I was violently sick earlier.

Blinking, I try to adjust my eyes to the darkness, and it is then that I hear the sound and catch the brief flicker of a tiny light.

I try to focus, hear the click again, and this time when the light comes, it briefly illuminates the area around it, and I see Duncan sat on a chair, watching me.

He has a lighter in his hand and every few seconds, he is igniting the flame.

Why the hell is he just sitting there in the dark?

'Duncan? Please let me out.' My tone is pitiful, but I am desperate.

There is no reaction at all. How long has he been there?

As my eyes gradually adjust to the darkness, I can see him clearer. He continues to sit and watch and flick the damn lighter. It's almost as if he has zoned out.

I try again. 'Duncan, please. I am so cold.'

My voice breaks on the last word and I don't know if that is what finally stirs him, but he slips the lighter in his pocket and gets up, moving towards me.

Is he finally going to let me out?

It takes me a moment to see he has something in his other hand. A big, plastic bottle that he is now uncapping. For one foolish moment, I think he is going to at least offer me a drink, but then he is tipping it over the crate, the liquid pouring through the bars and soaking me to the skin. I try to recoil, but there is nowhere to go. And to my horror, I realise it isn't water, the heady fumes of petrol crawling up my nostrils, the awful taste of it in my mouth.

Finally I understand. The crate, the lighter, the dousing of petrol.

He is going to burn me alive.

Terror chokes me as he takes out the lighter again. 'No, please, Duncan.' My tone is pure panic. 'Don't do this. Please. I'll do anything.'

He had said he would kill me if I left him. His words had scared me, but I think part of me hadn't believed it was true. Now, trapped here in the garage with no escape, I am begging for my life. My sobs turning to screams as he clicks the lighter.

'I warned you what would happen, Mica,' he finally speaks. 'I told you I would kill you if you ever left me.'

'I'm sorry. P-please give me another chance.' Snot is dripping from my nose, my eyes stinging from the mix of petrol and tears. 'Please, Duncan. Please. I'm so sorry. I didn't mean it.'

He takes a step closer and I flinch, squeezing my eyes shut and hugging my legs tightly, certain this is it. Waiting for the anguish and the pain as the fuel ignites.

When seconds pass and nothing happens, I finally dare to open one eye. The flame has gone and Duncan is dropped down on his knees in front of me.

'One more chance,' he tells me sombrely. 'But I will make you regret it if you ever betray me again.'

'I won't,' I quickly assure him. 'I will never betray you, and I will never leave you again. I promise.' And in that moment, I mean it.

This isn't the life I want, and I hate living in this house. Most of all, I despise the man in front of me. But fear is a great motivator and tonight, I have witnessed exactly how wicked Duncan Stone is.

I wait for him to let me out, my heart sinking when instead, he stands and heads to the door. 'Good, I will hold you to that,' he says, turning back. 'Goodnight, Mica.'

This time, as the door closes, I don't call out. Instead, I accept my fate, and as I sit there in the dark and sob quietly, I know I am too afraid to ever try to leave him again.

# 19

***

## NOW

The body of Anya Mitchell was recovered from undergrowth close to a fishing lake in the village of Little Plumstead, less than five miles from where she had last been seen by Callie.

Or Nico, as he had claimed to the police.

Their lie was spiralling and Callie wanted to take it back. What if they thought he had something to do with what had happened to Anya? Because although Vince hadn't used the M-word, he had said to Nico that they were treating her death as suspicious.

'We stick to the story,' Nico insisted when Callie raised her concerns.

They were back at Stable Cottage and what had started out as a day filled with hope, after he had shown up unexpectedly, catching her off guard with his admission of how he really felt, had taken a dark and unwelcome turn. The lunch she had been looking forward to now put on hold.

Anya had been just eighteen years old, and although she had a troubled past, her whole life had been ahead of her. She hadn't deserved this.

As for Nico, he had been her mentor and her friend. Callie

knew he was reeling, and probably in too much shock to grieve, yet he was still putting her first, seeking to reassure her about the inevitable police investigation.

'I can tell them the truth, that it was me.' It had been bad enough lying to the police about who had seen what when they thought Anya had run away, but now she was dead, it was so much worse. Callie couldn't let him cover for her. 'They're going to want to speak with me anyway, I imagine. I'm living here right next to the woods, so I might as well own up that that I was the one who saw her.'

The idea of doing so terrified her. Not that she planned to let Nico know. She wanted to prove to him that she was strong, and that she could be there for him too.

'It's not going to work, Callie.'

'Why not? I just have to stick to the story that I'm your cousin. They won't do an identity check, will they?'

It would still be a lie. Just a much smaller one.

'I honestly don't know,' Nico admitted. 'I've never been in this situation before. But I'm pretty sure you'll come under more scrutiny when they realise you lied to them in the first place. They're going to want to know why you didn't admit it was you in the woods.'

He made a fair point, and it was one she hadn't considered.

'If the truth comes out about who you are, you know there's a chance Duncan will find out you're alive.' His tone softened. 'You've already been through so much. Please don't take that risk. If not for you, then for me.'

He was right. Deep down, Callie realised that.

She wanted to be brave for Nico and to protect him back, but the risk was too great. Over the months she had been at Willow Brook Farm, she had gradually learnt to relax. At first, she had been constantly looking over her shoulder, fearing Duncan would catch up with her, but now she dared to believe that perhaps she really was free. And she wanted a future without fear. Now, more than ever.

So they went ahead with the lie, and when, a few days later, the police paid her a visit, she told them she was Callie Adams and that she hadn't seen or heard a thing.

If the detective constables noticed her hands were shaking slightly, then they said nothing, seeming to buy her story that she was staying with Nico for a while as an extended holiday. And, to her relief, they didn't ask for any form of identification.

They had more questions for Nico, but when she pushed for details of what those were, he casually brushed over the topic, telling her it was nothing to worry about.

She just hoped he wasn't a suspect.

At the moment, it was all anyone was talking about. Who could have wanted to hurt Anya Mitchell? And it wasn't just Nico who was in shock. Jodie and Toby had both worked with her too, and their mood was subdued. Toby even taking a rare couple of sick days. Callie knew this was hitting him hard.

'It's all going to work out okay,' Nico assured her now.

And she hoped like hell he was right.

After Anya's body had been found, he had tried to persuade her to come and stay with him in the house. 'Just temporarily,' he had been quick to add, clearly picking up on her reluctance. 'We don't know what happened and I don't like you being out here alone in the cottage. It's too close to where you saw her that last night.'

Callie didn't like it either, but she was scared of things going too fast with him, remembering how quickly she had moved in with Duncan. Although Nico was nothing like him, she was still rebuilding her confidence and reclaiming her identity. It was important to her to maintain her independence.

'I have the cameras,' she told him lightly. 'And you're still close by.'

She could tell he didn't like it, but he didn't push her, and it was one more thing she appreciated about him. He cared about her safety, but equally he respected her decisions.

Ten days after Anya's body had been found, a man from a local travelling community that had been living in the woods was arrested for her murder. The police were working on the theory that she had simply been in the wrong place at the wrong time.

The news came as a shock, but it was tempered by relief.

Callie had still felt she was hampering the police investigation by not coming clean. At least if it had been a random attack, it meant the man she had seen Anya in the woods with must have been uninvolved.

Free of guilt and also of the fear they might come under further police scrutiny, she relaxed enough to start really appreciating time alone with Nico. This thing they had started, that they were tentatively exploring together, might not have happened at the best time, but it was something they were both invested in.

She began joining him for dinner most nights, and they found common ground in the kitchen. Neither of them was the best cook, but they enjoyed attempting new recipes and learning more about each other. And at the end of each evening, Nico walked her back to Stable Cottage, where they would enjoy lingering kisses on the porch. At other times, while when they walked in the woods together, he would reach for her hand. Other than that, he seemed content to let her set the pace.

She appreciated his patience. For so long, she had felt unworthy of love, conditioned to believe she was clumsy and stupid and pathetic. Duncan had always made sure she was less than his equal; she had been his pity project.

Everything with Nico was different. The way she sometimes

caught him quietly watching her. How he was interested in what she had to say, even laughing at her occasional bad jokes. And each time he kissed her, she was aware of the urgency. He was careful not to push things faster than she was comfortable with, but she understood how badly he wanted her. That it would take just one word from her to move things to the next level.

Aware she held that power both scared and strengthened her. He was intoxicating, and while she didn't want to rush things, her control was slipping. She didn't think she could hold off for much longer.

She studied him now from the doorway of the stable as he worked with Red in one of the paddocks, sitting long and lean in the saddle, muscles working in his shoulders as they took one of the jumps he had set up. There was a clear bond between man and horse, and she could see from the way Red's brown eyes followed Nico as he dismounted, that he trusted him completely.

It had been different when the horse had first arrived. Nervous and unpredictable, he had taken unending patience and hard work to tame, and Nico had been so good with him.

Just like he was being with her, Callie supposed, for the first time seeing the similarities.

Later that evening, as he went to leave the cottage, she caught hold of his hand, stopping him. 'Stay with me.'

He hesitated, and she could see he was torn between need and responsibility for doing the right thing.

'Are you sure?'

He needed reassurance, so she linked her arms around his neck and pulled him close, kissing him firmly on the lips and breathing him in, the scents of horse and leather and his musky natural odour tingling her senses.

'I've never been more sure,' she whispered against his ear, biting gently at his lobe.

She heard his intake of breath and he tensed in her arms, but only for a moment, then things were moving fast as his hands stroked down her back to cup her arse and he was lifting her off the ground. Callie wrapped her legs around him, holding on as, between frantic kisses, he clumsily stepped inside, kicking the door shut behind them and moving through to the bedroom.

Perhaps it should have been a little awkward with bashed heads and noses, Nico dropping her inelegantly on the bed before they began tugging at each other's clothes, and maybe she should have wanted things to slow down given everything that had come before, but it wasn't and she didn't, as caught up in the moment as he was.

'Wait, I don't have a condom,' he said, stopping abruptly.

Callie paused, considering the bathroom cabinet. They did need one since she was no longer on the pill, and she remembered seeing a pack when she had moved in.

'Stay here,' she instructed, easing away.

When she returned with the foiled wrapper, Nico propped himself up with his elbows, his eyes widening, and her cheeks immediately burned.

'I never put them there. I assumed they had been yours.'

'Not mine.' But then he groaned. 'Laurel.'

And that made perfect sense. It was exactly like Laurel to prepare for every eventuality. Had she hoped that Callie might hook up with her brother?

She went to him now, straddling his lap and tipping her head back when he started to trail kisses down her neck, and thoughts about whoever had supplied the condoms were gone.

They knew each other well enough now that there was no shyness. They were both laughing and encouraging each other, until lust and need mingled, the following moments hard and fast and almost desperate.

It was only in the aftermath that Callie remembered the dogs, bolting upright in bed. 'We left them shut outside.'

For a moment, Nico looked confused, but then he was leaping out from under the sheets and tugging on his jeans, while Callie grabbed his T-shirt. Slipping it on, she followed him through to the front of the cottage, watching as he opened the door.

Shyla was waiting patiently on the porch, but there was no sign of Dash or Chester and Callie's heart caught. But then there was a rustling sound in the bushes and they came charging out from the wooded path, tongues lolling and excited to see their humans.

Nico was just ushering them all through the door when the sound of an engine had Callie looking up. Headlights dazzled as the vehicle they belonged to bumped along the track and her guard immediately shot up, nerves jittering in her belly.

'It's okay.' Picking up on her unease, Nico gave her hand a reassuring squeeze.

Was it? It was gone ten thirty and he was here with her. She couldn't think of anyone else who would have reason to visit the cottage this late on a Thursday night, unless it was the police. Or...

No, she refused to consider Duncan. She had been here now for nearly four months. She had to believe she was safe.

Still, as the engine grew louder, she clung on to Nico, not able to get a good look at the car until it reached them.

Realising it was Faith, the tension ebbed out of her, curiosity taking its place. The woman looked unusually pale and worried, and her perfectly coiffed, blonde hair was messier than usual, as if she had been raking her fingers through it.

'Is everything okay?'

'I'm sorry to come over so late, Callie. I was hoping you would know where Nico was. I stopped by the house, but I didn't realise he was here with you.'

As she spoke, Faith's eyes glanced over at Nico, taking in his bare chest and feet, and no doubt his bed-ruffled hair, before she glanced back at Callie, her focus on the T-shirt, which was too big for her and hanging around her bare thighs.

Callie could see she had questions and for a moment the worried look turned to one of curiosity and sly amusement, before Faith seemed to check herself.

'What's wrong?' Nico's tone was a little impatient as he tried to pull her back on track.

'It's Ethan.' The worried look returned. 'He went out for a drink with a client earlier and he hasn't come home.'

'The pubs haven't shut yet. Have you tried calling him?'

'Of course,' Faith snapped, before apologising. 'I'm sorry. I didn't mean to take it out on you. It was an early drink. He knew I had dinner on the table waiting for him. I've called him a few times, but he's not picking up.'

'Which pub?' Callie asked, hovering and a little self-conscious.

'The White Heron, down in Brundall. I've already been over there and apparently, he left hours ago. I was hoping he might have come here to see Nico.'

'I'm sure he's fine,' Nico reassured her. 'Where's Olive? Please tell me you haven't left her at home alone.'

'Of course not!' This time, Faith didn't apologise for her snappiness. 'What kind of mother do you think I am?' she huffed. 'My friend is watching her. Look, just help me find him, please?'

'Okay,' Nico sounded resigned. He wasn't as worried as Faith. 'Go wait in the car. I will be out in a couple of minutes.'

When Faith's gaze darted again between him and Callie, and she looked as if she was about to ask what might be an awkward question, he gently shut the door in her face.

'That was unexpected,' he said, turning to Callie.

It was. Faith had caught them red-handed and Callie wasn't sure what the implications of that would be. 'I don't think you'll get away with telling her you were here to fix the shower,' she joked, trying to make light of it, relieved when Nico's lips twitched.

'No.'

'We're supposed to be cousins.'

'Adopted cousins,' he corrected. 'Technically, there's nothing wrong with that. Your cover is safe.'

Callie hoped so. She hadn't come this far to blow it now.

'Do you think Ethan's okay?' she asked, changing the subject as she followed Nico through to the bedroom. Chester and Shyla were both hot on their tail, but Dash was already in there and had settled himself down in the middle of the bed, looking up as he gave a big yawn.

'Mate, get down,' Nico told him.

'He's fine.'

Shaking his head, Nico fished on the floor for his socks. 'So, here's the thing with Faith,' he said, sitting down on the edge of the bed as he pulled them on. 'Don't get me wrong. She's a sweetheart and she has a good heart, but she can sometimes be hard work. She and Ethan have been together since they were kids and she does like to have things on her terms. Ethan loves her to bits, but sometimes he just needs a break and a bit of downtime to himself. It's for his sanity.'

'So this has happened before?'

'Not for a while. I would imagine it's to do with Anya. They're both pretty upset about her death. I know they thought a lot of her. Faith had taken her under her wing a bit, and Ethan, well, he doesn't show it much, but he has a vulnerable side. I think this has affected him more than he's letting on. So, I'm gonna go with Faith and we will figure out which pub he is in. If I know Ethan, he will be in the Ram, propping up the bar.' He paused, the side of his mouth curving up. 'You look really good wearing my T-shirt, but I'm going to need it, I'm afraid.'

Callie nodded. 'Are you going to come back here? I mean, tonight,' she asked, peeling the cotton shirt over her head and handing it to him.

Nico's gaze lingered on her face before doing a slow sweep all the way down her naked body, then back up again. He tugged her towards him, running his fingertips down the curve of her back, making her nerve endings tingle, before pressing a kiss to the tip of her nose. 'I'm absolutely coming back.'

He left her with Shyla and Dash, Chester running around excitedly when he realised they were staying, and told her, as he did every night, to keep the door locked.

Callie didn't need the reminder. What had happened to Anya had been enough of a warning that even out in the sticks you weren't safe.

Although she fully intended to get back in bed as soon as Nico returned, it didn't hurt to tidy up a bit and, after dressing, she spent a moment straightening the sheets, before spotting the condom wrapper. It was still on the floor and had been knocked slightly under the bed. Dropping to her hands and knees, she reached for it, managing to push it further out of reach.

She stretched her fingers out, ducking her head down when she couldn't see it. Towards the back wall, something glinted on the carpet.

A piece of jewellery?

It wasn't hers. She had left all of her valuables behind: the chain her dad had given her a few Christmases back, the earrings Phoebe had bought her for her birthday one year, and, of course, all of the lavish gifts from Duncan, the make up presents for the times he hurt and abused her. At least for the times before he decided he no longer cared about winning her over.

Curiosity had the better of her, which is why Callie ended up on her belly, shuffling her way forward until her fingers closed around the prize. After managing to wiggle her way back out – not as easy as going in – she sat back and studied the delicate bracelet in her hand. It didn't look expensive, but it was pretty. Thick, black string threaded with tiny rose quartz stones and a silver dog tag that read, *You've got this*. Who did it belong to?

Not Nico. The bracelet was feminine in style and would have been too small for his wrists.

Had someone else stayed here since him?

Or perhaps it had belonged to an overnight guest?

While it wasn't pleasant thinking about the past women he had slept with, particularly in this bed, she wasn't foolish enough to believe he had been celibate, and after her sobering relationship with Duncan, she wasn't prone to jealousy.

Deciding she liked the mantra on the bracelet, that it suited her own journey, she unfastened the clasp and slipped it on. The owner couldn't have missed it or they would have returned to look for it.

She did have this. And, from now on, whenever she wobbled and the doubts crept in, she would look at the dog tag and remember.

Still, as she drew back the curtain in the living room, peering out at the darkness and wondering how much longer Nico was going to be, aware that he wasn't in the main house and she was currently here at the farm all alone, she couldn't help the shiver that crept up her spine.

# 20

---

'I know you're not going to like what I'm about to say,' Faith began. 'But—'

She didn't get to finish as Nico interrupted her.

'Then don't say it.'

Briefly removing her attention from the road, she glanced over at him. His face was shadowy in the darkness, but she could still see the stubbornness of his jaw and the slight scowl of his mouth. Aware she was watching, he turned to her and gave her a pointed look, eyebrows raised.

'She's your cousin, Nico.'

'Adopted cousin.'

'That's still family.'

'And my business, not yours. How about we focus on your family and find out where Ethan is?'

Ouch. She swallowed her retort, reminding herself he was helping her. From the scene she had disturbed, she knew he would rather be back at Stable Cottage with Callie.

That night they'd joined Nico and Callie for dinner, she had suspected something was going on, but tonight had confirmed it. Did Laurel and her parents know the pair of them were seeing each other? Faith wondered what they would think.

She knew Nico had endured a rough childhood. He was one of her closest friends and she didn't want to see him get hurt. And she liked Callie too. If the woman would loosen up a little, the pair of them could become good friends.

She resented his insinuation that she wasn't focused on Ethan. Of course she was worried about him – heck, she had been worried enough to drop Olive off in the village with one of her friends while she went out looking for him. Nico and Callie were a distraction. She liked solving a good mystery, and always appreciated having something to take her mind away from bigger problems.

After the shock news that Anya's body had been found, they had all felt numb. She had been welcomed into their lives and Faith had treated her like family. As for Olive, how did they tell their ten-year-old daughter that the girl she had idolised was dead? That the police suspected murder?

Everyone knew each other around here and Faith was aware they were all looking at each other with suspicion. She had thought Nico's stable hand, Toby, might have been taken in for questioning. The boy had doted on Anya and had a big crush on her, and Faith knew Anya sometimes took advantage of his good nature. It wasn't a stretch to suspect that one day, she might push him too far.

And Ethan was right. Even though she liked Vince's partner, David Arthur, she knew the police often looked close to home. David hadn't been in Vince's life for long, and he did have a close friendship with Anya.

Both men were feasible suspects, so it had come as a surprise when a stranger had been arrested, and although it had been a relief, it had also brought with it delayed shock.

As a coping mechanism, Faith had thrown herself into various projects with a couple of the other school mums. She only worked part-time since Olive was born, doing a few hours a week in the local estate agents, and liked to keep herself busy. Ethan should have done the same. But he wasn't wired that way, so instead he dwelled. He had been drinking heavily again just lately and that worried her.

Nico didn't seem so concerned and she hoped it was because he knew where his best friend might be.

He instructed her to drive to the Ram – a pub she had only been to once or twice over the years – and she was relieved when following him inside to find Ethan at the bar.

Seeing them approach, he greeted Faith with far more enthusiasm than he had done in a while, throwing his arms around her. 'Here she is, everyone. My beautiful wife.'

'I've been calling you,' she hissed, grateful when Nico helped her get him off the bar stool and manoeuvred him outside. He was steaming drunk.

Back in the car, Ethan on the rear seat, chatting away and slurring his words, her temper rose a notch. As always, he was acting irresponsibly and she was the one having to deal with the aftermath.

She loved him, she did, but sometimes she wondered if he appreciated all she did for him. He had been absent around Olive recently and Faith needed him to step up. They were supposed to be a partnership, and she was sick and tired of carrying his slack. Tomorrow, when he had sobered up, they needed to talk. She simply couldn't go on like this.

Luckily, he fell asleep before they reached the farm and finally she had a moment of peace.

'Are you going to be okay?' Nico asked as she pulled up outside the cottage. She assumed that was where he wanted dropping, and her guess that Callie was expecting him back was confirmed when the woman opened the front door and wandered over to the car.

'Yeah, I'll be fine. I'm just tired.'

'You found him okay then?' Callie asked, peering into the back seat where Ethan was now snoring loudly.

'We did. Emergency over.'

'Are you going to be able to get him in the house by yourself?' Nico asked, as he got out of the car, going round to join Callie.

'If I can't, he will be sleeping in the car, which is perhaps what he deserves. Thank you for tonight, Nico.' Faith glanced at Callie and smiled. 'And I'm sorry I disturbed your evening.' They had both been good to her. She wouldn't say any more about the cousins thing.

'It's fine, honestly.' As Callie spoke, there was a light breeze picking up and it caught a few strands of her hair, blowing them into her face. As she raised her hand to push them back, Faith caught the glint of the bracelet on her wrist, her eyes narrowing as she recognised it.

'Where did you get that?'

For a moment, Callie looked confused, but then she realised what Faith was looking at. 'Oh, this? I found it under the bed.'

'You did?' Nico sounded surprised, catching hold of her hand and taking a closer look at the string of quartz stones.

'It's pretty, isn't it?'

'It looks familiar,' he said.

It was, and the last place Faith had expected to see it was on Callie's wrist.

'It should do. It was Anya's.'

Nico and Callie both stared at her.

'I know because I gave it to her at Christmas.' Faith remembered how the girl's face had lit up. 'I wanted to do something nice for her.'

'But how did it get in the bedroom of the cottage?' Callie sounded confused.

Faith stared from her to Nico, her mystery-solver mind working overtime. 'That's a very good question.'

## 21

Rob was insistent Duncan was clutching at straws believing Mica was alive, but deep down in his gut, Duncan knew the truth. He had clung to hope before noticing the picture frame, but now he was certain. There was no other explanation for why it had disappeared.

The two of them had argued over it when Duncan had refused to let Rob bag up her things. Rob hadn't been happy about it, convinced this was just a delay tactic. He even made the ludicrous suggestion that perhaps she had taken the picture into the sea with her.

Duncan didn't buy it. Now he knew the frame was missing, everything was starting to make sense. It explained why she had left her things on the rocks at Hope Cove. It had been a clue for them to find and throw them off her track, and it was why they had never been able to find her body.

The whole thing had struck him as odd from the start. He remembered Mica telling him early on in their relationship that drowning scared her, and she had really freaked out the time she hadn't washed up his favourite coffee mug properly, a little grime still clinging to the bottom of the cup, and he had been forced to hold her head under the soapy water to teach her a lesson. She had been an emotional wreck, suffering what appeared to be a full-on panic attack. Why would she choose that way to die?

No, she had deceived him and was sneakier than he had realised. Certainly more cunning. She had planned this in great detail, while tricking him into giving her a longer leash, leading him to believe she was fully compliant and wouldn't betray him again.

Knowing that she had made him look a fool had him raging.

She couldn't have just disappeared. Someone had to have helped her. She had left with nothing and he still had her passport and driver's licence, all of her bank cards, and even her phone. The only thing she had taken was the damn picture frame.

But where the hell would she go?

It wasn't back to Watford. He had seen Juliette, Aarna and Tracy at the memorial service. The cheeky bitches had dared to show up, that hoity cow, Juliette, shooting daggers at him as soon as she saw him.

It had crossed his mind that perhaps Mica had secretly patched things over with them, but he had arranged to have them discreetly tailed, soon realising they had nothing to do with her disappearance.

And he knew and trusted Michael Parker and his daughter, Phoebe. Mica's family had been easy to win over from the start. Mica had a conveniently cool relationship with her father and sister, which had made it easier to isolate her. Duncan knew how to read and manipulate people and Michael and his wife, April, Phoebe and her boyfriend, Ed, they were all on his side.

That left him at a loss. There was no one else Mica was in touch with.

There would be a clue somewhere. He just needed to find it.

He had already been through her emails, texts and WhatsApp messages, and checked her social media accounts. It was something he had done routinely throughout their relationship, wanting to keep tabs on anyone she might be speaking to and the nature of those conversations. He kept a list of her passwords written in a notebook and she was wise enough not to change them, having learnt the consequences of doing so a while back.

There weren't many messages, certainly not personal, and nothing to suggest where she might have gone. Instead, he turned his attention to her banking transactions. He didn't need her passwords for those. He had full control of her finances, having made her close her own account and allowing her shared access to one of his. Although he kept an eye on her spending, he didn't often scrutinise what she spent. Now he paid each purchase careful attention, looking for any kind of pattern.

That was how he noticed the cash withdrawals. They had started up about five months before she vanished, and she had been clever, taking out money whenever she went out, but never too much in one go. Small amounts that if questioned, she would be able to come up with a reason for. If she was going to run, she would need cash. The amounts only added up to about £400, but it would have given her a head start.

He looked back to the first withdrawal. It had been in late September and he tried to recall if there had been anything odd with her behaviour.

Nothing stood out and, if anything, she had been affectionate and loving towards him. He remembered thinking just how far they had come. Yes, she still displeased him at times, but she was less wilful and made a concerted effort not to provoke him. He still punished her now and again, but that was more for kicks, and to remind her to keep towing the line.

If anything, he had been forced to get creative in finding fault with her. The glitter of fear in her eyes, realising she had done him wrong and that she was about to pay for it, gave him a rush like no other. He lived for those moments.

He scrutinised her purchases now. Apart from grocery shopping and a new dress for a charity event he insisted she get, there was nothing. And then as the month drew to an end, there were Christmas gifts. Token ones for her family and then the one she had bought him.

She had commissioned an artist to paint the view of the gardens from the rear of the house, and he remembered being touched by how much effort she was putting into arranging it. She had even taken photos to the artist to ensure everything was perfect.

Oksana Harding. That was the artist's name, and the painting was a good one. It hung in his study on the wall above the desk.

Mica had originally seen the artist's work on social media and after visiting her studio and buying a framed print of the Dart Estuary, one they were both fond of, she had reached out to Oksana again about doing the personalised painting.

Knowing it was a gift, he had cut her some slack. He hadn't read their message exchange or complained about her visits to the woman's studio.

Rob had gone with her, so he knew where she was.

Curious now, he opened Mica's Instagram page and scrolled through her messages. There were none to Oksana, which surprised him and had him looking for the woman's page.

He found her immediately, noting she had several thousand followers. There was an email address and a phone number, but after spending time checking the phone's call log and Mica's inbox, he could see she hadn't made contact with Oksana.

Yet she had met with her a few times and the painting was hanging up in his house.

Looking back at the cash withdrawals, they had started around the same time.

Was this Oksana Harding somehow involved?

Paying close attention, he stalked her online, looking for some kind of clue.

It was on her open Facebook profile that he joined the dots.

A photo from a year ago of Oksana and another woman whose grey-blue eyes looked familiar. In the picture, they were hugging and the caption beneath read,

Date night.

The woman was tagged.

Laurel Adams.

## 22

---

BEFORE

We are out to dinner in Duncan's favourite restaurant, sat in his preferred window seat, when I hear my name called, and, as always, I am dressed as he has instructed. My hair is worn up and tied back in a knot as he likes it, showcasing the sapphire earrings he gave me as a gift after he forced my head into the toilet bowl for leaving a stray hair on the floor of the shower, and I am wearing the cashmere dress he picked out. The wool is too warm for the late-summer heatwave we are having and I am uncomfortably hot. He always chooses high necks and long sleeves, as they are better at hiding the bruising.

I am careful with my words, letting him lead the conversation and agreeing with him on everything. I don't complain when he orders for me, and I ease out a breath of relief when the waiter takes our drinks order, and my request for table water isn't overruled.

I have learnt that Duncan intentionally tries to get me drunk if we are out so it gives him an excuse to punish me. Depending on his mood, I can lose either way, as sometimes he gets shitty with me if I am not drinking.

*Do you realise how much I just paid for this bottle? You are an ungrateful little bitch. Where the hell are your manners?*

Of course, he never says those things in earshot of anyone. As far as the public are concerned, he dotes on me and spoils me rotten. Because I am not a celebrity and he claims to value his privacy, I am lucky that most people don't know that much about me. There was some initial interest from the press when we were first dating and I moved in with him, but I guess I am too boring for them to waste column inches on now, so that is why I am surprised that someone is calling me across the restaurant and not him. I am simply Duncan Stone's placid and rather dull fiancée.

That's right – fiancée. He proposed to me a couple of weeks ago, producing a rock that was supposed to impress me. Instead, it filled me with dread. Fiancée means marriage, and marriage is permanent, but what choice did I have?

He asked the question in a restaurant full of people and when he dropped to one knee, the whole room gave us a round of applause. Somehow I managed to smile and pretend to be excited, but the tears I cried weren't of joy, as he and our fellow diners assumed.

I knew there was only one answer to his question. No wasn't an option. I was going to be Mrs Stone whether I wanted to or not.

Mrs Mica Stone.

A name I never wanted and one that doesn't belong to me.

It's not the one being shouted out now, though.

No, the woman is calling, 'Callie.'

And despite the poshness of the restaurant, she has no qualms about raising her voice. I see Duncan bristle and I'm afraid to look over to see who has recognised me.

I am afraid of everything these days.

It was the cage that broke me. Six months ago, when he locked me in that tiny, cramped crate and threatened to burn me alive. I knew he had a sadistic streak, but I didn't realise what monstrosities he was capable of, and although he hadn't ignited the petrol, I saw his face and I know he had considered it.

I had spent all night in the garage, freezing cold, certain the fumes from the petrol would have made me throw up if my stomach wasn't already empty, every part of my body aching from the position I had been forced into. But that wasn't the worst of it. No, the worst was knowing at some point, he would come back, and I had no idea what he would do next.

It was as daylight was breaking, light creeping under the garage door, that I was unable to hold my bladder any longer. As I peed myself, my shame was complete. I knew I had lost all sense of self-worth. The only blessing was the petrol fumes overriding the stench of my urine.

When I heard his footsteps approaching the door, I squeezed my eyes shut and began to beg for mercy. I had never been so scared in my life.

I don't know what I was expecting, or how much worse I thought it was going to get, but he caught me off guard by unlocking the door to the cage. Somehow, I had resigned myself to the fact he intended to keep me in there.

'Come on, get out.'

I didn't need to be asked twice, but climbing out wasn't as easy as getting in. I had been in a cramped position for so long and in icy temperatures. My muscles had groaned as I attempted to move them and I'd cried out in agony. That was when he lost his patience, reaching in and grabbing hold of me, the pain excruciating as he forced me from the cage.

As I lay on the floor, curled back in a ball and sobbing, he scrunched up his nose. 'You fucking stink, you filthy cow. Get upstairs and clean yourself up.'

I still remember how I felt that morning. Terrified and humiliated. And broken.

He hasn't locked me in the crate since, but it is still there in the garage. A reminder of what will happen if I ever try to betray him again.

I won't. I have learnt my lesson.

So when the owner of the voice calling me across the restaurant comes bounding over to our table, and I hear Duncan's quiet hiss of breath, I instinctively stiffen, my hands trembling.

'Callie Parker, I bloody knew it was you.'

Now she has spoken more than one word, her voice is recognisable, and surprised, I look up.

'Laurel?'

What is she doing here in Dartmouth?

Laurel Adams was my roommate at university, and for a long time, she was my closest friend. We are still connected on Facebook, but have drifted apart over the years, which is a shame as at one time, we were inseparable.

She hasn't changed, her wide eyes huge against the pixie cut framing her face. It suits her personality, which is loud, enthusiastic and inquisitive, in the best possible way. We had some brilliant adventures at uni, all instigated by Laurel. Everyone loved her and she loved everyone back in turn. She is the least bitchy and most thoughtful person I know and her overconfidence is tempered by her kindness, a trait she inherited from her parents. Seeing her now, I realise just how much I have missed her. How the hell did I let this gorgeous spark of a woman slip out of my life?

Overcome with emotion, I want to push my chair back and hug her, but I am aware Duncan is watching us, and he isn't happy. He doesn't allow me to have friends and he has gradually isolated me from the ones I had, and Laurel will have already incensed him with her couldn't-give-a-shit, mishmash of an outfit, a shapeless dress patterned with all of the colours of the rainbow, teamed up with her faithful Doc Martens. It is everything I love about her, and everything he hates, and he is sneering slightly as if she smells bad. She doesn't.

Laurel takes the decision away from me, diving in to embrace me, squealing as she does so, and I struggle to keep my emotions bottled down. I am so happy to see her, but also terrified of Duncan's reaction.

His tone when he speaks is amicable enough, but I can detect the ice beneath it. 'Mica, are you going to introduce me to your friend?'

I ease back from the hug, nodding like a puppet. 'Um, of course. Laurel, this is my fiancé, Duncan.'

'Hi,' he tells her, slipping on his public face. The one with the killer smile that will fool her into believing he is a nice guy.

She glances in his direction with her big smile. 'Hey, it's good to meet you,' and I can see him sit up a little straighter. I realise he is getting ready to take charge of the conversation, to charm her then dismiss her, as he does with everyone else, but he only manages to hold her attention for a split second before it is back on me. 'Fiancé? Cal? You're getting married?'

Maybe she doesn't recognise him, or perhaps she just doesn't care. Laurel has always treated everyone the same, regardless of status, and she doesn't get starstruck. Right now, she is just excited to see me.

Duncan won't be happy. He is the important half of our relationship, the one people want to talk to. The scowl is already darkening his face.

'Yes,' I tell her. 'To Duncan. Duncan Stone.' I gesture to him again, to make sure she realises, desperate to make him a part of the conversation.

'I know who he is, silly,' she laughs, winking at Duncan. 'But

I'm sure he realises he's the lucky one, for bagging you, right, Dunc?'

Oh fuck. I had forgotten about her tendency to shorten everyone's name.

'It's Duncan,' he immediately corrects her.

'Okay, cool, sorry Duncan.' Her apology sounds flippant and she gives him a chill-your-beans look, before shaking her head, seeming a little amused.

'And Cal here,' Duncan says, his tone a little sarcastic, 'now prefers to go by Mica.'

For the first time, Laurel takes a moment to really study him. 'Oh she does now, does she?' she asks teasingly. 'Mica. That sounds posh.'

I want to cry, my excitement at seeing Laurel is dampened by what is happening between her and Duncan. She is reading him wrong. He isn't a man who can laugh at himself and he is going to make me pay for this when we get home. I need to fix it.

'How come you're in Devon?' I ask, trying to keep my voice steady. 'Are you on holiday?'

If she notices the tremor in my tone, she doesn't say. 'Yes, well, kind of. My ex lives locally and we're still close. I've been staying with her over the summer. That's the beauty of freelancing. You can work from anywhere and it gives me a change of scenery from Billericay.'

'What is it you do?'

The question is from Duncan, who has slipped his mask back into place.

'I'm a graphic designer.'

I'm not sure if it's my imagination, but Laurel sounds a little off with him when she answers. As if she's not a fan.

But that can't be true. Everyone loves Duncan.

She isn't interested in him, though.

'We should meet up, Cal. You live here now, right?'

I nod numbly as she excitedly chats away.

'This is just too cool. We have so much to catch up on.'

I want nothing more than to catch up with Laurel, but Duncan isn't going to let me.

How do I tell her without upsetting her? She isn't going to understand.

I look between her and Duncan, unsure how to answer.

Luckily, I am saved by the waiter bringing over our drinks. He glances at Laurel and then at Duncan. 'Will this lady be joining you tonight? Should I set another place?'

I swear I see mischief in Laurel's eyes and I know she is considering saying yes, before Duncan snaps, 'No. She was just leaving.'

I had assumed she was already dining here and I am about to ask the question, but realising, she smiles and shakes her head.

'I was walking past and spotted you through the window. I was sure it was you and I had to come in and say hello.' She turns to Duncan now. 'So, Callie's number. Am I allowed to have it or is she too important to speak to me now she's dating a celebrity?'

She is being facetious, no shade thrown at me, an amused smirk on her face as he chokes on the wine the waiter has just poured him.

I am in shock, while the waiter's lips twitch.

'Laurel,' I beg. 'Please don't do this.'

Duncan looks furious and when he eventually speaks, his words are clipped. 'Mica can give her number to whoever she likes. She doesn't answer to me.'

The biggest load of bullshit he has ever spoken, but still he sounds convincing.

Laurel turns to me, eyebrows raised expectantly, and I see Duncan glaring at me behind her back, warning me to say no.

Much as I want her to have it, the risk is too great. If he puts me back in the crate again... I remember how it felt, trapped in that tiny cage, and I start shaking just thinking about it.

'I'm sorry,' I say, looking down at the table. 'Things are so busy, I don't have time to meet up. It was lovely to see you, though.'

There is a long, heavy silence, and I can feel the weight of her disappointment before eventually, she answers.

'I'm sorry too.'

* * *

The first slap catches me off guard.

After Laurel left, Duncan was tight-lipped and I could see he was struggling to keep his temper under control. I was safe while we were in the restaurant, but my stomach was already flipping with nerves, knowing things would change once we were in private. So he surprised me, when his mood seemed to lift as we ate dinner. Perhaps it would be okay. After all, I had done as he'd wanted and I hadn't given Laurel my number.

Rob had picked the two of us up after the meal, and as we drove home, Duncan chatted with him about golf and politics. Two subjects that always had me switching off. I didn't mind. It gave me time with my own thoughts, as I stared out of the window at the dark countryside, and I was relieved Duncan seemed relaxed and content.

The pair of them were behind me as I pushed open the front door and I turned to ask Duncan if he wanted me to pour them both a nightcap, as he often finishes the night with a brandy or a whisky.

That is when he hits me.

The backhanded crack against my cheek is hard enough to knock me off my feet. As I fall to the floor, he says goodnight to Rob, as if it hasn't happened.

Rob carries on talking, ignoring me.

He is despicable.

The metallic taste of blood coats my tongue and my cheek stings. I think Duncan's ring caught my mouth because my bottom lip is starting to throb. I can hear Chester whining from the kitchen, where Duncan insists he stays these days. At least it's not the crate, so it was a compromise I accepted.

'Get upstairs,' he orders, shutting and locking the door.

I want to go to my dog, but I know better than to question him, pulling myself up from the floor as quickly as possible and fleeing for the bedroom.

It wasn't my fault Laurel spotted us in the restaurant and I didn't give her my number. I want to protest and plead my innocence, but I know he won't listen.

Duncan has his own narrative and nothing I can do or say is going to change that.

I am stupid, I am thoughtless, I abuse his generosity and kindness. He is a good guy, but he can only be pushed so far. I have heard it all before. Apologising and accepting whatever is about to happen is safest. If I am docile, sometimes he goes easier on me.

I hear his footsteps on the stairs while I am in the bathroom bathing my split lip.

'Mica. Come here.'

I am not fool enough to keep him waiting and dread coils in my belly when I step into the bedroom and find he has removed his belt.

'I'm sorry about what happened tonight.' I dip my head in shame.

'It's a little late for apologies. The damage has been done.' His tone is calm and he sounds almost reasonable. I know this is when I should fear him the most. When he loses his temper, he lashes out, but at times like these when he is thinking clearly, he is cruel and calculating, and the punishment will often be worse.

Later, as we are lying in bed, and I am propped onto my side, the most comfortable position with my back and buttocks covered in painful welts, he snuggles up behind me.

'I love you, Mica. No one cares about you more than I do.' His breath is hot against the back of my ear as his hand creeps round to caress the underside of my breast, and I fight the instinct to recoil. 'Everything I do, it's for your own good. I hope you realise it doesn't give me pleasure to hurt you.'

I don't acknowledgement him. Instead, I pretend I'm asleep. And, not for the first time, I wish to hell I had never met him.

## 23

I never got my car back. From what I overheard Duncan tell Rob at the time, he had arranged for my Polo to be taken from Phoebe's straight to the scrapyard. I had been devastated, but over the following months, Duncan eventually relented and allowed me to have another car.

When he presented it to me, he told me it was because I was slowly earning back his trust, and he could reward as easily as punish. It was because of my behaviour I was getting a new car. Not that I believed him. I know it suits Duncan for me to be mobile so I can run chores for him. Pick up his dry cleaning or nip to the supermarket.

And, of course, the new car came with a compromise. It has cameras and a tracker fitted so Duncan knows where I am at all times. Because, apparently, having Rob tail me everywhere isn't enough.

That is what he is doing right now, having followed me to Plymouth, where I have been sent by Duncan to find a suitable dress for an event we have been invited to. Rob is not discreet as he parks across from me, and I do my best to ignore he is there.

I hate clothes shopping. It's something I used to love, a pastime I would enjoy with friends, usually making an afternoon of it with lunch or cocktails, but these days, I am alone and my confidence has taken such a hit, I have to pluck up the courage to venture out of Dartmouth.

I know a chain-store outfit won't pass Duncan's seal of approval, so I head to a couple of the boutiques, relieved when the first dress I try on fits okay. It's black, as had been requested, and covers enough of my flesh that it won't reveal any of the scars and bruises. It's been ten days since he whipped me with the belt and the marks are still visible.

It's an easy purchase and as I leave the shop with my bag, spotting Rob sat waiting on a bench outside looking bored, I change my plan to rush home.

To hell with him. This isn't my idea of fun either, but I will make him suffer for a little longer.

I know I can't afford to stay out all day. There are chores to be done around the house. Duncan notices if things are untidy or out of place. I have to keep everywhere in pristine condition. But for an hour, I will wander. I can always use the excuse I was looking for a bag or shoes if I am questioned.

Rob follows me, a scowl on his face – I'm sure I've never seen him crack a smile – and as I disappear into another store, he settles himself down on a bench to wait.

The clothes and accessories are all pretty, but none of them interest me. There was a time where I would have been in my element and could have wasted half an hour in here, but as I glance over racks of clothes and display tables of colourful bags and costume jewellery, I realise the shop is no more than a hiding place, a brief escape from my everyday hell.

Knowing I can't stay in there indefinitely, I start to leave, my eyes widening in horror as I spot Laurel hovering just inside the entrance. She is studying a pair of boots and I'm pretty sure she hasn't seen me, which is good. After our last uncomfortable encounter, I don't want to run into her again. Plus, if Rob sees me talking to her and tells Duncan, there will be hell to pay.

Realising there is no way of passing by without her spotting me, I break into a clammy sweat, wondering what the hell I am going to do.

A woman walks past me and I see she has just left the changing room. Without giving it any thought, I grab a random item from the nearest rack and head for the safety of the cubicles, forcing a smile for the assistant standing by the entrance.

As I disappear inside, I swear I hear Laurel calling my name.

There are three cubicles and all are empty, so I pick the end one, hanging the green top I brought in on a wall hook and dropping my bags to floor, then sinking down onto the stool to wait. Even all these days later, my arse hurts from where the belt lashed it, a reminder I can't risk upsetting Duncan again.

Minutes tick by and my panic grows. How long should I stay in here? What if Laurel spots me when I leave? And what about the assistant? She is going to wonder why I am taking so long. I'm an idiot. I should have brought more clothes in with me.

I hear the sound of footsteps. Another customer, I assume. But then a figure pauses the other side of the curtain and I wonder if it's the assistant coming to check up on me. I wait for her to ask if everything is okay.

What I don't expect is for the curtain to pull back, exposing my hiding place, and for Laurel to be standing the other side.

She looks me dead in the eye, her expression determined. 'You and I need to talk.'

I'm immediately on my feet, grabbing the green top. 'I'm sorry. I don't have time. Duncan's expecting me back.'

'Callie. Wait!'

'I told you. I don't have time.'

I try to push my way past her, but despite being three inches shorter and at least twenty pounds lighter, she's surprisingly strong. Blocking my way and refusing to move.

'What has he done to you?'

'What?'

'You know who I mean. Duncan? What has he done to you?'

How does she know about the bruises? I am always so careful to conceal them. Panicking she can see one, I redden and cling to denial.

'He hasn't done anything to me.' I force a laugh. 'Though he's going to wonder where I am if I don't get home soon. I promised him I would only be gone a couple of hours.'

'I saw the two of you together, Cal. Sorry, I forgot, it's Mica now, isn't it?' she says sarcastically. 'And that is not a healthy relationship.'

She saw us for five minutes. How dare she judge how we are together? Anger chokes me. 'My relationship is none of your business. You know nothing about Duncan or how things are between us. He's a good man.'

'A good man who won't let you catch up with one of your best friends?'

'That was my choice, not his?' I feebly protest, knowing full well I don't have a good reason, if she presses me, for why I didn't want to exchange numbers.

'Of course it was. I know his type. I saw how he was with you. You looked half afraid to open your mouth in case you upset him. Is his ego that fragile?'

'His ego is fine, and I need to go.' I try to push past her again, my panic spiking when she refuses to move. Rob is going to wonder what the hell I am doing. What if he comes in here looking for me? The thought has my belly flipping with nerves. 'Let me go.

I have a security tail waiting outside for me. You can't force me to stay here.'

'I'm trying to help you,' she says, sounding so reasonable.

'You're not helping me.' I can feel the hysteria rising, tears pricking at the back of my eyes. 'You don't understand how it is. I have to go. I'm late. I have to go now.'

She studies me for a moment, her expression softening. 'Jesus, look at you, Cal. You're trembling just talking to me. What happened to my gorgeous, strong, capable friend?'

'I'm still here,' I snap, ashamed she can see through me.

'Prove it to me then. Have lunch with me.'

'I can't! I just told you I need to get home.'

'Okay then. A drink one night this week,' she pushes.

'Laurel, I can't. I'm busy.'

'Next week then or the week after. Breakfast, lunch, dinner or just a coffee. You pick. Just tell me when is good.'

She is trying to force my hand, knowing it's impossible for me to agree, and I drop my head unable to look at her. 'I can't. I'm so sorry. I just can't.'

'You can't, or Duncan won't let you?'

The pause before I answer is a mistake and it speaks volumes. 'I can't,' I repeat flatly, relieved when she steps back to let me pass.

'Is he just controlling or does he hit you too?'

Heat floods my cheeks. Am I really this transparent? How come then no one else notices how things are? I tried to go to Phoebe. She believed Duncan. I have considered going to the police. And I'm sure if I reported what he did to me, he would find a way to manipulate the situation, to twist it back on me again.

I can't go back in the crate.

I don't realise I'm crying until she hands me a tissue, and knowing I need to pull myself together before I can leave the store,

I have no choice but to wait. I dab at my eyes and will the tears to stop.

'It's not as bad as you think it is,' I tell her, unable to hide the tremor in my voice.

There, I've conceded my relationship with Duncan isn't great. I'm just not admitting how awful it is.

Laurel smiles sympathetically and I hate her pitying me. She knows. Somehow, she has figured it out. She has always been astute and able to read people.

'I'm guessing if I contact you on Messenger, Duncan will read it,' she says.

When I don't confirm or deny, she continues.

'I'm staying with Oksana Harding. She's an artist and she has a place on the river with a little art studio attached. I'm at the house every weekday afternoon.'

'Laurel, I need to—'

'Just let me finish, Cal. This is important. She has a website and she's on Instagram too. You can get the address on either. If you change your mind about letting me help you, or if you just want to talk things through, come and find me.'

I sniff and nod. I have no intention of meeting up with Laurel. It's too dangerous. 'Thank you.'

'Oksana Harding. Remember it.'

I look at her one last time before I leave, knowing I won't see her again. 'I will. I promise.'

'I don't want this life for you, Callie. You deserve better.'

Her words ring in my ears as I leave the store.

I don't want this life either.

## 24

---

NOW

Callie had been wearing a dead girl's bracelet.

She couldn't shake the thought as Nico slept soundly beside her, just as it was playing on her mind that Anya had been in the cottage at some point.

Learning Faith had given Anya the bracelet as a Christmas present, Callie had taken it off her wrist, handing it back. It wasn't hers, and the quote she had found inspirational now felt redundant. Anya hadn't *got this*. Her life had been cruelly taken from her.

Callie had moved into Stable Cottage mid-February. Had Anya lost the bracelet before or after? Was she the mystery intruder who had touched Callie's things?

If so, it made no sense. Anya had been the most aloof with her of everyone and Callie barely knew her. Why would the girl be so interested in her?

Unless she had figured out Callie Adams and Mica Parker were the same person.

No, it wasn't possible. Duncan was more often than not photographed alone and the press had never been interested in her. Plus, along with the name change, she looked different.

Gone were the designer dresses and she seldom wore make-up these days. And her hair was always worn loose now and naturally wavy, instead of being straightened to within an inch of its life.

Would Anya really have recognised her?

It was a stretch, but she supposed it was possible. Was that why Anya had broken in? Was she looking for proof of who Callie was?

What if she had been spying for Duncan?

The unwelcome thought, as preposterous as it was, popped into her head.

No. She was stretching things too far.

But Anya was dead. Was Duncan somehow involved in what had happened to her?

It was ridiculous and far-fetched, but the seed was planted, and the longer she lay there, the more it was snowballing out of control. As much as she tossed and turned, and tried to shake the thought, sleep wasn't forthcoming.

Did Duncan know she had come here? Was he watching her and getting ready to pounce?

It would be his style to lurk in the shadows while he toyed with her. He liked playing games.

She fought the urge to get up and check the front door was locked. Although she was sure she remembered twisting the key, Nico had been distracting her at the time, trailing kisses along her jawline and down her throat, and they had both been eager to get back to what they had earlier started.

For a while, he had kept her occupied, patient and giving and tender. So different to Duncan. It was afterwards, in the quiet darkness, that her mind had started working overtime.

No, the door was locked. She shouldn't doubt herself. And they had a canine army on the floor around the bed. If anyone tried to break in, the dogs would alert them.

Still, she stewed and she fidgeted, her movements eventually waking Nico.

'Are you always this restless in bed?' he asked, his voice husky with sleep.

'Sorry. I didn't mean to wake you.'

'It's fine. I'm a light sleeper anyway. Is everything okay?'

When she didn't answer him, not wanting him to think she was a fool, he propped himself up on his elbow, a lot wider awake as he looked down at her. He ran his free hand gently up and down her arm.

'Something's bothering you. Talk to me.'

'It's nothing. I'm just being paranoid.' She tried to make a joke of it. 'And laying here in the dark doesn't help.'

'So what's playing on your mind. You know if you say it out loud, it won't seem so bad.'

Callie wasn't so sure about that.

'Is it about Anya?' he pushed, his intuitive brain already racing to the root of the problem.

'She was here, Nico. In this bedroom.'

He couldn't deny what was fact, and to his credit he didn't try to, nodding in agreement. 'I don't know why. I offered it to her when she first started working for me. I said she could stay here, have her own space, but she didn't want it. Despite her relationship with Larissa, I think she felt an obligation to look after her.'

'So why was she here?'

He shrugged. 'Maybe she changed her mind, but was too proud to say. I guess I must've missed the bracelet when I was getting the place ready for you.'

'Do you really think it's that simple?'

He was silent for a moment. 'Yeah, I do. And it's not something that should be bothering you in the middle of the night.' He smiled at her, his hand moving up to cup her cheek and his thumb brushing across her bottom lip. 'It happened before you moved in; you're worrying about nothing.'

'But what if it didn't?' Callie's voice was a whisper.

She watched his reaction, saw him frown.

'I don't understand.'

'What if it didn't happen before I moved in?'

'Callie—'

'No, listen to me, please.' She pushed herself up so she was facing him, mirroring his pose. 'I told you someone tried the door the first night I arrived, and remember how I thought someone had been here going through my things?'

The frown deepened. 'You think it was Anya?'

'I didn't imagine it, Nico. Someone was here and it would make sense, given that I found her bracelet.'

Seconds ticked by as he considered her words. 'But why?'

'What if she recognised me?'

'No, she didn't. I know Anya. She spoke her mind. If she had suspected who you were, she would have said something. If not to you, then to me.'

He sounded firm in his defence of the girl and Callie hesitated, considering her next words.

'Was there a reward?'

'A reward?' He looked confused. 'For what?'

'To find me.' She saw the realisation dawn and quickly pushed on. 'I know Duncan. He wouldn't have just accepted it when he was told I had drowned. Not without a body.'

It was a lot to put in front of him, especially given that he had just woken up, and she watched the flicker of different emotions on his face as his brain switched through the gears.

'Wait, you think Anya figured out who you were and approached Duncan?' he asked, eventually. His tone was carefully neutral.

'I don't know what to think. It's possible though, right?'

'So, what, you're saying you think he killed her?' Nico's eyes widened and she could see he was taken aback.

Callie dropped her gaze, a little embarrassed. 'Him or Rob Jolly. Is it really that big a stretch?' she asked, picking at a frayed edge on the duvet.

He took his time answering, which at least told her he was considering what she was proposing. 'Anya went missing weeks ago and the police have already made an arrest,' he said eventually.

'But what if they have the wrong man?'

He fell silent again. 'They must have evidence,' he pointed out eventually. 'Besides, if any of this was true, it would mean Duncan has known where you are for a while. Why would he not have come forward?'

'It could be a trap.' Her voice had dropped to a whisper again, remembering how Duncan had liked to trick her, to have her believe she could change the outcome, then enjoying the moments when he took all hope away.

Nico's expression softened and he reached out to run his fingers through her hair.

'I get it, okay. He did some godawful things to you, and it's easy for your imagination to run riot, especially in the middle of the night. It's understandable you're worried and scared he might show up, but I honestly don't think Anya was in contact with him. I can't explain how her bracelet happened to get under your bed, but I'm sure there is an innocent explanation. I don't believe he's here in Norfolk either. But I want you to feel safe, so I'll stay here with you while we figure this out, either on the sofa or in this bed, whatever works for you, or you can come and stay in the house, okay?'

He was so logical, his words making sense. 'Okay,' she agreed.

'I won't let anyone hurt you, Callie.'

She believed him. Nico radiated a steady inner strength, which gave her hope, remembering he'd had his own difficult past. She didn't know the details, but Laurel had told her he had once been volatile and angry at the world for the shitty hand it had dealt him.

'How do you do it?' she asked, reaching for his hand and entwining their fingers. 'You're always calm and reasonable, and you seem so confident in your own skin too. Laurel says you weren't always this way.'

Her words seemed to surprise him and for a moment, she wasn't sure if he was going to answer, but then he asked, 'You know about my mother?'

'Not really.' It was the truth. She hadn't been given all the details. 'I know you were alone when Paul and Janice took you in.'

There was another hesitation. This time, he pulled his hand away and settled back down against the pillow.

Worried she had pried too much, she quickly backed off. 'We don't have to talk about it. I'm sorry. I shouldn't have said anything.'

'It's okay, Callie, I'm going to tell you. Come here.' He unfolded his arm, indicating for her to lie down with him, letting her get comfortable, before tugging her close. 'My mum was twenty-one when she had me. She was living at home and didn't have the best relationship with my grandparents. I never knew who my dad was, other than his first name was Luca. He was a holiday fling. A local she met in Italy – hence my name. He's not on the birth certificate and they never stayed in touch, so I doubt he knows I exist.'

'That can't be easy,' Callie sympathised, feeling him shrug it off.

'It is what it is. It used to bother me, but not so much now. We lived with my grandparents in Cumbria until I was six, then Mum met Kevin. He was older and had been discharged from the army. Mum was besotted and, despite my grandparents' disapproval, we moved away with him to live in Kent. He wasn't healthy for her to be around. She was easily influenced and he had plenty of vices. He was also lazy, supposedly retrained as a painter and decorator, though he hardly ever took on any work. Either he had an injury or the jobs just weren't there. My mum worked, but she struggled to pay the bills and put food on the table. Then, when I was nine, my grandparents were killed in a house fire and, as their only child, Mum inherited everything. That was when things went downhill.'

'How so?'

'Mum and Kevin both had addictive personalities and Kevin liked to gamble. I think the inheritance lasted them just over a year. When the money was there, everything was great. They were both full of smiles and life was all holidays and presents, but then it was gone and, shortly afterwards, Kevin left. Mum was devastated and she blamed me.'

'What?' Callie shifted her head to look up at him. 'How the hell was it your fault?'

'It wasn't, but she was young and saddled with a kid she had never wanted in the first place. She was alone, unhappy and penniless. Other women her age were out having fun. She saw it that I was holding her back. That's why she started lying about who I was to the men she met, pretending I was her younger brother. She hated being alone and was desperate to meet someone else.'

'And did she?'

'Yeah, she met Harvey.' There was the faintest hint of bitterness in his voice.

'And he thought you were her brother?'

'At first, yes, and when he found out the truth, he threatened to leave her. Instead, she left me.'

It shouldn't have come as a shock. Callie knew he had been alone, but still she had to hold in her gasp. 'How old were you?'

'I was twelve.'

'Seriously?' That was messed up. Her own family dynamics weren't great, but at least she had been an adult when her dad had moved back to the States. 'You were a kid. That's not even legal.'

'I didn't tell anyone for ages. I guess I was too embarrassed. I woke up one morning and she was gone. She'd left me a note on the kitchen table telling me to look after myself and she loved me, but couldn't do the whole parenting thing any more, and there was an envelope with £50 in it.'

'You were all alone.' Callie's heart squeezed and she reached up to touch his cheek. In that moment, she had an overwhelming urge to look after him, horrified at what his mother had done.

'I tried to carry on as normal, going to school, trying to eke the money out on food, but gradually, my supplies dwindled and the envelopes of utility bills were piling up. I didn't have money for those and I was terrified of the landlord coming to kick me out. It turned out she had paid two months' rent in advance, but I didn't know that at the time. Of course, he did come knocking eventually and after dodging him for a couple of weeks, I was too afraid to go home. I used to hide in the school changing room after football practice and sleep there.'

This was so much worse than Callie had realised, and it couldn't be easy for him to talk about. Thank God he had crossed paths with Paul and Janice Adams.

'That's when you met Laurel, right?' she asked, keen to push him on to happier memories. She remembered some of what her friend had told her. Laurel had been at Nico's school, a couple of years below him. Her first year of high school. There had been a bully who had targeted her and, hard to believe it now, she had been scared of him.

'Yeah, I didn't really know her at the time, but I'd seen her around and heard one of the other kids picking on her. He was in the year below me. One night after school, her mum was late to pick her up and the spiteful little prick was with his two friends. They had her surrounded and had emptied her school bag over the ground. I told myself it was none of my business and it was safest to stay in the changing room, but then I heard her crying.'

Laurel was so headstrong, Callie couldn't imagine her being reduced to tears. 'You intervened, right?'

'Yeah, it was three of them and she was a tiny girl. It wasn't fair. I climbed out of the window and went over to confront them. I made sure they left her alone.'

He was playing it down. Laurel had told Callie how he had kicked their arses and that they never gave her any grief again. Although she knew the rest, she listened as he explained how he had made Laurel promise never to reveal his hiding place. But, worried about him, she had told her parents anyway. Initially, Nico had been mad at her and frightened too, but it turned out to be his saving grace. Paul and Janice Adams had taken charge of the situation, insisting on giving him a bed and a decent meal, then contacting the authorities. It took some manoeuvring, but they were eventually allowed to foster Nico, while steps were taken to track down his mum. She had been found living in a bedsit with Harvey in Cornwall, but died after being hit by a car while fleeing the police.

Eventually, Paul and Janice had adopted Nico, and even though by then he was in his teens, they treated him as their own, giving him exactly the same opportunities as Laurel.

'How did you feel when your mum died?' Callie asked now. She knew the emotion of grief she had experienced with her own mother, but this had to be different.

Nico shrugged again, tracing light circles on her arm with his finger. 'Sad, angry, but mostly numb. She was my mother, but she hadn't been a mother. If that makes sense.'

'It does.' Callie reached up and kissed him. 'Thank God you met Laurel's parents.'

'They're my real family. Sometimes blood doesn't matter. It's the people who are there for you. And it's because of them I got the opportunity to work with Teddy. Paul was doing Teddy's accounts when he lived down in Kent and I was with him one day when he went out to see him. It was the first time I had been around horses, but I felt a bond straightaway. Teddy recognised it and offered me an apprenticeship.' He smiled at Callie. 'So there you have it. The story of my life.'

It was a sad one, but with a happy ending, and realising everything Nico had overcome, to see what he had achieved, and the person he was today, gave her hope. He had defeated his demons. Was it possible she could defeat her own?

It also struck her that Nico and Duncan had both risen from nothing. Their stories were similar and they had both pulled themselves out of the gutter, finding success, but how differently it had shaped them. Duncan using his past as an excuse for cruelty, while Nico tried to be a good man.

Talking helped and this time when she closed her eyes, Callie drifted off to sleep. Her dreams plagued her, though.

Duncan was in them, and he was at Willow Brook Farm. She kept trying to run from him, to hide, but he kept finding her.

Then, eventually, she was safe and back in bed in the cottage.

*The weight of the mattress dipped and she was aware of Nico leaning over her, tenderly brushing her hair back. His breath was warm against her ear, but he didn't smell right, and as he spoke, she froze, realising it wasn't his voice. Terror choked her.*

'You think you can escape,' Duncan whispered. 'But I will find you.'

## 25

After dropping Olive off at school on Friday morning, Faith headed into Brundall to see Vince Mitchell.

She had left Ethan at home, sleeping off his hangover. Later, they were going to have to talk about his drink problem, which was becoming steadily worse. Faith put him and Olive above everything. Was it so much to expect him to do the same back?

Parking outside Craft Angels, she fished the bracelet she had given Anya out of her purse and studied it. She had taken her time picking it, wanting it to be perfect. The pretty quartz stones, glinting in the sunlight, signalled strength, while the message on the dog tag was meant to encourage, to let Anya know she could handle everything life threw at her.

How wrong she had been about that.

She had bought the bracelet, but didn't want to keep it, not wanting the reminder of everything that had happened. Instead, she planned to give it to Vince. Larissa might have been Anya's mother, but Vince was the one who had loved and cared about her most. She also wanted to ask a few questions, curious as to how the bracelet had ended up at Stable Cottage.

Getting out of the car, Faith went into the store, embracing Vince warmly and telling him how sorry she was. Although she had been there in the early days after Anya went missing, joining in the searches and trying to offer support, she hadn't seen him since the body had been found. 'Ethan and I are here if you need anything.'

That started the tears and she waited patiently as Vince removed his glasses to dab at his eyes, then blew his nose.

'Is everything okay?' David wandered through from the back room of the shop. Seeing Faith, he nodded a hello to her.

Ethan wasn't a fan of David, but Faith had never had a problem with the handsome Ghanaian. He and Vince had only met a year ago, and he had a quiet and calming presence, which was good for the somewhat scatty and melodramatic Vince.

'I'm sorry, I didn't mean to upset you,' Faith apologised.

Vince shook his head and finished blowing his nose. 'No, it's fine. Everything is starting me off at the moment. It's not just you. I just can't believe she is gone.'

There wasn't much Faith could say, and as her own emotions stirred, she wondered if she had made a mistake in stopping by. Instead, she asked about the investigation. 'Is there any further news?'

Vince shook his head. 'Not really. We know it was a blow to the head that killed her. The police think her body may have been moved. I just don't understand why anyone would want to hurt her.'

'It's awful, Vince. I wish there was something I could say to make it better.' Remembering the bracelet, Faith held it out to him, waiting as he swiped at his eyes again, before slipping his glasses back on.

'This is Anya's,' he said, taking it from her and peering closely at it. 'Where did you get it?'

'Callie found it.'

'Callie Adams? Nico's cousin?' he sounded surprised. 'Where?'

*She's more than his cousin*, Faith was tempted to say, but bit her tongue. She had promised herself she would stay out of it. 'It was in Stable Cottage, under the bed apparently.'

Both Vince and David were gawping at her. They hadn't expected that answer.

'How did it get there?'

'I honestly don't know, Vince. I'm guessing she must have lost it at some point. Do you remember when you last saw her wearing it?'

He shook his head, but she could see he was thinking about it.

'She had it on at Christmas,' David said, finally joining in.

'Yes, that's when I gave it to her. But you haven't seen her wearing it recently?' Faith pushed.

'I don't think so. Did she used to stay at the cottage then?'

'Not that I knew of. Callie's been living there since February.'

David looked thoughtful. 'So she must have left it there between Christmas and before Callie moved in.'

'And it was under the bed, you say,' Vince asked, double-checking.

'That's what Callie said.'

'But why would Anya have been in the bedroom?'

Faith and David exchanged a look as Vince pondered. For a worldly-wise man, he could be naïve when it came to his niece.

The question was one she had already given thought to – or, rather, she had wondered who Anya had been in the bedroom with.

The police had arrested a traveller who had been living in the woods, but Katy Matthews, who was one of Faith's school mum friends, was married to a sergeant and said the police were wondering if they had the wrong person.

If it was true, they were going to be looking more closely again at the man Anya had been seen with that last night. Faith was considering whether to mention Toby's name, suggest that perhaps he had been in the cottage with Anya, when David spoke.

'Do you think Nico had anything to do with her disappearance?' he asked, and Faith looked at him in shock.

'No,' Vince was quick to protest. 'Not Nico. He adored Anya. He would never hurt her.'

'You're too trusting, Vince. She spent a lot of time with him. You have no idea how honourable his intentions were towards her.'

Well, this was going in a direction Faith hadn't anticipated. Nico was Ethan's best friend and she knew he had nothing to do with what had happened to Anya, but the bracelet had been found in the bedroom of his cottage.

'Perhaps we should hand it over to the police,' she suggested. 'They will soon be able to eliminate Nico from their enquiries.'

'If he is innocent,' David pushed.

Faith gave him a tight smile. 'I'm sure he will be.'

# 26

BEFORE

Chester is the breaking point.

I tried to be as compliant as I can, but Duncan grows bored and when he does, his sadistic side comes out to play. Sometimes it is a beating, other times he gets creative, and just recently he has been using my dog, knowing how much it upsets me.

I will never forgive myself if anything happens to him. Chester never asked to be brought into this situation. He and I had a happy life together before I met Duncan.

This is all my fault and I need to get him to safety. If that means rehoming him, then so be it. The idea of giving my dog up is unbearable, but I know I have to be brave. I will miss him terribly, but having him safe is a priority.

Much as he dislikes Chester, I doubt Duncan will allow me to rehome him. He will lose one of the threats he likes to dangle over me. And between him and Rob, they watch me like a hawk. I can't just take Chester away.

I remember back to my conversation with Laurel. It was over a week ago I saw her in Plymouth and I've had no intention of making contact with her, but now I need her help. A couple of nights ago, Duncan fed Chester and I realised just how much danger my dog is in.

At the time, I was making dinner and when he offered to fill his dish, I thought he was having a rare kind moment. Thank fuck I spotted the glint of silver in the food, moments after Chester had started tucking in, pulling the bowl away from him.

'Is something wrong?' Duncan had asked innocently.

I fished in the food, pulling out the razorblade, for a moment my anger choking me. 'You put this in here?'

'Mica, don't be ridiculous. I love Chester. It was obviously already in the food. We'll complain to the supermarket.'

He gave me a look that was a dare to challenge him and, knowing better, I immediately backed down.

'You're right. I'm sorry. I didn't mean to accuse you.'

My hands were shaking as I wrapped the sharp blade in tissue, before throwing it in the bin. Ignoring Chester's whines, I checked the bowl thoroughly before putting it back down on the floor.

'Can I help with anything else?' Duncan asked cheerfully.

'No, no. I have everything covered. But thank you for offering.'

'Then for goodness' sake smile. The crisis was averted. Chester lives to see another day.'

I listened to him witter on, ignoring his attempts to goad me, but all I could think was, he had just tried to hurt my dog.

I casually looked Oksana Harding up on Instagram later that evening, perusing some of her posts and giving them an obligatory like. Laurel and I don't follow each other on this site, but I knew she might be looking out for a sign that I had viewed Oksana's page. She was the only way I could think to get Chester to safety. I didn't know how. Only that I was going to need help.

'What are you up to?' Duncan asked, as he walked into the bedroom and caught me off guard.

'I'm just on Instagram.' I swallowed, my mouth dry, and when he held out his hand for my iPad, I passed it over.

My heart thumped as I watched him, knowing I was on Oksana's page.

'Is this a friend of yours?'

'No, I've never met her. I saw a post of one of her paintings and thought how pretty it was.' His expression was unreadable as he scrolled. 'She does local scenes in Devon,' I added. 'They're really good, aren't they?'

Eventually, he nodded. 'Yes, she has a talent.'

'I could drive down there, maybe buy one of her paintings for the house if you like?'

He immediately looked up, eyes narrowing, and I wondered if I had overegged it.

'We could go together,' I quickly added, knowing he was unlikely to want to.

I watched him consider, before dismissing the idea. 'You go. I don't have time. You can put it on my credit card. Be careful what you choose, though. I don't want some monstrosity hanging up in the house.'

I breathed a sigh of relief, hoping I wasn't making a terrible mistake.

That's where I am going now, to Oksana's studio, a pretty little annexe attached to a house, tucked away in a spot by the river. I had hoped Rob might have other plans, but no, he is right there in the rear-view mirror as I pull into the small car park, the trademark scowl on his face.

My heart drops like a stone when he gets out of the car and follows me to the studio. I had assumed he would wait outside for me as he usually does. How am I going to talk to Laurel if he is there?

I break my rule of ignoring him, holding the door for him and forcing a bright smile. 'Good, you're coming in. You can help me choose which painting to buy.'

Oksana is recognisable from her Instagram page as she wanders through from a room at the back of the studio, her caramel brown hair framing a heart-shaped face and almond-shaped eyes hidden behind stylish, dark-rimmed glasses. She smiles warmly and introduces herself, asking if we need any help.

'I'm just browsing, thank you.'

Rob stands by, bored, as I wander around the studio. This will be a wasted opportunity unless I can make him leave.

'I am torn between these three,' I say eventually. 'I could do with your opinion.'

He glances up from his phone, looking irritated.

'This is important, Rob, please. I have to make the right choice.'

'Okay. That one.' He points to the second canvas I showed him.

I make a point of hesitating. 'Do you think so? But where would I hang it? What do you think? In the dining room or the living room?'

He rolls his eyes and I can tell I am annoying him.

'I have several more paintings out back,' Oksana pipes up. 'If you would like to see them.' Does she realise who I am? The smile she gives me suggests she might. 'Choosing the right artwork isn't something you should do in a rush. You need to take your time and let each piece speak to you. You will know when it's the right one.'

I look at Rob, who doesn't hide his exasperation. This isn't his bag at all.

'I'll wait in the car,' he mutters, shaking his head as he leaves the shop.

I wait until the door closes before looking at Oksana.

'Is Laurel Adams here?'

She doesn't look surprised, instead giving me a wink. 'Come on, Callie. I'll take you through to see her.'

\* \* \*

I know I need to be honest with Laurel if I want her to help me, but it isn't easy.

I am so embarrassed by the mess I'm in, the things I let Duncan do to me, and I despise myself for not being stronger. This time, I manage not to cry, but I do hang my head in shame when she asks again: does he hit you?

I promised there would be no more secrets as I was driving over here, but it takes a moment before I can bring myself to acknowledge the truth.

Oksana has returned to the studio to give us both some privacy, and also to keep a lookout so she can alert us if Rob returns, and knowing it is just the two of us, I am eventually brave enough to show Laurel some of my scars and I can see she is horrified.

'You have to go to the police,' she begs me.

It's not an option. Duncan is well connected and there are too many people who will turn a blind eye to protect him. 'I can't. I'm trapped. If I leave, he will find me and he will kill me,' I tell her. 'But I need to get Chester out.'

She's not happy I'm staying, but she agrees to help me with Chester, and my shoulders sag with relief.

When I return home an hour later, I have a painting I hope will appeal to Duncan, and a plan to help my dog.

A couple of days later, I take Chester for a walk around one of the local parks. We have been here before and it's a great place to exercise dogs off the lead. Thankfully, Rob stays in his car. Although the park is surrounded by woodland, he has an uninterrupted view of us while we are in the main field. I go through the motions of throwing Chester's ball, letting my boy fetch and return, his eyes never leaving the prize, and all of the time I keep glancing at the trees.

Eventually, I spot Laurel. She is standing a little way back on one of the wooded paths, a leash in her hand, and she gives me a nod.

This is it. The moment I have been building up to. I glance towards the car park. Rob appears to be studying his phone and I know I can't waste the precious seconds while he is distracted. I throw the ball again, but this time my aim is off, and it goes bouncing into the woods, my gorgeous goldy charging after it and disappearing into the brush.

I watch and I wait, and I consider everything that could go wrong. If Laurel doesn't manage to get to Chester before he finds the ball. If he makes too much fuss when she clips on the leash. Or if Rob comes over before Laurel and Chester have managed to get away.

I leave it a couple of minutes, then I glance back at the car, where he is still looking at his phone, before heading to the edge of the wood.

And then I see them. Chester is with Laurel, and he is agitated, straining at his leash when he spots me. I rush over to him and drop to my knees, pulling him into a tight hug. 'It's going to be okay, baby. Laurel is going to take care of you.'

'Callie.' Laurel's tone is urgent and I glance up at her. 'I know you said you can't leave, but there has to be a way. Come back to the studio when you can. Tell Duncan you have commissioned a painting for him. It will buy us more time.'

'I can't. It's too dangerous.'

'Please, just think about it.'

There isn't time to argue with her, so I nod, needing her to drop the subject.

Of course I won't go. It's not worth the risk.

I press a kiss to Chester's furry cheek, tears blinding my vision as she leads him away. I knew this moment was going to break my heart, but it's worse than I imagined. I want to go running after them, to stop them, but then I remember the razor blade and I know I have to let him go. Laurel has promised me she will find him a safe home, somewhere he will be loved, and I believe her.

When Rob comes charging into the woods a few minutes later, they are gone and I am still crying.

'What the hell are you doing back here?' he demands, his face red with fury.

'I can't... find... Chester.' I am gulping between sobs and this part is not an act. I am devastated my boy has gone.

He looks at me like I am stupid. 'What do you mean, you can't find him?'

'I threw the... ball. It... went... into the woods. He was... he was looking for it.'

I demand he helps me search for Chester and he does briefly, but soon gives up.

'He's not here,' he says, irritated. 'We should go.'

'But I can't. I can't leave without him.' I manage to inject just the right amount of panic into my voice.

Frustrated, and unsure what to do, Rob calls Duncan.

As I suspect, I am ordered home.

'For fuck's sake, Mica. He's just a stupid dog,' Duncan later complains as I start crying again at dinner.

I want to stab him with my fork, such is my hatred for this man. I know Chester is safe, but this reinforces how little Duncan cared about him. There is no attempt to try to find him and he won't let me register his disappearance anywhere. Not that I want to – I need it to be as easy as possible for Laurel to rehome my dog.

The house feels empty without Chester and my mood is at rock bottom. I honestly don't know how much of this I can take.

I can't run. Duncan won't ever stop trying to find me while I am alive.

The thought stops me, and I give it some consideration. Maybe it's my way out.

The seed of an idea is planted, and it's bold. I'm not sure how I would even begin to pull it off.

Laurel said she will help me, though. Is it possible this could work?

Duncan won't stop looking for me while I'm alive. But what about if I am dead?

# 27

The day I leave Duncan starts the same as any other, waking early in the bed we share and hoping like hell I can quietly get up and dressed before he stirs.

He is a big fan of morning sex and I have to pretend I am enjoying it, when really I feel like I am dying inside. It is becoming harder to mask my true reaction.

Luckily for me, he is still snoring when I sneak from the room and by the time he appears in the kitchen, I have coffee ready for him and eggs poaching in boiling water.

I try to relax as he walks over and pecks me on the cheek, forcing cheer into my voice when I speak. 'Good morning. Did you sleep okay? Breakfast will be ready in a couple of minutes.'

'You know how to look after me,' he comments, squeezing my bum before going to sit down.

He seems to be in a reasonable mood and my shoulders relax slightly.

Duncan's state of mind governs how my day will go. If he is agitated or in a grump, he will find a way to take it out on me, but if he is even-tempered, he will be more willing to loosen my leash. I need him to be okay with my plans for the day. If not, escape will be impossible. I have been planning this for weeks. It has to work.

'Well, I know you have your big meeting today,' I say lightly. 'I wanted to make sure you get a decent breakfast.'

He was approached before Christmas to be the face of a major charity campaign, one I know he hopes will further boast his profile and potentially bring in other opportunities, and he is heading to Bristol this morning to finalise the details.

That is why I have chosen today, knowing he will be away. Though, of course, Rob will be here keeping an eye on me, and Duncan will be tracking my car and phone, and checking the cameras.

A couple of days ago, the date of the meeting was almost changed, and the bottom nearly fell out of my world.

I haven't spoken to Laurel since before Christmas, having no reason to visit Oksana's studio now the painting is complete, but last week, I had commented on one of Oksana's paintings on Instagram, saying how much I liked it. This was my signal to Laurel that the date we had chosen for my escape was still on.

If anything changed or went wrong, there was no way to warn her. Luckily, after a few terse conversations between Duncan and his campaign team, it was decided that the date was finalised.

The toaster pops and I fill a plate with food, bringing it over to the table. As Duncan tucks in, I pour two mugs of tea then take a seat, watching him shovel a forkful of egg into his mouth.

He likes me to sit with him at breakfast, even though I have nothing but tea. Often, the aroma of food is torture to my empty belly, but he forbids me from eating anything until lunchtime. Apparently, he is concerned about my weight, even though I am the lightest I have ever been.

Today is different. I couldn't stomach the food if I tried.

'What do you have planned?' he asks between mouthfuls.

On another day, he would tell me what I am doing, so it's a relief he is asking.

'I was thinking about going shopping. I know we're out to dinner on Friday and I thought a new dress might be nice. If that's okay with you, of course. Then I might go for a walk on the beach. I'm caught up with housework and just need to clean the kitchen.' I am babbling and I force myself to stop. I don't want him to be suspicious.

He pauses eating and studies me across the table, silent for a moment before he answers. 'Get some new underwear too. Something to pad your tits out a bit. I swear they're disappearing.'

They are. Because he is forcing me to lose weight.

I nod. 'Any preference on colour?' I ask.

'Red,' he says without hesitation. 'Something I will want to take off you later.'

The idea makes me feel sick, but I force myself to smile. 'We can celebrate your new deal,' I say. 'Is there anything special you would like me to get in for dinner?'

'Let's not jump the gun. I haven't signed yet. We can discuss it when I'm on the way home.'

A short while later, I kiss him goodbye, and as I watch his car disappear down the driveway, I hope to hell it is the last time I will ever see him.

I finish cleaning the kitchen, then go upstairs to change. I know Rob will be watching me on the cameras, so it is no surprise when an hour later, he is already in his car, waiting for me to leave.

As I drive into the town centre, nerves jitter in my stomach and my hands tremble against the steering wheel. There are many things that can go wrong today. What if Laurel can't make it for some reason? What if Rob realises what we are up to?

I head to a little boutique I know, select a dress and walk

towards the fitting room. It's exactly 10.30 a.m. The time we agreed to meet. What if she isn't here?

'Callie?'

I hear her voice behind me and want to cry with relief.

I don't. We have a long way to go for this to work.

She follows me into the fitting room and hugs me tightly before going over our plan and reassuring me everything will be okay. 'It's all in place, Cal. I will be waiting for you where we agreed. And Nico will be at the train station in Norwich.'

Fresh nerves surface. Somehow, she has roped her brother into helping; a man I barely remember and who I am now going to be dependent on for the foreseeable future.

If today goes according to plan.

I hand over my plastic bag of possessions for safekeeping, then leave the changing room and buy the dress, for no other reason than to keep our charade up for Rob. I don't bother with the underwear though, as I have no plan of seeing Duncan again to wear it.

Rob is waiting outside the shop and trails me back to the cars, before following me as I drive to Hope Cove, where I have been going for regular weekly walks over the last few months.

If Rob follows his usual routine, he won't come down to the beach; instead, he will head to the pub that overlooks the cove for a coffee.

When I first started coming here, he would watch me like a hawk, but familiarity leads to complacency and now he is confident he can take his eyes off me for a few minutes.

What he doesn't realise is I picked this place purposely because there are several points where I can exit the beach into the woods.

I see him disappear inside the pub and realise this is it. My moment of opportunity.

The beach is empty, unsurprising for a cold, February morning, and I sprint across the sand to the rocks, knowing I am now out of sight. I quickly remove my coat and boots, leaving them in a pile, then drop my handbag beside them, then finally I remove my engagement ring, setting it down before clambering over the rocks and in between the trees. The wooded ground is hard under my socked feet, but it's a small price to pay for the freedom that is so close now.

I am aware of my heart beating fast, the noise echoing in my ears, and my breathing is ragged, but I am scared to slow down. I focus on reaching the road, wondering if Rob has realised I am gone yet. What if he is looking for me? What if he finds me before I reach Laurel?

When I finally spot her car, I sob with relief, dropping into the passenger seat.

'Did it all go okay?' Laurel asks. 'He didn't see you?'

'I don't think so.' My whole body is shaking. Adrenaline rattling through me. Probably shock at what I've just done. I focus on my breathing and clutch my hands together in my lap to try to stop them from trembling, as Laurel drives a couple of miles before pulling the car off the road into a wooded clearing.

We both get out and she hands me a carrier bag of clothes. Jeans, a loose-fitting jumper, a dark anorak and trainers. 'Hopefully they will fit.'

I nod, quickly stripping and get dressed in the new clothes. They are not the kind of thing 'Mica' would wear. The jeans worn and the trainers scuffed. The anorak is a little too big, but it is warm and will disguise my figure. The last item in the bag is a wig. A blonde bob that she helps me put on. I stand still as she adjusts it to frame my face, my stomach churning.

The crunching of a twig has me jumping, and we both turn to see what made the noise.

Nothing is there. Still, the panic must be clear on my face.

'It's okay,' Laurel reassures me. 'He's not going to find you.'

I want to believe her.

We are mostly silent as we drive to Totnes. Laurel, who is usually a chatterbox, seems to realise I need a moment to take everything in.

Has Rob found my things on the beach yet? Has he alerted Duncan?

When we pull up at the train station, she hands me my plastic bag and a mobile phone. 'Your train ticket is on here. You'll need to scan it at the barrier,' she says, showing me, before giving me a hug. 'It's going to be okay, Callie. Nico will keep you safe.'

And then I am leaving the safety of her car as I head on the first leg of my train journey, wondering what the hell I have just done.

# 28

NOW

It didn't take long for Duncan to realise Laurel Adams was no longer in Dartmouth.

He had suspected she wasn't, remembering she had said she was staying with her ex for a change of scenery. That had been months ago. Still, he had made Rob tail Oksana Harding just to be sure. When he knew for certain Laurel had left, he started making discreet enquiries, learning she was back in Essex.

Convinced she was the key to finding Mica, he had driven up to Billericay with Rob, arriving late on a Friday afternoon.

They parked a ten-minute walk from Laurel's house: an older-style, detached property set in a large garden and with few close neighbours. It offered plenty of privacy. After approaching on foot, and ensuring she wasn't home, Rob picked the lock on the French doors and they let themselves in. They took their time familiarising themselves with the layout of the house before settling down in the dark living room to wait for her.

She kept them waiting. Eventually, rolling up courtesy of a taxi at 2.30 a.m.

As she walked into the hallway and Duncan heard her lock the door, he smiled, anticipation thrumming through him. Since Mica had been gone, he had missed this: the thrill to intimidate and to be in control.

Rob started to get up, but Duncan urged him to sit. He didn't want to rush this moment, and he was enjoying listening to Laurel wandering through the house, gulping down a glass of tap water, then flipping the switch on the kettle, before disappearing upstairs, where he heard the shower running. Going through the little routines that were familiar and safe before he turned her world upside down.

A short while later, she was padding back down the stairs and straight into the lounge, flipping on the lights, and freezing in horror when she spotted the pair of them.

The next few moments played out in slow motion.

Laurel fleeing the room and charging straight for the front door – she was quick and would have made it if they hadn't already pocketed the key – Rob following after her and wrestling her to the ground, then the sound of her screams before he taped up her mouth.

She fought like a tiger, all teeth and claws, and with surprising strength for such a little thing, before he managed to overpower her. Ten minutes later, they had her upstairs in the bedroom, her hands bound together and the surplus rope pulled over the top of the door and tied off to the knob. The result had her hanging from her wrists, her toes barely scraping the floor, and the side of her face mashed against the wood.

Duncan knew it wouldn't be comfortable, but that was good. The more pain she was in, the quicker he would get answers. She knew where Mica was and he didn't plan to leave until she told him.

He sat down on her bed, hatred burning through his veins as he remembered the disrespect she had shown him in the restaurant. Even if she confessed and gave him an address, he would not go easy on her. Laurel Adams had tried to make him look like a fool and he was going to enjoy watching her suffer.

She was thrashing against the door, fighting to free herself as she watched Rob moving around her bedroom opening wardrobes and pulling out drawers, emptying the contents over the floor as he searched for any clues that might help them.

'You know why I'm here,' Duncan told her, his tone calm but firm, drawing her attention back to him. 'Mica isn't dead, like she tried to lead everyone to believe. You helped her, didn't you?'

Unable to answer him, she shook her head.

'I know you're lying and you're going to tell me where she is. This will be easier for you if you cooperate.'

Her nostrils flared as she mumbled something into the tape. Whatever she said was unintelligible, but the fury on her face told him it had been some kind of insult.

'Fine. Your choice.'

He unzipped the duffle bag at his feet, slowly removing items and laying them on the bed beside him, making sure she got a good look at everything. Her eyes bulged as he took out his Japanese kitchen knives and placed them beside the screwdriver and pliers.

'You might want to save some of your energy,' he commented as she continued to struggle. 'If you're not going to tell me what I need to know, then we have a long night ahead of us.'

He picked up one of the knives, along with a fresh reel of tape, and went over to her, and her feet kicked against the door as she tried to pull away.

'Let me explain how this is going to work,' he told her, his tone rational, as if they were just discussing what to have to for dinner. 'In a moment, I'm going to remove your gag and ask you questions. If you answer them, then I will cut you down. If you don't tell me what I need to know, I'm going to tape up your mouth again and hurt you. When I've had some fun, we will try the questions again.'

She stilled, wide eyes staring at him, and he could see she was trying, and failing, to keep her breathing steady.

'Are we clear, Laurel?'

For a moment, he didn't think she was going to answer him, but then she gave him a jerky nod.

This was a good start.

Her eyes followed the knife as he stepped closer, and as he peeled off the tape, she gasped for air.

'Please,' she managed between gulps. 'I don't know what you're talking about.'

Duncan gave her no warning, his gloved fist cracking into the side of her face. Her teeth cracked together, and had the rope not been anchoring her, she would have dropped to the ground. Instead, she blinked at him, stunned, for a moment unable to react.

'This won't work if you lie to me.'

'I'm not... lying,' she managed.

He peeled off a length of tape and she started struggling again.

'No, please. I'm telling you the truth. I haven't seen her since that night in the restaurant. No. NO!'

He silenced her with fresh tape, glancing over at Rob, who sat on the bed with her phone. 'Anything?'

'I need a password.'

'I'm sure Laurel here will oblige once I've shown her what happens when she messes me around.' His comment was met with more struggling and frantic, muffled yelling. 'See if she has her passwords written anywhere.'

He studied the woman before him. She had changed into pyjamas after her shower. Red checked bottoms and a Rolling Stones *Voodoo Lounge* T-shirt. Nicking the knife into the material of the top, he sliced it open, exposing her bare back.

Leaning in close behind her, he spoke quietly against her ear. 'I love my Japanese kitchen knives. They're really sharp, which gives me plenty of precision when slicing. Let me demonstrate.'

He held her in place against the door to quiet her struggles as he cut the blade into her flesh. She flinched and bucked hard against him as the thin, red line began to bleed.

Pressing his mouth against her hot skin, he licked at the dark rivulets dripping down her back.

She was shuddering against him and that was good. The more frightened she was, the easier she would crack.

He took his time, creating lots of little nicks, some of them no bigger than papercuts, forming a patchwork of red. At first, she was frantically kicking at the door and struggling against him, but by the time he decided to give her some respite, she was hanging limply, her face damp with tears.

He peeled off the tape again. 'Where's Mica?'

Instead of answering, she turned her head to look at him, then spat in his face, giving him a challenging glare when he snarled at her.

He wiped at his cheek, frustrated. He had been convinced she was going to tell him.

Furious, he taped up her mouth again, then used the cheap bottle of whisky he had brought to douse her wounds. She didn't like that and he knew if she wasn't gagged, she would be screaming in agony.

'I'm in,' Rob exclaimed. He had been focused on the phone and a little notebook he had found, paying no attention as Duncan tortured Laurel.

'Check her WhatsApp and her email. Messenger too if she has it,' Duncan instructed. 'Remember Mica's friends used to call her Callie.'

While Rob searched through the phone, Duncan amused

himself by cutting off Laurel's pyjama bottoms, laughing at the cute little boy shorts she was wearing. They were a shocking pink and covered in zebras. He tugged them down to her knees, wanting purely to humiliate her, rubbing his big hands over her cheeks and giving her a hard slap, which in turn brought on renewed struggles.

Did she think he was going to rape her?

As tempting as it would be to fuck her arse, he had no intention of leaving semen for the police to find. Still, he continued to torment her into believing that's what he was going to do.

'Are you ready to talk yet?' he asked.

'We need to find out who Nico is,' Rob said.

'Why, have you got something?' Losing interest in Laurel, Duncan wandered over.

'There are a lot of messages back and forth between them. None of them mention Mica, or Callie, but she sent him one the day Mica vanished telling him she hoped everything went smoothly. It could be coincidence.'

'Or not.' Duncan went back to Laurel, ripping the tape from her mouth. 'Who's Nico?' he hissed.

He had to give her credit. She was a tough little thing. It took another couple of hours and he had to get creative before she finally broke down and confessed Nico was her brother and he had helped Mica. Still, she refused to give up their location.

Duncan was incandescent with rage. Mica leaving him was bad enough, but the idea she was with another man was unthinkable. When he did finally get his hands on her, he was going to make her regret crossing him again. This time, there would be no further chances.

'I think I have it,' Rob said eventually. He had turned to Google after finding several pictures on Laurel's social media of horses. On one of them, she had captioned:

So proud of my brother and the work he has done transforming this once frightened gelding into a champion.

'There's a horse trainer in Norfolk called Nico Adams.'

'That has to be him. Is there an address?'

As Rob continued tapping at his phone, Laurel whimpered. Her reaction suggested they were on the right track.

'Willow Brook Farm. It's in a place called Strumpshaw, which is a few miles southeast of Norwich.' Rob looked up. 'It's out in the countryside, lots of land. The perfect place for someone trying to hide.'

'So we'll head up there now,' Duncan decided. Dawn had already broken and the time on Laurel's bedside clock read 5.55 a.m. By the time they had finished here and driven to Norwich, it would be mid-morning. 'I'll walk back and get the car. You make this place look like there's been a burglary, take a few valuables, then deal with her.' He nodded to Laurel, who hadn't given up the fight. 'It's been fun, but I need to go catch up with Mica. I'll tell her you said hi.'

She glared back at him through bruised and puffy eyes. Not much longer and Rob would put her out of her misery.

Duncan whistled to himself as he headed back to the car, concocting a plan in his head. Once they found Willow Brook Farm, he wanted to stake the place out and learn exactly where Mica was hiding. When he pounced, there could be no room for error. He wanted her in the car and on their way back to Devon by no later than this evening. Anyone who got in the way would be treated as collateral damage.

Once he had her home, within the walls of The Old Rectory, he would decide exactly how he was going to take his revenge.

## 29

Nico was down at the stables with when he saw the police car pull up outside the house and, curious why it was there, he jogged over to meet it.

The two uniforms were already on the doorstep about to ring the bell when he arrived. He didn't recognise either man and neither of them looked a day over twenty, which had him feeling old. One of them was smooth-faced and lanky, while his shorter, stockier colleague had bum fluff above his upper lip, in a pitiful attempt at a moustache.

'Hey, can I help you?'

'Are you Nico Adams?'

'I am.'

'We have a few further questions for you about Anya Mitchell,' the taller one said, not cracking a smile.

'Okay.' This was unexpected, given they already had a man in custody, but he would help them however he could. 'Do you want to come inside?'

'Would you mind accompanying us back to the station?' Bum Fluff asked politely.

Nico glanced between them, trying to gauge the nature of the questions they wanted to ask. The fact they wanted him to go to the station suggested things were more serious than he had anticipated. Should he be worried?

'Am I under arrest?'

'No, but we would like to speak with you.'

Callie chose that moment to open the front door, her wide, blue eyes blinking in surprise when she saw the two constables. She had stayed at the house with Nico last night and he had left her sleeping in his bed. 'What's going on?'

'They just want to talk to me,' he assured her, not wanting to cause any alarm.

It didn't work. 'Why?' she squeaked, the panic clear in her tone.

'They have a few more questions about Anya.'

Having heard visitors, Dash pushed his way past her legs, running up to sniff the two uniformed officers. Bum Fluff immediately bent down to make a fuss of him, while his lanky colleague took a step back, eyes widening when Shyla and Chester appeared too. He obviously wasn't a dog person.

'Shall we go?' he asked, seeming keen to get away.

'Go where?' Callie demanded. 'Are you not talking inside?'

'They want me to go to the station with them,' Nico told her quietly, rubbing his palms up and down her arms to try to calm her.

'Why? Are you under arrest?'

He shook his head. 'No, it's just to talk.'

'Do I need to call anyone?'

'There's no need. I'll be back soon, I promise.'

She didn't look convinced and as he left her, getting into the back of the police car, unease crept into his gut. He wasn't entirely convinced it was a promise he would be able to keep.

* * *

Callie couldn't settle with Nico gone.

Why had they taken him in for questioning? An arrest had been made for Anya's murder. They had no need to talk to him again.

She paced, agitated, knowing the dogs needed a walk, but if she strayed too far from the farm...

No, they would have to wait. She had to stay close in case there was any news.

She was still in the house when Faith showed up. Olive was in the car with her and Callie remembered it was Saturday. Time for Olive's morning riding lesson.

For once grateful to see them, she was out of the front door before Faith could ring the bell. Olive was already charging down the path to the stables to find Jodie and Faith's eyes widened in surprise when she saw Callie.

'Hi. Is everything okay?' she asked as the dogs pranced around her.

'It's Nico. The police have taken him in for questioning.'

'What, why?' Faith blinked, looking shocked.

'Something to do with Anya.' Callie let out a shaky breath. 'I don't understand. I thought they had arrested someone.'

'I heard rumours the police think they might have the wrong person. I don't know how true they are.'

She had? How come Callie didn't know this? If Faith was right, it made things ten times worse. The police would be looking for a new suspect if the traveller was innocent. Was that why they wanted Nico? Were they going to charge him with Anya's murder?

Her mind was jumping ahead.

They didn't have anything on him. He had been Anya's

employer and her bracelet had been under the bed in Stable Cottage, but Callie lived there. Nico hadn't in a long while.

*And they think he was the last person to see her in the woods.*

That, right there, was a reason to suspect him.

She would come clean. If they arrested him, she would tell them the truth.

'I should call Ethan and let him know,' Faith decided. 'He can try to find out if Nico needs a solicitor.'

'Okay.' Callie looked guiltily at the dogs as Faith updated Ethan. They had been so patient, but Dash was whining now, not understanding why they hadn't gone for a walk. 'They need to go out,' she told Faith when she ended the call. 'But I don't want to leave the house in case there is any news.'

Faith nodded, understanding. 'It will do you good to get some fresh air, Callie. Go and clear your head and keep your phone close. I'll stay here and if there is any word from Nico, I promise I will call you.'

She was right and by taking the dogs out, Callie would at least be doing something, instead of pacing and generally being useless.

Leaving Faith in the house, she took the dogs, heading towards the woods. Nico didn't like her walking in them alone, but she wanted to stay close to the farm.

As she let them off their leads and threw a ball for them, she kept checking her phone. The signal was a little patchy out here and she didn't want to miss any news.

Nico had told her not to worry, but she couldn't shake the ominous feeling that her carefully constructed house of cards was about to come tumbling down.

\* \* \*

Faith was waiting for the kettle to boil when she spotted the black BMW 7 Series pull up next to the paddock that ran alongside the road. When it was still there ten minutes later, her curiosity got the better of her. It could be entirely innocent, but her protective motherly instinct had kicked in, and she decided to wander down and check it out. It was a quiet lane and saw little traffic. It wasn't a place people stopped.

As she neared the car, she saw the window was open and she spotted a man with a shaved head and dark shades sitting in the driver's seat. He was looking at something on his phone.

'Are you lost?' she asked, startling him. That was the beauty of walking on grass. It softened your approach.

He didn't answer her straightaway, turning to talk to someone sat in the passenger seat.

'Is this Willow Brook Farm?' the driver asked, his tone not at all friendly.

He must be one of Nico's clients. The car was expensive and so were the sunglasses he was wearing.

'Yes, the entrance is about quarter of a mile up the road. If you're looking for Nico Adams though, he's not here.'

'When will he be back?'

'I have no idea.' Faith kept her tone cool. The man's brusque attitude had her back up.

He turned to talk to the passenger again, their voices too low for her to hear what they were saying.

'Can I help with something?' she asked abruptly, reminding him she was waiting.

He stared at her through the dark glasses. 'Are you his wife?'

'No. My daughter is having a riding lesson.'

She didn't point out that Nico was a good friend; it was none of his business.

He nodded, closing the window. No thank you. No goodbye.

'You're welcome,' she muttered and started to walk away.

'Wait.'

She heard the door opening and turned back, ready to give him a mouthful about his rudeness. It wasn't the driver, though. His passenger was walking around the front of the car, flashing her a killer smile. There was something familiar about that smile and his chiselled jawline, but with his hair hidden beneath a baseball cap and dark shades covering his eyes, she couldn't place him.

'I don't suppose you've seen this woman, have you?'

He held out his phone, and despite the make-up, the straightened hair and the stunning dress – which she would put money on was Vera Wang – Faith recognised Callie.

'Her name is Micaela Parker. She goes by Mica, or sometimes Callie. I'm trying to find her.'

Faith's head was about to explode with questions. First and foremost, why had Nico introduced her as Callie Adams if her name was Parker, and why did a woman dress like a charity case if she owned designer labels? She kept her thoughts to herself, though. This pair had her alarm bells ringing.

The driver, despite being well dressed, reminded her of a thug, and yes, Mr Smooth in front of her radiated sex appeal, even if she couldn't see his eyes, but why were they parked here on the side of the road, and why were they looking for Callie?

To buy herself time, not sure if admitting she knew her was a good idea, she widened her eyes and dumbed down on her intelligence.

'Are you the police? Is she an escaped felon?'

She managed to look and sound both impressed and concerned, and he grinned, seeming amused. His perfect, white teeth looked as if they had been professionally done.

'No, no. Nothing for you to worry about. She went missing a few months back and we're trying to locate her. She has a lot of mental health issues and she hasn't been taking her medication. We're just worried for her safety and need to get her back to the hospital.'

Was he telling her the truth? He sounded convincing.

Still, Faith wasn't sure.

'Poor girl. I wish I could help you, but I've never seen her.'

She could see the man was disappointed. 'Of course. No worries.'

He was so familiar, even his voice, and she wished she could place him.

'Do you have a card?' she asked. 'You know. In case I do come across her. I could give you a call.'

He seemed to consider, before answering 'No.' Then, changing his mind, he rapped his knuckles on the driver's window. 'Give her one of your business cards,' he ordered as the window wound down.

The lout in the driver's seat grumbled, but did as told, and after wishing them luck, Faith watched them drive away. As soon as the car had disappeared, she glanced at the card.

*Rob Jolly Security Services*. There was just a mobile number beneath. No website or email address, and nothing to tell her who the sexy man was.

Her mind working overtime, Faith wandered back to the house, hoping Callie might be back. She was desperate to find out why the woman had lied about her name and also who the men were.

Frustratingly, she was still out, and while re-boiling the kettle, her curiosity got the better of her. She typed *Micaela Parker* into Google. Several hits came up for different women with that name, but none of them were Callie. Remembering the shortened name the man had given her, she tried *Mica Parker*.

There were at least half a dozen images of Callie, impeccably dressed and coiffed to within an inch of her life. In a couple of them, she was with the sexy stranger and Faith realised who he was the moment she saw his picture.

Duncan Stone.

She had bloody known he looked familiar. The dark glasses had hidden those piercing blue eyes of his.

Was Callie his girlfriend? If so, what the hell was she doing here with Nico?

Duncan had said she had mental health issues. She really did if she was foolish enough to give up a super-hot catch like Duncan Stone. Faith would give her the opportunity to tell her side of the story before deciding who to trust.

When Callie eventually arrived back with the dogs, the first question out of her mouth was, 'Have you heard from Nico?'

Christ, the poor woman did have it bad for him. Was that the deal? Had she left Duncan for Nico?

Was she mad? Nico was cute and everything, but he didn't have the perfect symmetry of Duncan Stone.

'No word yet. I'll make you a cup of tea.'

Callie wandered through as she was pouring the drink. Faith handed it to her, then topped up her own mug.

'You had a visitor while you were out,' she said casually.

'I did?' Callie looked up, and there was worry in her blue eyes. 'Who?'

Faith grinned, feeling a little smug, and ready to get all of the gossip. 'You're a sly one, Micaela Parker. Fancy not sharing with me that your boyfriend is Duncan Stone.'

# 30

It took Callie a moment to register that Faith knew her real name, and the second Duncan Stone was mentioned, the mug she was holding slipped from her fingers; hot tea and shards of porcelain hitting the floor.

He knew where she was.

Willow Brook Farm was no longer a safe haven. She had to go.

Her shocked brain was telling her to run, but her feet weren't complying. Instead, she stood there staring at Faith as panic rattled through her.

Where would she go? How could she escape him?

And then there was Nico. She didn't want to leave, but by staying here, she was putting them both in danger.

She must have looked petrified because Faith was staring at her wide-eyed and she had fallen silent. When she did eventually speak, her tone was sympathetic.

'You've been hiding from him, haven't you?'

Her words were the kickstart Callie needed. 'I have to go. I need to get away from here before he comes back.'

Her things. She should get back to the cottage and pack what she needed.

But Chester? She looked at him contentedly sitting on the sofa next to his best buddy, Dash. Was it safer to take him or kinder to leave him here? She loved him and would do anything for him, but she had no idea where she would go, if she would even have a roof over her head, and he was getting old. Taking him would be stressful for him and dangerous for her. But if he stayed with Nico, he had all he needed.

If Nico was coming back.

No, she couldn't think that way. She had to get to safety, then she would call the police and tell them she was the one who had seen Anya that night.

It took a moment to realise Faith was calling her name, but it wasn't until the woman pulled her back from the front door as she was about to leave, that she registered.

'I can't stay here. I need to go,' she repeated, trying to shake her arm free.

'Callie,' Faith said, this time more firmly. 'He doesn't know you are here.'

'He doesn't?' She paused, studying the woman's face for any sign she was lying.

'No. Everything felt off, so when they asked if I'd seen you, I lied. It was instinct. I figured I would talk to you first.'

She had said 'they'. That meant Duncan had brought Rob with him. No surprise there.

Unsure what to do, if it was safer to stay or to leave, Callie stood there like a rabbit caught in headlights.

'Love, you're shaking.' Faith seemed genuinely worried about her. 'Look, let me make you another drink. We'll sit down and you can tell me what's going on, then we can decide the best way forward.'

When Callie hesitated, Faith quickly added, 'I just want to help you.'

Maybe it was best to stay. At least for a little while, until she had figured out what to do.

Callie nodded, numb inside, and let Faith guide her to the sofa.

* * *

Half an hour later, Callie had told her everything and Faith was in complete shock.

The sick bastard. It went to show you never knew what people got up to behind closed doors. And she had watched all of Stone's movies too. That one adapted from a Jack Foley book was her favourite. She had honestly thought he was a genuine person.

Callie had shown her a couple of her deeper scars, ones that would never fade, seeming to need to convince Faith she was telling her the truth. After learning about her sister and how she had taken Duncan's side, Faith understood why.

She had seen the haunted look in Callie's eyes and felt her hand trembling in her own as she talked. She believed her and she was going to help her. Faith looked after those who mattered. Olive came first, closely followed by Ethan, then her parents and sister. Nico was high on the list too, and now she would add Callie. She hadn't deserved any of this.

Faith had told Stone she didn't know her, but it was possible he might come back, and it was a risk they couldn't take.

Until Nico returned and they could discuss what to do next, she needed to keep Callie safe, and the best way to do that was to take her home.

They had to leave the dogs, as they would upset the family cats, but they put food down for them before leaving and Faith promised that if Nico didn't return later, she would come back in the morning and feed them herself. She would also give Jodie a call and arrange for either her or Toby to call in and check on the horses.

'We're going to tell Ethan,' she said, pulling into the driveway of her house in Cantley, and waiting until Olive was out of the car. 'I can't keep this from him. But your secret is safe, I promise. We're going to help you, Callie. Stone won't find you here.'

During the short drive down country roads, Faith had kept a close eye on the rear-view mirror and knew they hadn't been followed.

Inside, she made more tea, then, after sending Olive upstairs to play, she called Ethan through from his study. As Faith updated him, he looked just as shocked as she had been.

'It goes without saying you can stay with us for as long as need-ed,' he spoke eventually to Callie. 'I honestly had no idea you had been through all that.'

'Nico will be back later. Won't he?' she asked, looking worried.

Ethan rubbed a hand over his jaw. 'Honestly, I don't know. I tried calling, but they wouldn't tell me anything. I don't know how seriously they are treating this.'

'But he didn't do anything.'

'I know that. You know that. But it's a case of convincing the police.'

'It was me!' Callie blurted the words and Faith and Ethan exchanged a confused look.

'What was you, love?' Faith asked gently.

'In the woods the night Anya went missing. I was the one who saw her. Not Nico.'

Faith wasn't surprised, remembering back to the night they'd had dinner at Nico's. She had known something was off with his account of things.

Ethan looked taken aback, though. 'Why haven't you said anything about this before?'

'Nico made me promise. He said it wasn't safe and the police would look at me too closely if I said it was me. We didn't mean any harm. I told him what I saw and he pretended it had been him.' Callie shook her head in regret. 'Now they're talking to him and thinking he might have murdered her. I don't know what to do. I should call them.'

'Is that safe?'

'No. But I can't let Nico get arrested for this.'

When Faith had first realised who Callie was, she had been intrigued and excited for gossip, but learning the truth about Duncan Stone had shocked her. It would be safest to sit tight and wait for the outcome of Nico's interview. If the police did arrest him, then they could talk about intervening.

She ran a soothing hand over Callie's hair and squeezed her shoulder in comfort. 'It will be okay. We're going to figure it out, I promise.'

## 31

'You should have stayed in the bloody car,' Rob grumbled for the third time. 'If she recognised you—'

'Relax, she didn't.' At least, Duncan was pretty certain the woman hadn't.

But yes, it had been a spur-of-the-moment action he now regretted. He shouldn't have given her Rob's card either, but it was too late now, and he didn't need to keep being reminded.

He was so close to getting his hands on Mica now and the anticipation was making him cocky.

Normally, he was such a calculated man, and smart enough to cover his tracks, but his control had slipped. He needed to rein it in. He couldn't fuck this up now.

Even with Mica and the marks he had left on her, he had always made sure they wouldn't be seen. Clothing mostly took care of that, and if the bruising and other injuries couldn't easily be explained away, he would take her phone and car keys, confining her to the house until they had healed.

Not that he had believed she would ever dare tell anyone what he did to her. The night in the dog crate had scared her half to death and kept her compliant. And he had made sure she knew about his old friends, the ones Rob kept close.

Shortly after the crate incident, he had invited a few of them over to dinner, encouraging them to share tales of some of the terrible things they had done. Later that night in bed, he had warned her if she ever told anyone the truth, his friends would come for her.

That was why he was so stunned she had dared to defy him.

He was going to have to come up with something really spectacular to make her realise she couldn't double-cross him like this.

'What if she alerts this Nico fella that we were here?' Rob pushed, not letting the slip up drop.

Irritation bristled. 'She won't. She was just there for her daughter's riding lesson. I doubt she knows him well.'

Though she had known he was away.

How long was he going to be gone, though? Hours? Or maybe days? And was Mica with him?

The idea that his fiancée might have been intimate with another man had jealously raging inside of Duncan. When he got his hands on her, he would make her pay.

After leaving Willow Brook Farm, they headed into Norwich to pick up a few supplies and grab some lunch. Later this afternoon, they would return to the house. Hopefully, Nico and Mica would be home by then. If not, they would wait.

He didn't doubt for a second that he could take care of Nico. Laurel Adams had been a tiny thing and the photo on the mantel that he had seen of her with her parents, suggested that they too were slight of build. It must be a family trait. And while Duncan didn't know much about horses, the few jockeys he had met were tiny. Why Mica had left him for a puny horse trainer, he couldn't fathom.

He recalled his mother's words. Once he found the right one, he must never to let go. He didn't intend to, and he wouldn't leave here without her.

* * *

There had been no word from Nico and Callie was struggling to settle.

She believed she was safe here. Duncan wasn't going to know she was with the Stuarts, and their home with in the middle of nowhere, but knowing he was close by terrified her.

What if Nico was released and Duncan and Rob were waiting for him at the house?

She needed to warn him, but her messages were unread and her calls going to voicemail. It was nearly 3 p.m. He had been with the police since 11 a.m.

Faith insisted on changing the sheets on the guest-room bed. 'You'll stay with us tonight. If they let Nico leave this evening, then he can come and stay here too. It will be safer for both of you.'

Callie didn't try to protest, grateful for Faith's kindness. 'Thank you. Is there anything I can do to help? I feel like I'm in the way.'

'I need to take Olive to her friend's house. They are having a sleepover tonight. I was going to prepare a chicken casserole for the slow cooker. You can start chopping the vegetables if you like.'

'Okay.' It was a job that would keep her occupied and she followed Faith into the kitchen.

'Help yourself to more tea or coffee if you want. Olive's friend, Issy, lives just down the road in Brundall, so I won't be long. And don't worry. You're safe here. Duncan won't find you.'

Faith and Olive both shouted goodbye to Ethan, who was still in his study, and then they were off, Olive excitedly chatting about her sleepover as they left the house.

Trying to shake the tension out of her shoulders, Callie started chopping carrots, onions and celery, and told herself everything was going to be okay. She had come this far and she couldn't give up now.

Ethan wandered through as she was putting the veg in the saucepan and he flicked the switch on the kettle. 'She's got you working hard, I see,' he laughed good-naturedly.

'I'm happy to help. You're both being kind, letting me stay here.'

'Nonsense. Nico would do the same if Faith was in trouble.' He put a teabag in his mug. 'Can I make you a drink?'

'I'm fine, but thank you.'

As he opened the fridge, she heard him swear.

'Is everything okay?'

He held up the almost empty milk bottle. 'I don't suppose my wife said if she was going to pick up milk on the way back.'

'No, sorry.'

Ethan had his phone out and, moments later, she heard him talking to Faith.

'Did you realise we were out of milk?' There was a pause. 'Well, can you get some?'

She must have been on her way back, because when Ethan next spoke, he sounded a little agitated.

'It will take you five minutes if you turn round now.'

Another pause.

'Okay, thank you. I love you, pickle.'

Callie stopped chopping. She had heard that odd term of endearment before.

'Anyone would think I had asked her to go the moon,' Ethan joked.

'You called her pickle,' Callie commented, trying to figure out why it was so familiar. Had Ethan used it in front of her before?

He shrugged. 'Just a silly nickname.'

The edge of a memory was there, but she couldn't reach it. The woods. She had been walking Chester.

Suddenly, she realised.

Anya and the hidden man she was talking to. She had heard him speak.

*It's nothing, pickle. Come on, let's get out of here.*

'It was you.'

She didn't mean to blurt the words, but in that moment of realisation, she was shocked.

Ethan didn't appear to understand, though, blinking at her. 'It was me what?'

'Nothing. Sorry. I'm getting confused.'

She focused on wiping the chopping board as her mind went into overdrive.

Ethan had been in the woods with Anya. He had been the last person to see her before she died.

Had he killed her?

She wasn't safe here. She needed to leave.

Her phone was upstairs in the guest bedroom charging. She would go and get it, then make up an excuse to step outside.

She forced a smile for him. 'I'm just going to nip to the loo.'

He was watching her, but didn't react other than to nod.

Leaving the kitchen, she quickly headed for the stairs, running up them and into the bedroom to get her phone, her heart thudding.

She wasn't overreacting to this, was she?

If Ethan had nothing to hide, he would have told the police he had been with Anya.

And he knew they were talking to Nico, that his friend was in trouble. Why hadn't he spoken up?

Had he been having an affair with Anya?

Oh God. Poor Faith.

And he knew Callie had seen them because she had confessed earlier that it hadn't been Nico in the woods.

She needed to get the hell out of his house. Where to, she had no idea. She only knew she needed to run.

She unplugged her phone and turned to leave. Jumping when she saw Ethan standing in the doorway.

'You know, don't you.'

She froze, staring at him, and he shook his head regretfully as he stepped into the room.

## 32

'Were you having an affair with her?' Callie asked, trying to buy herself time. If she could keep him talking, then maybe the opportunity would arise for her to get away. At the moment, he was standing between her and the door. If she made a run for it, he would catch her easily.

'I never meant to. I never meant for any of it to happen. She babysat for Olive one night and I gave her a lift home. She instigated it. Of course I had noticed how pretty she was, but I wouldn't have done anything if she hadn't encouraged me.'

So he was blaming Anya, who conveniently was no longer here to defend herself or offer a different version of the story. Callie bit down on her rising anger. She was grateful for the stronger emotion overriding her fear, but couldn't afford to show Ethan how she felt. Not while she was trapped. As hard as it was, she needed to appear sympathetic.

'So she seduced you?' she asked, almost choking on the words. They were talking about an eighteen-year-old girl, and what was Ethan? Maybe thirty-nine, forty?

'I love my wife, but you have to understand, Faith and I have been together since we were teenagers. I'm not gonna lie, at times my marriage is hard work. She's so headstrong and sometimes she forgets I have needs too. Since we've had Olive, she's lost interest. We used to have a great sex life, but these days, I'm lucky if it's once a month. Even then I can tell she's not that into it.'

Poor, hard-done-by Ethan, playing his tiny violin. Callie wanted to vomit.

'I didn't mean for Anya to seduce me. It was the first time in a long while that I felt noticed and really wanted. I just had to have one taste. She was intoxicating. Once we started, I couldn't stop. I knew it was wrong, but I needed her. We used to meet at Stable Cottage. I took one of Nico's spare keys. It was lying around in a drawer in his kitchen. He had no idea it was missing.'

'That's why her bracelet was under the bed,' Callie said, realising, before another thought came to her. 'Was it you trying to get into the cottage the night I arrived?' she demanded.

Ethan shook his head. 'No, that was Anya. I couldn't meet her that night. Lucky, I guess, as I hadn't realised Nico had moved you in there. That could have been awkward.' He gave a humourless laugh. 'Faith caught me off guard with her parents coming over for dinner. I didn't get a chance to message Anya, to tell her I couldn't make it.'

So that first night when Callie had been terrified, it had been a teenage girl at the door? She might have felt foolish for her overreaction if she wasn't so scared.

'She wasn't happy about that,' Ethan continued. 'And she was livid when she found out you had moved in. But, in a way, I was relieved. I thought it would put an end to things. She wanted me to leave my wife. She threatened to tell her. To go public about our affair.'

He took a step closer to Callie, holding his hand out to her, and she backed up again, this time hitting the dresser. What was he going to do to her? He wasn't just going to let her leave.

'I'm sorry,' he told her, his voice dropping to a whisper. 'You can't tell anyone.'

\* \* \*

Faith stood outside the bedroom door listening to her husband's confession and she backhanded tears from her eyes.

She had arrived home with the milk, surprised when Callie and Ethan weren't downstairs, but then she'd heard voices from the first floor and wandered up to find them, overhearing Ethan talking about Anya.

*Of course I had noticed how pretty she was.*

*My marriage is hard work.*

*I just had to have one taste. She was intoxicating.*

*I needed her.*

His words cut her deep. Her husband detailing their sex life and his affair with an eighteen-year-old girl. Someone she had let into her home and tried to help repeatedly.

Anya's betrayal stung.

Faith was about to step into the bedroom and put an end to this, but then she heard Callie's chilling question, 'Did you kill her?' followed by Ethan's sob, and her heart dropped.

*No, Ethan. Please. No. Please tell her you didn't.*

'It was an accident,' he said, his voice so low, Faith was having to strain to hear him. 'I tried to break things off, but Anya wasn't having it. She threatened to tell my wife and to go to the police and say I raped her. I had to meet her, to try to persuade her to stop. That was when you saw us in the woods. I thought I had talked her around, but then she went to leave. I didn't mean to push her. It was an accident.'

Faith closed her eyes, clenching her fists together, his words devastating her. She remembered their marriage vows. *For better, for worse. Till death us do part.*

Why had he betrayed her?

'You need to tell the police,' Callie begged. 'They think it was Nico.'

'I know, and I'm so sorry, but they can't find out.'

'Ethan, please. You're scaring me.'

Faith needed a weapon, realising how much danger they were in. The heavy vase her late mother-in-law had given them sat on the cherry-wood console table at the top of the stairs, and she went over to pick it up. Perhaps it was fitting. It broke her heart what she was about to do, but she had to stop him.

'Callie, come back!' Ethan's frantic tone had Faith turning as Callie made a run for safety, charging out of the bedroom with him in hot pursuit.

Faith raised the vase, heard the hard crack as it hit bone, and she took an involuntary step back. For a moment, there was a deathly silence.

'I didn't want it to come to this,' she apologised, hugging the vase to her chest. 'You didn't leave me with any other choice.'

'Faith. Thank God you came home. I was really scared there.'

Slowly, she raised her gaze from the figure on the floor to the one standing in the doorway of the bedroom, her throat burning with bitterness, as she took in her husband's shocked face. She had willed him to stop talking, to not give away their secrets. 'You stupid, stupid man. What the hell did you do? We made a promise. Never tell anyone.'

'She'd already worked out it was me.' Ethan's tone was panicked. 'I didn't know what to do. I thought if I explained, that if she realised it was an accident, she would—'

'She would what, Ethan? Take pity on you?' Faith shoved the

vase into his arms and started to pace. 'I liked her. I genuinely liked her. But now look what you've made me do. I was going to help her, until you ruined everything.'

'I'm sorry.'

'Yes, of course you're sorry. You're always bloody sorry. Sorry you had an affair with Anya. Do you know how hard it was to stand there and listen to you tell Callie our marriage is hard work and that you found that little slut intoxicating? That you couldn't resist cheating on me? After all the sacrifices I've made for you! It's always me, isn't it? Always me having to clear up the messes you make.'

Even after Faith had helped him deal with Anya, he couldn't hold it together. Disappearing on drinking binges and leaving her terrified he might spill their terrible secret.

She looked down at Callie with regret. A quick check of the woman's pulse told her she was alive, but out cold for now. In a way, it would have been kinder if the smack to the head had killed her. At least she wouldn't have suffered.

Part of Faith considered hitting her again and putting her out of her misery, but she couldn't bring herself to do it, not when it was someone she had liked.

It had been different with Anya. The silly girl had betrayed her, so when Ethan had called, after allegedly being out with a client all night, confessing that Anya had fallen and hit her head, and panicking, unsure what to do, Faith had rushed to help him.

Anya had still been alive, and she had woken before Faith had bashed her in the head with a rock. At the time, she had been furious at the betrayal of both her husband and the girl she had treated as a younger sister, and she hadn't hesitated. Then, while Ethan fell apart, she was the strong one, instructing him to help wrap Anya's body in the bin liners she had brought. It had taken an effort to drag Anya back to where the car was parked, but at least it was in a secluded place and they weren't interrupted as they bundled her into the boot.

'What are we going to do with her?' Ethan had demanded, on the verge of hysteria.

'Shut up and let me think!'

She had considered and rejected a number of potential dumping sites before settling on Little Plumstead. The woman who microbladed her eyebrows lived on the new estate and she was always complaining about the overgrown state of the lake and woods. It was owned by a management company, who were supposed to maintain it, but didn't. Faith had been for a walk around there with another friend after visiting the Walled Garden Café on the edge of the estate for coffee and cake one afternoon and it had been full of stinging nettles, which made the paths difficult to access. Could they get Anya's body into the lake?

She had driven to the village, turning into Witton Lane and passing a number of houses before they reached the woods.

There was an entrance further along and, leaving Ethan, who was frankly being useless, Faith had tackled the metal gate herself, relieved when it opened and she could get the car through. Shining her torch ahead, she had scoped out the area, trying to get her bearings, and wandering a little further into the clearing, the crunch of her feet against stones and twigs helping quieten the thumping beat of her heart.

She had soon realised getting to the lake was going to be impossible. To the right was a narrow, overgrown path that they would struggle to access, while a couple of large vehicles were parked a little further along the track to the left. Travellers, she'd thought, knowing they couldn't risk being seen.

In the end, they had worked with a bad situation, carrying the body into the trees and hiding it in undergrowth behind a utilities building. Faith rationalising that it was a part of the woods that was unlikely to be used by dog walkers.

Well, hadn't that bitten her in the arse? Anya's body, she had heard, had eventually been sniffed out by an inquisitive German Shepherd.

Still, she had managed to stay low-key, keeping away from suspicion, occupying her mind by focusing on the mundane. If she had something else to think about, then it kept her from remembering that she had murdered an eighteen-year-old girl.

Meanwhile, Ethan's way of coping was to numb his memories with booze. It wasn't easy to forgive him, but she had promised to stand by him for better or for worse. She would not let her daughter grow up knowing her father had betrayed them or that either of her parents had gone to prison.

'Is she dead?' he asked now, panicked as he stared at Callie. Blood gushed from a wound in her head, so he could be forgiven for thinking that.

'No, she's not,' Faith snapped.

'But you're gonna take care of her, right?'

He looked at her pleadingly and she understood exactly what he meant.

'I'm not going to kill her. I have enough blood on my hands from Anya.'

'You can't leave her alive.'

She got such a kick from the look of panic on his face that she almost told him yes.

Unfortunately, if Ethan went down, so did she, and she couldn't leave Olive. And sadly, that's what it came down to. Callie versus Olive.

She didn't want to kill Callie, so there was only one other solution.

Reaching into her pocket, Faith fished out the card Duncan

Stone had given her and tapped Rob Jolly's number into her phone.

It rang twice before he answered with a terse hello.

Duncan Stone was a dangerous man. Faith understood that. And she needed to play this carefully. He could either be the worst mistake she had ever made or the solution to all of her problems.

'I want to speak to Mr Stone,' she told him brusquely.

'Who is this?' came the equally abrupt reply.

This was where she risked everything, revealing her identity to a man who might be the Devil. 'My name is Faith Stuart. I met you earlier at Willow Brook Farm. Tell Mr Stone I lied to him. I do know Micaela Parker and I have her here. I will hand her over, but I need assurances.'

There was a pause, during which time she heard hushed voices.

'What do you want?' he asked eventually.

She drew in a breath, reminding herself that this was for her family, and apologising silently to Callie. 'I want a guarantee that you will make her go away, and that she will never bother my husband and I ever again.'

More hissed whispering, then Jolly came back on the line.

'Mr Stone says you have a deal.'

## 33

Callie awoke convinced she was in Nico's house and her first cohesive thought was remembering he had been taken in for questioning. The second was that her head was hurting, a dull, heavy thump bashing her skull when she tried to move, and her mouth was horribly dry and chalky.

She cracked open one eye and saw two figures ahead of her. They appeared to be arguing.

Where was she?

It took a moment, but then the missing hours came back to her. Faith seeing Duncan. Going back to the Stuarts' house. Learning that Ethan had been having an affair with Anya.

He had killed her.

That last lightning bolt hit her brain like a jackhammer.

Nico. She had to save Nico and tell the police the truth. In order to do that, she needed to get the hell out of here.

In her head, she tried to get up, but her body didn't comply. For a moment, she thought it was because she was too groggy, but when she tried again, she understood her limbs weren't working.

Her arms were jerked back, something holding them in place. As feeling gradually returned, she felt the bite of whatever restraint was binding them behind her back.

Had Ethan done this to her? He had said she couldn't tell anyone. Had he knocked her unconscious?

And why had he tied her up? What did he plan to do to her?

The arguing couple became clearer. Ethan and Faith. They were through a doorway in the living room of their house, which meant Callie was in the hall. Ethan had his hands in his hair and was pacing, Faith going after him and poking a finger at his chest when he turned.

Callie tried to speak, to get Faith's attention and warn her, but her words came out muffled. That was why her mouth was so dry. Some kind of cloth was pressing against her tongue, forcing her lips apart.

Her head was thumping and she was convinced she was going to be sick.

She needed to get Faith's attention so the woman could untie her.

Struggling, Callie managed to pull herself into a seated position, bile climbing into her throat and her vision swimming. As she willed the nausea to pass, she started picking up on pieces of the conversation.

'I can't believe you did this!' Faith sounded so angry.

Did she already know?

'Please, Faith. You have to understand. I didn't have a choice.'

'Do you have any idea what kind of danger you've put our family in?'

'It was your idea to call them.' Ethan sounded panicked. 'If you had taken care of her, they wouldn't be involved.'

Faith laughed, without humour. It was a hard, derisive sound.

'Do you think I like having blood on my hands from clearing up your fuck-ups?'

Blood on her hands? But Ethan had killed Anya.

Callie's heart thumped.

And what did she mean by clearing up his fuck-ups?

Had it been Faith?

No. She had been cut up about the girl's murder. They had been friends.

And Ethan had been having an affair with Anya.

Callie thought back to upstairs. Ethan had chased after her when she ran, but she'd had a head start. He had hit her with something heavy, but when she had been talking to him, his hands had been empty.

Had Faith been the one to hit her?

Her head was a muddle of part truths and theories. All she knew was she had to somehow get out of this house.

She tested the bond around her wrists, but there was no give. Whatever was tethering them felt softer than rope, though. Exploring with her fingers, it felt like a belt, or possibly a necktie. She searched for the knot, fingers fumbling when she found it.

'I'm not doing it again,' she heard Faith telling Ethan. 'They want her, so let them have her. It solves our problem and keeps them happy.'

'But what if she gets away again? If she goes to the police—'

'Damn it, Ethan. You were there when I made the call. They're on their way. It's a bit late to start with the "what ifs". Callie told me he will kill her if he gets her back and she sounded pretty damn convincing. They promised they will take care of her and we have to trust they mean it.'

Callie tensed at the mention of her name. Who had Faith called? Had she contacted Duncan? She recalled the woman telling her she had taken Rob Jolly's card. At the time, she had suggested they go to the police, but now it seemed Callie was being offered up as a gift. She had become a danger to the Stuarts and they wanted rid of her.

Nerves trembled through her and she struggled to breathe, sweat beading on her forehead. Was this why they had tied her up? They needed to keep her subdued until Duncan and Rob arrived.

A wave of dizziness and fresh nausea swept through her.

*Focus, Callie. Breathe through your nose.*

Faith and Ethan were no longer a safe haven. There was no one she could trust except Nico and Laurel, and neither of them were here right now. She had to find the courage to help herself.

Refusing to give into the fear that threatened to overwhelm her, she tried to focus on the knot. She needed Faith and Ethan to keep fighting. If she could get her wrists free, she would make a run for safety. The key was in the front door, so even if it was locked, she stood a chance of getting out before they realised.

She needed to do it before Duncan arrived. With no idea how long she had been unconscious or when Faith had made the call, she knew that could be at any moment, and she fought the urge to sob.

She could be brave. She had to be brave.

But then Ethan was moving to the window and peering out, and when he turned back to Faith, his face was pale. 'I think they're here.'

Blind panic had Callie trying to climb to her feet. She stumbled once, managed to right herself, then was blindly heading towards the kitchen. The wooziness of her head injury together with lack of balance from having her hands tied behind her back worked against her, and as she fell forward, arms caught her.

'I'm sorry, Callie.' She heard Ethan's voice, and he sounded genuinely remorseful, except for the tremor, which told her he was afraid too.

Coward. She wanted to scream the word. He was throwing her to the wolves.

Faith was already at the front door and Callie struggled against Ethan as it swung open. Seeing Rob step into the hallway, followed by Duncan, fresh terror rattled through her and she fought with renewed vigour.

*This can't be happening.*

She wanted to look away as Duncan moved towards her, but she couldn't, caught in his cold, blue stare. As he reached out a hand to touch her cheek, she tried to recoil.

*Please don't let this be real.*

'I've missed you, Mica. We have a lot to catch up on.' His smile was both cruel and gloating and the dread of what came next nearly made her pee herself.

As she was handed over to Rob, his vice grip on her arm made her realise she was going nowhere. Meanwhile, Duncan turned businesslike with Faith, asking for Rob's card back.

'We were never here,' he instructed.

'But you'll make her disappear. We have your word.'

Duncan smirked. 'You won't ever hear from her again. You protect me, I'll protect you. But, if you betray me, I'll make sure you regret it.'

'We won't. I promise.' Faith's gaze slid to Callie. It was the first time she had acknowledged her since the truth had come out, and her expression was carefully blank. There was no sign of the compassionate woman Callie had believed her to be. 'I'm sorry it's come to this. It's not personal.' Faith might as well have been a robot. While Ethan looked like he was going to fall apart at any moment – not out of any remorse for their actions, but from self-pity – she showed no emotion. Her voice detached and monotone. 'I have to put my family first. If you had kids, you would understand.'

Seriously? She was trying to justify her actions? Rage choked Callie and for a moment, it was a welcome relief from the fear. She cussed through the gag, a string of expletives, telling Faith exactly what she thought. The words were muffled, but the woman's eyes widened, suggesting she understood them clearly enough. The bitch had the gall to look offended, her mouth stretching into a thin line.

Callie had built a new life here, rediscovering who she was and taking tentative steps towards a future with a man she was slowly falling in love with. Without her defence, Nico could end up being charged with Anya's murder, and he would never know the truth about the couple he considered to be his two closest friends. Frustration mingled with regret for what could have been, with fear for what her immediate future held, and with anger for the couple who had betrayed her.

'On that note,' Duncan said briskly, 'we'll be on our way.'

As he reached the front door, a phone started vibrating and he froze, turning around and casting his eyes over Faith, Ethan and Callie.

'Whose is that?'

'Um, mine,' Ethan told him, reaching into his pocket.

'Do not answer it!' Duncan snapped, loud enough that Ethan almost dropped the handset.

There was silence as everyone waited for the phone to stop.

'Who was it?'

Ethan's eyes darted from Faith to Callie, eventually landing on Duncan, as he answered. 'A friend of mine.'

'Which friend?'

There was another quick look at his wife before he answered. 'Nico.'

'Nico,' Duncan repeated, looking at Callie, and from his expression, it was obvious he knew exactly who Nico was. His attention switched to Faith. 'Why would Nico be calling your husband?' His tone had turned suspicious. 'Does he know Mica is here?'

'No, no, of course not.' For a moment, the tremor in Faith's voice betrayed her nerves, but she quickly recovered. 'Ethan told you. They are friends.'

And if Nico was calling him, did that mean he was back home?

Callie's question was answered moments later when a WhatsApp message followed the call.

'Give me your phone,' Duncan demanded. He held his hand out and Ethan hesitated before complying. Duncan read the message aloud. 'Have you or Faith heard from Callie? She's not picking up.' He stared from Ethan to Faith. 'You said he was away, right?'

When Faith nodded, he tapped out a reply, reading it out as he typed. 'Maybe she's in the shower. Everything okay?'

The reply came back. 'Yeah, long day, but I'm now heading home,' Duncan relayed, before going back again. 'I'm sure she's fine and will be waiting for you.' He slipped Ethan's phone in his pocket. 'I'll be needing this.'

Ethan didn't protest, instead looking at the floor.

'Are we good to go?' Rob asked. He had stayed quiet so far, letting Duncan lead the conversation, and Callie could hear the impatience in his voice.

Duncan looked between Faith and Ethan again, as if trying to weigh up whether he could trust them. 'We're good,' he confirmed.

Rob's fingers dug in Callie's arm as he pushed her through the door and she tried to jerk away as he led her towards the car. She was no match for him, though, and he bundled her into the back easily, fastening her seat belt.

The door slammed shut and the aniseed scent of the air freshener he favoured wafted into the air. It was chillingly familiar, making her nightmare all the more real. It transported her back to The Old Rectory with its dark, high-ceilinged hallway and Duncan's clipped footsteps echoing as he came to find her. She couldn't go back there, but how the hell was she supposed to get away?

They were both in the front seats now, Rob starting the engine, and she fought against the wave of claustrophobia at her trapped position, convinced she was about to have a full-scale panic attack. She couldn't breathe with this cloth in her mouth and her arms were aching from how they had been forced behind her back. The afternoon sun was beating down on the window and sweat beaded on her upper lip and pooled under her arms.

She mumbled to try to get their attention, desperately in need of water.

Duncan might not give her any, but she had to try.

If he heard her, he ignored her, instead speaking to Rob. 'I don't trust those two.'

'Do you want them taken care of?' Rob asked casually, as if offering to kill two people was normal to him. Because that's what Callie assumed Duncan wanted done. And despite hating Faith and Ethan for turning on her, for what they had done to poor Anya, and for how they had betrayed Nico, she remembered they had a daughter and her heart broke for Olive, knowing how it felt to lose a parent.

'Make it look like some kind of domestic. An argument that got out of control.'

'Got it.'

'Then come and meet us at Willow Brook Farm. You can bring the family car. They won't be needing it.'

'You're going back there?' Rob sounded surprised. 'Why?'

Duncan turned and glanced at Callie before he answered, wanting to be sure he had her attention, and when he spoke, his words chilled her to the bone.

'I want to meet the man who stole my fiancée.' He gave Callie a twisted smile. 'And then Mica is going to watch while I kill him.'

## 34

Callie wasn't responding to his calls and messages, and Nico couldn't shake the feeling that something was seriously off.

It had been odd for Ethan not to pick up his call too. Usually, he preferred talking to texting. Although he had replied on Whats-App, he hadn't asked anything about the police questioning, despite earlier bombarding Nico, demanding to know what was going on. Nico had seen all of the messages when his phone was returned to him, yet when he asked Ethan about Callie, it was as if Ethan had forgotten he was with the police.

It hadn't been an easy interview. After arriving at the station, the gravity of the situation had sunk in and he had decided he did want his solicitor present. There had been a wait for her to arrive and then the questions had seemed to go on forever.

All he could do was reiterate what he knew, aware that he had to protect Callie.

Eventually, he had been released under investigation.

Not an ideal outcome, but at least he hadn't been charged with anything – yet – and her secret was safe.

He had realised during the interview just how important she

was to him, and that he would do anything to keep her safe, so it was driving him crazy that she wasn't answering her phone, especially knowing she was at the farm all alone. Toby didn't work Saturdays and Jodie finished at two. Usually, Nico took care of the horses after she had gone, but they were going to be restless. Had Callie gone down to see them?

What if there had been some kind of accident?

He mused over different scenarios as he headed down to Guildhall in the city centre. There were still a few shoppers about as he went over to where the taxis were queued, but he took no notice. All he cared about was getting home to Callie and making sure she was okay.

\* \* \*

Vince was outside Stable Cottage when he heard the sound of an engine.

Although he didn't believe Nico or Callie had anything to do with his niece's murder, he had come to see Callie, hoping she would show him where Anya's bracelet had been found.

Unlike Vince, David was convinced Nico was guilty. It was something they had already argued over and it annoyed Vince that David had gone to Larissa with his suspicions. She wasn't the best judge of character and had immediately gone running to the police, demanding they arrest Nico.

They had already been told the police had doubts over the guilt of the traveller they had taken into custody. That meant Anya's killer was still at large. Distracting them with Nico was going to be a big waste of time.

Perhaps he shouldn't be so certain of the man's innocence, but his gut feeling was guiding him. He had known Nico for a while and Nico had always looked out for Anya as a big brother would.

Even a father figure at times. He had helped her build a life, believing in her and encouraging her, and proud of her achievements. It made no sense that he would want to kill her.

No. Whoever Nico had seen her with that last night was the guilty one.

Vince knocked again, but Callie wasn't answering and didn't appear to be home. It was as he was about to leave that he heard the engine, and not recognising the black car that pulled up outside the house, something in his gut had him taking a step back so he was mostly hidden by the cottage. He peered around the wall, spotting two figures emerging, the late-afternoon sun catching the red in Callie's hair. The man with her though wasn't Nico.

Whoever he was, he appeared to be steadying her, sticking firmly by her side as they disappeared towards the front door, and was he imagining it, but did she seem to be struggling against him?

Vince decided he would sneak up to the house for a discreet look to check everything was okay.

\* \* \*

The dogs were already barking before the door was unlocked and they came charging through into the hallway the second it opened.

Callie saw Duncan's nostrils flare in disdain, especially when Dash barrelled into him. He kicked out and the spaniel whimpered before retreating with a growl.

'Stupid animal,' he muttered, and that was when he spotted Chester.

The retriever's ears were pulled back and flat to his head, his tail between his legs, suggesting he clearly remembered Duncan, and not in a good way.

'Are you fucking kidding me? Another lie.' Duncan turned to

Callie, his pale-blue eyes hot with anger. 'I thought he ran away, Mica? That's what you told me, wasn't it?'

When she didn't react, he dropped the duffle bag he had brought with him, pushing his face close to hers and screaming the words again.

'Wasn't it?'

She flinched, spittle landing on her cheek, and trembled so badly, she could barely stand. He was staring at her, waiting for an answer, and she managed a nod.

'You sly, conniving bitch.' His fist came from nowhere, smashing into the side of her nose, and she heard the sickening crack before the pain registered. This time, she did fall, and unable to use her hands, her hip took the brunt as it smashed against the floor.

She blinked, her vision clearing, as her ears started ringing, and her face began to throb. Christ, she was going to be sick. She tried to push the gag from her mouth as Duncan disappeared through into Nico's living room, pulling a chair from the dining table into the middle of the room.

'Take a seat,' he told her, dragging her across and forcing her down.

Barking came from the doorway. Dash was the only one of the three dogs who dared get close, snapping at Duncan's leg and, from the yowl Duncan gave, biting into flesh.

'I need these fucking animals out of here.'

As he rounded up the dogs, kicking and pushing them out of the room, Callie tried to focus. She was aware of wetness dripping from her nose, and as it soaked through the cloth, the metallic taste of blood hit her tongue.

Her nose was becoming clogged and she was finding it more difficult to breathe. She tried to concentrate as Duncan returned. The door was open, but the dogs had gone. She could hear them and from the muffled barking, she suspected he had locked them in the kitchen.

He appeared calmer as he pulled another chair from the table and sat down facing her.

She needed to get away. If she stayed here, she was going to die.

Feeling for the knot again that bound her wrists, she discreetly tugged at it as he spoke.

'It doesn't pleasure me to punish you,' he said, as if it was a cross he had to bear.

'Let me go,' she tried to scream.

Whether he understood the words or chose to ignore her muffled plea, they were lost.

'I can't let this slide, though.' He ran a hand over his hair, looking conflicted. 'I love you, please know that, but you've done a terrible thing. And you've involved others. Do you realise how badly you have hurt me? How dangerous your mistake has been? It's going to cost lives. You understand that, right?'

He was deluded. Insane.

'Did Laurel put you in touch with Nico or did you already know him, I wonder.'

He knew Laurel was involved? Callie was trying her damnedest to keep a neutral expression, but her eyes had widened at the mention of her friend's name.

Duncan's smile turned smug. 'Yes, I know about Laurel. How do you think I found out you were here?'

*Oh God, oh God. Please let her be okay.*

She watched as he crossed the room to look out of the window, and while he had his back to her, she worked harder at the knot, relieved when she found a loop, pulling it loose.

'She's a spiky little thing,' Duncan commented, sounding almost impressed. 'I'll give her credit for that. She put up a good fight.'

A good fight? What exactly had he done?

He turned back to face her and she stilled. 'She was kicking and screaming to the end.'

The end? Was he saying Laurel was dead? That he had killed her?

Callie met his cold stare, tears leaking from her eyes, despite her best efforts not to react. Her nose was so blocked now and crying was only making it worse.

'It's your fault, Mica. You involved Laurel and now she's dead. And when Nico returns, you're going to have more blood on your hands.'

No. She would not let him kill Nico too.

She watched as he stuck his hand in his pocket and pulled out his dreaded dice. 'I'm going to take pleasure in ending his life. And you're going to watch while I do it. Shall we decide how I should kill him?' He laughed at her mumbled pleas. 'I'll choose for you, shall I? Evens, I stab him. Odds, I make him watch while I gut you, then I stab him?'

He rolled the dice on the floor. A three and a five. Eight.

'Evens it is then. That's good, Mica. Because I have much bigger plans for you.'

Callie ignored the fresh tremor his words brought. Somehow she had to get away from here and warn Nico.

Duncan reached for the duffle bag, unzipping it, and emptying the contents, and her attention was immediately drawn to a set of knives, their blades glinting in the light of the sun that was spilling through the window.

Oh fuck. She had to get out of here.

She tugged at her wrists with renewed force as he picked up a coil of rope and, as the material binding them loosened further, she managed to wiggle her left hand free.

That was when she ran.

She didn't hesitate, despite having no plan, no idea of where to go. She knew it was her only chance before he tied her to the chair.

To her relief, the front door was open, and tearing the gag from her mouth, gulping in much-needed air, she sprinted in the direction of the stables.

Behind her came a yell and then the sound of footsteps.

Duncan was stronger, but she was faster.

Unfortunately, she also had a head injury and a broken nose, and the dizziness made her stumble.

As she fell, strong arms caught her and she screamed.

Duncan clamped his hand over her mouth, dragging her with him back inside the house, barely reacting as she kicked and struggled like a feral cat.

'No more games.' he hissed, throwing her on the floor and kicking her in the stomach. As the breath whooshed out of her and she cried in pain, he reached for the rope again and caught a handful of her hair. 'You deserve everything that is about to happen to you.'

## 35

Nico's phone rang as his taxi headed away from Norwich and he frowned, not recognising the number.

'Hello?'

'Nico? It's Oksana... Laurel's ex.'

He remembered her. They had only met a few times, but Laurel often mentioned her in conversation. Although the relationship had broken down, the pair of them had remained good friends.

'Is everything okay?'

There was a pause. 'No, I'm sorry to have to tell you. I have some terrible news.'

He listened as she explained she had come up to visit his sister, and as she detailed the scene she had walked in on, numbness paralysed him.

'I'm sorry I didn't call sooner, but this is the first calm moment I've had. She's alive, Nico. God knows how, but she had a pulse. She's in a bad way, though. I've left a message for your parents to call me.'

'They did this to her over a break-in?' His head was pounding and he barely recognised his own voice. The idea that someone had tortured Laurel sat like a rock lodged in his throat. He needed to get down to Essex, but first he had to find Callie.

'That's why I needed to speak to you urgently. Laurel briefly gained consciousness and she mentioned you.'

'What did she say?'

'I don't know if this will make any sense,' Oksana told him. 'But she said, "Tell Nico. He knows." I don't know what the rest of sentence was, so I thought I should ask you what it is you're supposed to know.'

'I have no idea. Was that it?' he demanded. 'She didn't say anything else at all?'

'No, I'm sorry. She repeated it, but she was getting distressed and they had to sedate her.'

The cryptic words played on a loop in his head as he thanked Oksana and promised he would get down to the hospital as soon as possible.

*Tell Nico. He knows.* As the taxi pulled onto the A47, it occurred to him that maybe he was phrasing it wrong.

Oksana had said it as if 'he knows' was the start of a sentence. But what if it wasn't? What if Laurel had meant it, 'tell Nico he knows'?

Suddenly, her words took on a new meaning.

The break-in, the torture. 'He knows.'

Had Duncan Stone done this to her?

And if so, was he on his way to Norfolk?

Nico looked at his WhatsApp, noting that the message he had sent Callie was unread and she hadn't been active in the last couple of hours.

Had Stone found her?

He needed to get back to the farm, and fast.

\* \* \*

Vince had approached the house from the back and was creeping around the perimeter, peering in windows as he went, listening to the dogs frantically barking, and trying to figure out what was going on, when he spotted Callie charging out of the front door. She was running like her life depended on it and a moment later, a man came dashing out after her.

He looked familiar and it took a few seconds for Vince to realise who he was.

What the hell was Duncan Stone doing here?

He sounded angry, swearing as he chased her, and calling the name, 'Mica.'

Not Callie's name, so Vince didn't know why the man was using it, and for one bizarre moment, he wondered if this was something to do with a movie. There were no cameras, but a rehearsal perhaps?

Except Duncan Stone had retired from acting and Callie looked terrified. She also had blood crusting around her nose, suggesting she had hurt herself...

Or someone had hurt her.

Where was Nico while all this was going on? And should Vince call the police or try to intervene?

As he watched, Stone wrestled Callie to the ground, covering her mouth with his big hand as he dragged her back into the house.

Everyone loved Duncan Stone, but Vince had never been his greatest fan. Sure, the guy could act, but Vince thought he had dead eyes, and he remembered reading a couple of articles that the man had some shady friends and a bit of a temper.

What was his problem with Callie?

Curious, he stepped up to the window, peering in as Stone kicked her.

Acting without thinking, Vince barged into the house.

'Get the hell off her,' he demanded, grabbing one of Stone's beefy arms.

The man lashed out without even looking back, his arm hitting Vince full in the face, and he went flying backwards, hitting the wall, his glasses slipping off. As he fell to the ground, his ankle twisted and he let out an agonising scream.

Without the glasses, his vision was terrible, but he could see the figure looming over him, and heard Stone's deep voice.

'So, this is Nico, Mica. The man you left me for, you cheating slut.'

Vince didn't have a chance to correct him as Stone hauled him up by his collar and his fist smashed into his face. He was dazed momentarily, but then blinding pain hit, his nose throbbing as he cried out again.

'Let him go!'

Callie was screaming and Vince realised she was trying to drag Stone back. As the thug released him, he crumpled to the floor, howling as he landed on his bad ankle.

Stone turned his attention back to Callie and Vince watched helplessly wanting to intervene, but in too much pain to move. He needed to call the police. As subtly as possible, he pulled his phone from his pocket, grateful that his near vision was okay and he could see as he tapped at the screen. It took a moment, though, to realise his call wasn't connecting and that was when he spotted he didn't have a signal.

Dammit!

If he could manage to get back outside... His ankle was really hurting, though. Even crawling would be a struggle.

He swore silently at his phone, double blinking when a Facebook notification pinged up. His handset must have automatically connected to Nico's Wi-Fi. He had stopped for coffee a couple of times after they had been out looking for Anya and Nico had given him the password so he could message Larissa.

Knowing his network provider didn't support Wi-Fi calling, he quickly tapped out a WhatsApp message, sending it to both David and Nico.

Am at the farm. Pls call police. Callie in trouble.

As he stared at the message, waiting for the double ticks, an idea came to him.

Duncan Stone had an image to protect. What would his loyal fans think if they knew the truth about him, that he was a brute who beat up women?

Vince's hand trembled as he logged onto TikTok. He had nearly three thousand followers, which meant he could go live. He set his phone to record, then placed it on the floor beside him, the camera pointing in Stone's direction and hoping to hell it was picking everything up. The man had his back to him and Vince watched as he stood over Callie and kicked at her like she was a piece of rubbish.

'Leave her alone,' he demanded, trying to pull himself forward and yowling as pain stabbed his ankle.

Stone ignored him, his focus on Callie. 'You fucking disgust me,' he snarled, reaching down and grabbing hold of a clump of her hair when she tried to crawl away from him. She pleaded with him as he dragged her over to the chair, forcing her to sit down and yanking her arms behind her. 'You're going to watch me kill this piece of shit, then I'm going to deal with you. Perhaps when I put you back in the dog crate, this time I really will set you on fire.'

Vince was horrified. Stone was making this up, right?

'Please, stop hurting her.'

'Shut the fuck up, lover boy,' Stone snapped, not even bothering to turn round. 'I'll deal with you in a moment.'

'That's not Nico,' Callie sounded desperate. Vince could hear the fear in her voice, and could see her face was puffy and bloody from where Stone had hit her.

'Don't lie to me, you bitch.'

'I'm not lying. I swear. That's Vince.'

Stone swung around. 'So where the fuck is Nico?'

He scowled at Vince, rage twisting his features. As he went to take a step forward, another voice halted him.

'I'm right here.'

## 36

Nico took everything in.

Vince sat on his living-room floor, his glasses missing and looking terrified. The brute who loomed over him, Nico recognised as Duncan Stone. Then he looked at Callie. She was sat on the dining chair that had been positioned in the middle of the room, and seeing her beautiful face battered and bloody had an unfamiliar emotion twisting in his gut.

He realised it was rage.

He wasn't a violent man, and always looked for the peaceful solution, but Stone had done this to her. And before he had come looking for Callie, he had almost killed Laurel.

That was two women Nico loved and would do anything for.

Three sets of eyes turned in his direction as he spoke, and Callie choked out a sob that sounded both relieved and fearful.

'It's going to be okay,' he told her, before refocusing his attention on Stone. He had called the police the moment he had seen Vince's WhatsApp message, but no way was he waiting outside for them to arrive.

'You're Nico Adams?' There was still anger in Stone's voice, but also surprise. Apparently, Nico wasn't what he had expected.

'And you're Duncan Stone.' Nico took a step towards him, holding the man's stare. 'Film star, philanthropist, bully and abuser. I know what you did to my sister.'

Stone had the nerve to sneer. 'She deserved it. The conniving little bitch had it coming, persuading Mica to betray me.'

Nico clenched his fists and released a slow, steadying breath to clear his head. 'Her name is Callie, not Mica. And did she deserve this? What has she done to you that is so terrible, you had to use her body as a punching bag?'

'She left me. She lied to me and she left me.'

'Because you were already beating the crap out of her, you lowlife piece of shit.'

Stone's face paled, but his lips formed a grim line.

'You like an easy target, don't you?' Nico pushed when he didn't get a response. 'Callie, Laurel, poor Vince here. Do you get off knowing you are bigger and stronger, and that they can't defend themselves against you? You've been waiting for me. Well, I'm here now, so let's make this about us. No weapons, no cheap tricks, no hurting anyone else. Just you and me. Show me you're not the coward I think you are.'

Wanting to provoke a reaction, Nico took another step closer and gave the man a gentle shove. He might prefer peace over violence, but he knew how to use his fists. Growing up, he had been forced to defend himself or others on more than one occasion, and right now, he intended to give Stone a taste of his own medicine.

\* \* \*

The shove was enough to have Duncan throwing a punch. One that Nico easily blocked and gave him cause to go on the attack.

Callie had watched, terrified, as he'd pushed Duncan's buttons. Aware of what Duncan was capable of, and knowing that he wanted to hurt Nico, had her afraid for the outcome.

She had always thought of Duncan as being strong and powerful, but when pitted against someone of similar stature, he wasn't so tough. His jaw cracked loudly when Nico took the first swing at him and he staggered backwards, looking stunned by the force of the punch.

Although he was full of hard talk and insults as he recovered, he only managed to get one clean punch in before Nico went on the offensive again, angry and driven, and Duncan's attempts to defend himself were pathetic. When the telling punch came, it knocked him off his feet, and a kick to the gut had him curling into a ball.

It was a position Callie recognised and she knew from personal experience that he was trying to protect himself from further blows.

She had never seen this side of Nico. He was usually so calm and gentle, and she hadn't believed him capable of rage. Although his control had snapped, she wasn't afraid, understanding that his anger wasn't directed at her.

He was dragging Duncan to his feet now and pinning him against the wall. Duncan's pretty, movie-star face was covered in blood and those pale eyes of his were wide with fear, all of his bluster gone. He hadn't anticipated this outcome and Rob wasn't here to protect him.

'Give me one good reason why I shouldn't kill you,' Nico demanded.

And that was when the unexpected happened. A moment Callie thought she would never see.

Duncan begged.

'Stop. Let me go. Please.'

The room was silent as he spoke the words, his voice trembling and not much more than a whisper. Duncan Stone, the big, hard man who she had lived in fear of, had just pleaded for his life.

She glanced across the room at Vince, doubting her ears. Had he heard it too?

Movement behind him had her focus shifting to the door and, in that moment, she realised the nightmare wasn't over. Rob Jolly was striding across the room before she could open her mouth to warn Nico, and dragging him away from Duncan.

Callie found her voice, screaming for him to stop as Duncan slumped to the floor and Rob, having caught Nico off guard, punched him in the face.

He was bigger and stronger, and Callie knew how dangerous he was. As he shoved Nico to the ground, holding him down, his hands going to his throat, she looked around in panic. Duncan didn't appear to be a threat, still recovering from Nico's attack, while Vince was watching wide-eyed.

'We have to do something!' Callie yelled at him.

When he didn't react, appearing to be frozen in fear, she frantically looked for a weapon.

Her gaze landed on the large fireplace and the poker, and she stumbled towards it, grabbing hold of the iron rod and whacking Rob across the back, trying to get him to release his chokehold on Nico.

'Get off him.'

Rob ignored her, seeming to barely register the blows, until she bashed him hard over the head. Then he reacted, lashing out with one of his meaty fists, and she lost her grip on the poker as he sent her flying. Climbing off Nico, he turned to deal with her, and she scuttled backwards to get away, managing to grab the poker again and holding the sharp end up as a weapon to try to ward off his approach.

She heard Nico coughing, her relief that he was okay quickly turning to fear as she saw the look on Rob's face. Unsure whether to lash out or wait for him to get closer, she gripped the poker tight, but then the decision was taken away from her.

'Callie?' She heard Nico's voice, saw him try to stop Rob by grabbing at his ankles.

The move didn't halt him, but it did cause him to stumble and as he lost his footing, Callie tried to duck to the side.

She wasn't quick enough and as he fell on top of her, she heard a squelch and then a gasp. It wasn't until moments later when Nico pushed him away, and Rob rolled onto his back, the poker wrenching itself from her grip, that she realised it was impaled in his chest.

Her eyes widened in horror as he spluttered, his face pale and sweaty, and a red patch spread around the wound.

Nico had hold of her then, tugging her into his lap and folding her in his arms. 'Don't watch,' he told her. 'It will be over soon. The police are on their way.'

Perhaps she shouldn't, but Callie couldn't bring herself to tear her eyes away, as one of the men who had effectively helped keep her a prisoner died in front of her.

Her gaze went to Duncan, but he made no attempt to move, instead sobbing quietly. He was no longer the monster she had feared, she realised. He was pathetic.

'Is he dead?' Vince asked cautiously from the corner of the room, as Rob fell still, eyes staring towards the ceiling.

'I think so,' Nico told him, stroking a hand over Callie's hair as the sound of sirens echoed in the distance.

She glanced over at Vince, wracked with guilt that Duncan had hit him. 'Are you okay?' she asked, spotting his broken glasses on the floor.

He nodded and she watched as he reached for his phone, for a moment worrying that it was damaged too. 'I got him, Callie.'

At first, she was unsure what he meant, but then he held up the phone, managing a smile, and she understood. 'You recorded him.'

Perhaps it would be useful for the police, but she couldn't bring herself to be enthusiastic. She knew Duncan too well. He would lawyer up and find a way to make sure the video was never seen. He had a way of getting what he wanted and landing on his feet. The recording would probably conveniently disappear.

'Actually, I did one better.'

'What do you mean?' Nico asked, curious.

'I streamed him.' Vince's smile widened to a grin. 'The footage is already live. Duncan Stone is going to be trending all over TikTok.'

## 37

---

### EIGHTEEN MONTHS LATER

The public fall and disgrace of Duncan Stone was more epic than his meteoric rise to fame, and in the brief time before TikTok removed the video, it became one of the most streamed replays ever.

Only a few supported a man who was clearly seen beating up his ex-fiancée, and even those who initially tried to defend his actions – blaming everything from Callie deserving it to Duncan suffering from some kind of mental breakdown – quietened when the truth emerged about his quest to get her back and the casualties along the way.

Duncan had threatened Callie, telling her that he had friends who would kill her if she ever told the truth about him, and in the days that followed, she had been constantly looking over her shoulder. Whether it had been a lie or his lowlife friends simply decided to distance themselves, nothing happened, and as the weeks rolled by, she learnt to relax and rebuild her life without having to hide in the shadows.

Other women had come forward from his past with their own stories to tell when they heard of his arrest, and, eventually, even

Kacey Lewis spoke out against him, though she stopped shy of calling her relationship with Duncan abusive. Instead referring to him as broken and toxic. It seemed Callie had been one of many victims, and eventually, he was charged with a number of offences.

Rob's death was ruled as an accident, though Callie, along with Laurel, was investigated over whether they had perverted the course of justice, wasting the coastguard's resources. To their relief, no charges were brought, as it was decided they had both suffered enough.

Nico was Callie's rock through it all. She was now in counselling, as she dealt with the aftershocks of what Duncan had put her through, but it was Nico's quiet, unwavering support that gave her strength when she needed it most, making her believe she could tackle anything. In turn, she had been there for him too.

Learning the truth about Ethan and Faith had hit him hard. He didn't trust easily and knowing they had killed Anya, then had sent Callie to almost certain death, was a betrayal he struggled to reconcile with.

Callie wished she could give him closure, but the Stuarts had both died in the fire Rob had set so were never held accountable for their cruel and selfish actions.

That was tough for Vince too and initially, he had lashed out when Callie had admitted the truth, that it had been her in the woods the night Anya died. He needed someone to blame, she understood that, but still, she was relieved when eventually he chose to forgive both her and Nico, understanding the difficult position they had been in.

Nico had tried to protect Callie, and Faith had protected Ethan and Olive, she supposed, even if the secrets they were keeping had been monumentally different.

In the end, Faith had failed and Olive was the innocent victim of a terrible chain of events, losing both of her parents. Callie never saw her again and she heard that Olive, along with the family cats, who luckily had been outside when the fire was set, had gone to live with her aunt and cousins in Shropshire.

Looking out to the paddock now, where the young girl had once taken her Saturday riding lessons, she could see the field was bathed in light from the low December sun and she watched as the man she loved worked with his beloved gelding, Red.

She had first come here pretending to be Callie Adams, but now it was her name. Nico had asked her to marry him two months after Duncan's arrest, and as neither of them wanted anything fussy, they had wed in a quiet ceremony with Nico's family, Oksana and the dogs.

Juliette, Tracy and Aarna were the only friends she invited and it was important to Callie that they were there. Her old friends had reached out to her after Duncan's fall from grace, full of apologies, and she knew they all were racked with guilt that they had been quick to believe she had been responsible for the cruel message to Juliette. There was no bitterness on Callie's part. She knew Duncan had done everything possible to drive a wedge between them.

She hadn't wanted her family at the wedding, still struggling that she had been unable to turn to them for help. Phoebe refused to acknowledge her part in everything and together with her father blamed Callie for faking her death. They were upset she had lied, putting them through a memorial service, and that had been the death knell for their relationship.

As if she had been given a choice.

As far as she was concerned, Paul and Janice Adams were better parents to her than her father had ever been, and Laurel was the only sister she needed.

Callie had been convinced her friend was dead and she had wept learning what Duncan had done to her, but Laurel was a fighter and tougher than she looked. Her road to recovery had taken a long time, but she had finally healed both mentally and physically, and Oksana had been with her every step of the way. The two of them were dating again and closer than ever.

The build-up to Duncan's trial had taken forever and was something Callie was dreading. When she had finally given evidence, documenting the hell she had lived through, it was the most difficult thing she had ever done. Still, she had gone back to the courthouse with Nico, his parents and Oksana, sitting in the public gallery to give support as Laurel testified. When the jury had eventually returned a verdict of guilty on all counts, a burden had lifted.

Now they were waiting on today's sentencing verdict, and Callie was anxious as she tightly gripped Nico and Laurel's hands. She went from stunned to numb when Duncan was delivered a life sentence, barely aware as Laurel caught her up in a hard hug.

Outside the courtroom, she nipped to the loo, needing a few moments alone as the processed the news. Duncan Stone would never be able to terrorise her again. She was free.

She washed her hands and cooled her heated cheeks with cold water before going back to join her family.

Nico was waiting for her outside. 'You okay?'

Nodding, she went to him. 'I am now.'

He was silent for a moment, looking contemplative. 'He got life, Callie. That means you never have to worry about him again.'

'I know. It's still sinking in. I was shocked and now I'm relieved, but I'm working my way up to excited,' she grinned. 'So be prepared.'

'Come on, Cal,' Laurel yelled from further along the corridor, where she stood with Oksana. 'Mum is treating us to champagne.'

First, they had to get through the crowd of reporters who had swarmed outside the courthouse every day of the trial.

'Dad's gone to bring the car round,' Nico told her, picking up on her anxiety.

It would be the last time she had to do it. Keep her head down and focus on getting to the car. Then she could head back to Norfolk with Nico, where the dogs would be eager to see them. She could picture them now. Dash charging excitedly around them, a toy in his mouth, while quiet, even-tempered Shyla followed, and Chester brought up the rear.

Her gorgeous goldy was a senior now and he had arthritis in his back legs which slowed him down. Still, he was happy and Callie and Nico gave him the best life possible.

'Coming,' she told Laurel, tugging Nico's arm around her.

As she readied herself to face the crowd, she considered the parallels between the man she had married and the one she was finally free of.

Duncan and Nico both had it tough as kids, and their experiences shaped the men they had become. While they had gone on to have successful careers, Duncan had used his past as an excuse to do terrible things, while Nico had chosen empathy and kindness, wanting to help others. He had tried to help Anya and he had been there for Callie when she needed him most. Nico Adams had been, and would always be, her sanctuary, and by drawing on his strength, she had made sure that Duncan Stone would never be able to hurt anyone ever again.

# ACKNOWLEDGEMENTS

My thanks must firstly go to my brilliant publisher, Boldwood Books. To my editor, Caroline Ridding, for always believing in me and my stories, and for helping me to make them into the best possible versions. I love being on this journey with you. To my eagle-eyed copy editor, Jade Craddock, and proof reader, Emily Reader. To Amanda Ridding, Nia Beynon, Claire Fenby, Niamh Wallace, and the rest of the team for being a dream to work with.

Huge thanks go to my fab beta readers, Jo Bilton, Tina Jackson, fellow author pal, Trish Dixon, and Daniella Curry, and not forgetting my soul sister, Andrea Mummery, who also read for me. I hope I did both you and Red proud.

To Jonathan Kruger Curtis, who was my Devon Oracle, to Daniella and her daughters, Kaya and Kadyn Curry, for answering my TikTok questions, to my competition winner Tracy Novak, whose character appears in the book, and also to Leon Clements and Kacey Lewis for letting me borrow their names.

To my family, Mum, Paul, Holly (who helps me with those pesky police questions), Nicki and Victoria, for (mostly) not getting frustrated with me when my life revolves around writing deadlines, and the rest of my friends, who help keep me grounded: Paula, Ness, Shell, Caroline, Hannah, Krysia, Cheryl, Deano, Jerv, Christine, Emma and Louise, and anyone else I have missed.

I have a new group on Facebook, *The Keri Beevis Official Reader Group*. Please come find us. To Daniella, Jo, Bev Hopper, Tracy Robinson and Allison Valentine, who help me run this. Thank you.

You are all stars, and thank you to all of our wonderful members. I love how interactive you all are in the group.

A quick mention to my fellow authors, Val Keogh, Natasha Boydell, Charley Crocker and Amanda Brittany, and all of the lovely writers at Boldwood, thank you for generally being awesome and so supportive. As for bloggers, I hate singling people out, but I want to mention Mark Fearn (or Book Mark as you may know him) who I know hasn't had the easiest of years, and is one of the loveliest people in the book world. Thank you for your friendship and support. To the rest of the brilliant blogging community, a big thank you. Us authors are so lucky to have you shouting for us.

There are three groups on Facebook I want to mention who have been incredibly supportive of me over the last year or so. To the members of *Psychological Thriller Readers*, a huge thank you for taking a chance on my books, and also helping me pick dog names (that is Marissa Busk for Shyla, Danielle Boyd Jefferson, Kylah Burns and Karen Gordon for Dash, and Laurie Barker for Chester), to the lovely Christina Cook, who runs *Bitchy Bookworms*, and to Dawn Angels of *Psychological Thriller Authors* and *Readers Unite*, thank you for continuing to spread the word about me.

I think I have thank you'd myself out now, but one final shout-out to my lovely readers. I have said it before and will say it again: I write the books, but you breathe life into them. THANK YOU.

# ABOUT THE AUTHOR

**Keri Beevis** is the internationally bestselling author of several psychological thrillers and romantic suspense mysteries, including the very successful *Dying to Tell*. She sets many of her books in the county of Norfolk, where she was born and still lives and which provides much of her inspiration.

Sign up to Keri Beevis' mailing list here for news, competitions and updates on future books.

Visit Keri's website: www.keribeevis.com

Follow Keri on social media:

 x.com/keribeevis
 facebook.com/allaboutbeev
 instagram.com/keri.beevis

# ALSO BY KERI BEEVIS

The Sleepover

The Summer House

The House in the Woods

Trust No One

Every Little Breath

Nowhere to Hide

# THE
## Murder
# LIST

**THE MURDER LIST IS A NEWSLETTER
DEDICATED TO SPINE-CHILLING FICTION
AND GRIPPING PAGE-TURNERS!**

**SIGN UP TO MAKE SURE YOU'RE ON OUR
HIT LIST FOR EXCLUSIVE DEALS, AUTHOR
CONTENT, AND COMPETITIONS.**

## SIGN UP TO OUR
## NEWSLETTER

BIT.LY/THEMURDERLISTNEWS

# Boldwood

Boldwood Books is an award-winning fiction publishing company seeking out the best stories from around the world.

**Find out more at www.boldwoodbooks.com**

Join our reader community for brilliant books, competitions and offers!

Follow us
@BoldwoodBooks
@TheBoldBookClub

**Sign up to our weekly deals newsletter**

https://bit.ly/BoldwoodBNewsletter

Printed in Great Britain
by Amazon